my best
everything

my best everything

By Sarah Tomp

LITTLE, BROWN AND COMPANY
New York Boston

Little, Brown and Company

Hachette Book Group
1290 Avenue of the Americas, New York, NY 10104
Visit us at lb-teens.com

Little, Brown and Company is a division of Hachette Book Group, Inc.
The Little, Brown name and logo are trademarks of Hachette Book Group, Inc.

The publisher is not responsible for websites (or their content) that are not owned by the publisher.

First Edition: March 2015

Library of Congress Cataloging-in-Publication Data

Tomp, Sarah Wones.
My best everything / by Sarah Tomp. — First edition.
    pages cm
    Summary: When her father loses her college tuition money, Lulu works with Mason, a local boy, making and selling moonshine but their growing romance may mean giving up her dream of escaping her small Virginia hometown.
    ISBN 978-0-316-32478-6 (hardcover) — ISBN 978-0-316-32476-2 (ebook edition) — ISBN 978-0-316-32479-3 (library ebook edition)   [1. Moneymaking projects—Fiction.   2. Distilling, Illicit—Fiction.   3. Love—Fiction.   4. Family life—Virginia—Fiction.   5. Virginia—Fiction.]   I. Title.
    PZ7.T5979My 2015
    [Fic]—dc23

                                                                                    2013039870

10 9 8 7 6 5 4 3 2 1

RRD-C

Printed in the United States of America

For my mother, who asked the question.

(This is not the answer.)

1

The ingredients for moonshine are ordinary. Innocent.

Corn. Sugar. Yeast. Heat and time.

They could be the makings for something simple and forgettable. Like corn bread, bland and boring without butter and honey. But the same ingredients, thrown together in a particular way, lead to dangerous results.

You say it was all meant to be. You and me. The way we met. Our secrets in the woods. Even the way it all exploded. It was simply a matter of fate. Maybe if you were here to tell me again, to explain it one more time, then maybe I wouldn't feel so uncertain. But I'm going back to the beginning on my own. To see what happened and why.

The night you and I met, Roni and I sat on a crumbling stone bench in the graveyard behind Saint Jude's. We'd picked a spot beyond the church lights to mix our drinks. The tombstones already looked a little tipsy, crooked and lopsided under the dogwood trees. Bucky was inside, cleaning the floors. You were in there too, only I didn't know that yet. I didn't know the why until even later.

Drinking was supposed to be one of my last preparations for college. I'd let Roni convince me it was a necessary skill. "This way you'll have options, Lulu. You might actually want to take a break from studying sometime." She grinned. "Besides, everyone expects a hillbilly girl to know her way around a bottle."

I'd avoided alcohol all through high school, despite drinking being the main source of entertainment in town. I'd just said no, the way I'd been taught. I'd followed the rules. Kept my eyes on the future, my reward for being a good girl. With school over and done, I was stuck in Dale, Virginia, for one last summer. Then I'd be gone.

"I need to see the measuring line," I said, leaning in to read the markings on the plastic dispenser cup from a Children's Tylenol bottle. I poured precisely one tablespoon of vodka.

Roni laughed. "I guarantee you won't know exact measurements at a wild college party." She added a splash of juice, then handed me the cup. "This might taste strong. We need to get to the point."

The point was me gathering data. Figuring out how much I could drink. If I was going to do this, I was going to be good at it. I've always been an overachiever. The tangy juice felt both cool and warm going down. I said, "At least this juice is good for us. It has vitamins and antioxidants. Pomegranates and blueberries are both wonder foods."

"And you're a wonder dork," said Roni.

She was right, but I tossed a pebble at her anyway.

Roni pointed across the dark space. "This would be a good place for a wedding."

"In a graveyard? That's awfully pessimistic of you."

She laughed. "I meant Saint Jude's. The church is pretty, and there's that nice reception hall that leads out to the patio. The band could set up by the fence. It'd be sweet." She sighed. "But Catholics have too many rules."

I held out my cup for a refill. I liked the way I felt. Lighter and looser. Like I might float away as I walked barefoot through the dark graveyard, over and around the sinking stones. I knew the ghostly residents wouldn't be shocked by our experiment. Roni was right—Catholics have plenty of rules, but not when it comes to drinking.

Roni said, "I suppose we could have the reception at Monty's, like everyone else."

I stopped. Peered at her through the dim light. "Are you pregnant?"

"No!" Roni shook her cup at me. "I wouldn't be drinking. I'm not that dumb. But Bucky and I have been talking. We might get married anyway."

"Married? You can't get married." Maybe the vodka had blocked my censor button, but I'd always felt sorry for the girls who got married right out of high school. It seemed so dead-end, such a giving up on the future.

"Why not? I love Bucky."

That wasn't a why that made sense to me. Not then. I didn't believe in love.

Roni added, "I'm ready for real life. It's not like I'm going off to college."

I heard the missing in her voice. Knew she dreaded me leaving, but even more, Bucky. He'd been in all my AP classes, quietly earning grades almost as good as mine. He was only headed two hours down the highway to Virginia Tech, but Roni knew there were more than miles between here and there, more than hours between now and what might come. Bucky was way too smart to stay in Dale and pump gas so that other people could go places.

As I took another swallow, Roni said, "You better slow down, Lulu-bird. What happened to your scientific evaluation of the drinking process?"

We busted up laughing. Because that's really and truly how I'd described our plan.

Roni joined me on the tombstone where I'd settled. She said, "Beau Queen's been asking about you."

"What could he possibly need to know about me?" I heard the buzz in my words.

She smirked. "I was thinking maybe he could help with that other part of your education that's been sadly ignored."

I shook my head. "I'm done with redneck Virginia boys, Roni. I'm saving myself for California."

"You're such a snob, Lulu." She laughed as she said this, but she was right too.

I had my sights on the horizon. I was ready to ride off into the sunset. Away. Far away. Across the country and into another world. I was leaving the gritty mountain hol-ler of Dale and going to college in San Diego, a land of sun and sea and palm trees.

My restless anticipation kept me up at night. I'd lie in bed, listening to the downstairs clinking of Mom's all-hours baking, counting down the days until my escape. Eighty-five to go.

"I have to leave, Roni. I can't get stuck here. I just can't."

Roni knew me, knew my mother hadn't left the house once in the last three years. She understood that when someone's favorite place is an ancient graveyard on the forgotten side of a quiet town, that's a pretty solid sign they don't belong. All she said then was "You'll forget all about me when you're gone."

I threw my arm around her. "Impossible!" Then we lost our balance and tumbled backward off the granite stone, shrieking and laughing all the way down.

When we finally untangled our arms and legs, I stood up and picked graveyard moss from my curls. That's when you appeared. And I knew for sure and for certain, I was drunk.

The light shone behind you, hiding your face in the shadows. Something about your baseball hat in that orb of light looked like a halo. I grabbed Roni's arm. "Is that an angel?"

"Add hallucinations to your notes," she said, laughing again. Everything was hilarious.

Bucky's familiar wider frame appeared beside you in the shadows. He called out, "Hey, y'all done being miscreants?"

Roni leaped across the graveyard and threw herself into his arms, leaving me to pick up our trash and stumble toward the light. Where you still stood.

Bucky held Roni, who'd wrapped her arms and legs around him. He said, "Roni, Lulu, meet Mason. He works with me at the club." Bucky always worked several jobs—cleaning the church, helping at his daddy's gas station, and now that it was summer, at the Country Club.

You probably said hello, but I was too busy concentrating on standing in one place to notice.

"Mason's bike is messed up, so we're giving him a ride home."

I pulled Roni into the backseat as you loaded your bike into the bed of Bucky's truck. "Sit with me," I begged. I wasn't in any state of mind to sit beside some strange boy.

"How'd the scientific experiment go?" asked Bucky, climbing in.

He was making fun of me, but I didn't mind. At the time, I didn't mind much of anything. I just said, "Further experiments may be required."

"Lulu's drunk, Bucky," said Roni. "Really and truly. She didn't chicken out. And she's a fun drunk too." She sounded so proud of me.

We dissolved into giggles.

"Lulu's first time drinking," Bucky explained to you.

I can't remember much about that ride. At first Roni and I acted silly in the back while you and Bucky talked in the front. I remember when Bucky asked about your truck you said, "Piece of junk needs a radiator."

That's when my junkyard-girl instincts kicked in. I

leaned forward and said, "You should come by Sal's. I'm sure we have what you're looking for."

You turned and looked at me then. The way your eyes bored into mine, it felt like you were trying to read my deepest thoughts. I think that's the moment you reached inside me and changed the rhythm of my heart. Back then I thought I was simply drunk.

I talked over the rush of heat in my face. "You know Sal's. The junkyard? Sal's Salvage." That was another thing that sounded hilarious. Sal's Salvage. Especially when slurring.

Roni scooted closer beside me. Said, "Salvage might be your salvation!"

I added another one of Sal's junkyard wisdoms: "One man's junk is another man's saving grace."

"Junk is all in the eyes," agreed Roni.

"Junk is a matter of thunk," I said.

"I thunk it was junk, but it just needed a second chance."

"Sorry," Bucky said to you, shaking his head.

I said, "Really. Come by sometime. We'll find you a radiator."

"You work at Sal's?" you asked.

Roni said, "We both do."

When we first started working at Sal's, I didn't

advertise the information. Being a junkyard girl was not something I put on my college applications. I guess for some guys it's tough and sexy. That night, what with the way my eyes were wandering and mixing things up in my soggy brain, I couldn't read your reaction. I didn't care what you thought. I was already gone.

As we hit the town line, where the road turns rough and bumpy, I choked out, "How much farther?"

"Uh-oh," said Roni. "I think Lulu's going to puke."

Bucky stopped his truck, and I stumbled out, gasping for fresh air. Even through my wobbly vision I could see the stars, so many stars, now that we were a few miles away from town. The ground tipped beneath me. I staggered in circles.

Roni said, "Let it go, Lulu. Don't fight it."

I wish I'd listened. Instead, I willed myself not to get sick. Only some cheap white-trash hillbilly girl would puke on the side of the road. After a few minutes my stomach felt better, and I was more embarrassed than queasy. I was sure that meant I was sobering up.

We climbed back in, but I sat in the front and opened the window all the way, like you suggested, while you climbed in the back with Roni. I stuck my face in the rushing air and let the wind blow my curls any way it wanted.

Before long, there was no fighting it. You knew somehow. You leaned over the seat and shoved something into my lap. You even grabbed my hair away from my face. Then the puke came, bright and purple, right into your bike helmet.

You should have steered clear of me after that. But maybe you wanted to fix me. I was like a piece of wood, something to sand and shape. Or maybe the smell on my breath, the way I staggered and slurred, felt familiar. Maybe I reminded you of something you missed.

Like I miss you, right now.

There's a fine line between toxic and intoxicating.

2

I knew hangovers in theory but hadn't realized I'd feel so plain-and-simple awful the next day. I woke up in Roni's basement on the same lumpy sleeper sofa we'd always used for sleepovers, but I'd never felt like that before. I didn't know my brain could feel bruised. Like sloshing around in vodka had made it hit the walls of my skull. My eyes felt crooked and skewed, as if they'd fallen out and someone had put them back in the wrong sockets.

Roni was dressed and drinking a Coke by the time I rolled out of bed. Literally. I couldn't make myself go vertical. I didn't trust my tender stomach to make any sudden moves. From the floor I said, "Tell Sal I'm sick."

"Hello, but hell no," said Roni. "Today's going to be madness."

As much as I might want to, no way could we blow off Sal. Not with the losers from the Christiansburg Demolition Derby scheduled to be delivered that day.

On our way to the junkyard, Roni giggled. "Lulu Mendez fell off a tombstone last night."

"'Cause of you."

In a high and dreamy voice, she said, "I've had approximately four sips of alcohol, and now I'm floating." She swerved her Camaro back and forth across the empty road. Then she held up one finger and switched to her nerd voice. "Uh, I believe gravity is still working."

"I didn't say that!" I laughed, then whimpered. "Don't swerve. My stomach."

"Are you going to puke again?"

I suddenly remembered I'd thrown up in some boy's helmet. Again in his driveway. I vaguely remembered apologizing and asking for a hose, but I didn't remember actually using one. I hated the holes in my memory. "Did I mess up Bucky's truck? Is he going to kill me?"

"Nope. It all went in the helmet. Oh, lighten up, Lulu. It wasn't that bad. And it's not like Mason Malone is any angel. No matter what you thought last night."

I groaned and caught a whiff of my breath. I grabbed a

piece of gum from Roni's purse. I looked in the rearview mirror and wiped the mascara smears from under my eyes. I managed to fix my makeup, but my tangled curls were hopeless. "Who is that guy, anyway?"

"Mason? He's a couple of years older than us." She frowned, thinking. "He used to be heavier and had long hair. Kind of a waster. His girlfriend was the one who drove into the tree in front of the elementary school."

"He was Cindy D'Angelo's boyfriend?" Cindy had gone to Saint Jude's. I was on the flower committee when she died. Rumors said her accident looked like a suicide. Catholics say you aren't supposed to have a proper funeral if you commit suicide. It's a mortal sin and hard to fix with a penance. Especially since she might have been pregnant.

I'd been mesmerized by Cindy's death. All the stories— how you'd always been wild and crazy, but when she died you completely lost it—were both tragic and romantic, back when I was fourteen. Fast-forward to that particular morning, I figured you were simply messed up. A waster, like Roni said. At least there wasn't any reason to see you again. Any reason except what you call fate, that is.

Ten minutes later, as we officially left Dale and turned down the county road, we joined the line of cars headed to Sal's.

It's one of my theories that Sal's is what keeps people

living in Dale. Seeing as it's on the main road heading away from the river, people leaving town almost always go past it. The view from that road, no matter the time of year, is so pretty. Especially that spot coming out of the last long curve, where the silvery beech trees grow all lithe and graceful with the somber, steady hills behind them. That's a view that feels like hope and goodness, as if the whole world is right and strong. But then, all of a sudden, there it is: Sal's Salvage. Heaps of rusty cars. Noisy machinery. All of it ugly and old and worn out, and all wrapped up with harsh chain-link fences and barbed wire.

People must look back at Dale and think that's as good as it gets. So they turn around. They never get to the highway only one more half mile along. Just never see what else might be waiting. Mr. Palmer, who owns Corner Drug and is in charge of the Dale Chamber of Commerce, ought to pay an appreciation fee to Sal. Wouldn't surprise me if Sal set that up years ago.

By the time Roni pulled into the junkyard lot, the driveway was lined with tow trucks bearing beat-up, broken-down skeletons of vehicles.

Stepping out of her car was like entering a sensory battlefield. The blinding sun hit my eyes while the crusher and the dump trucks growled out of harmony. The heat and thick humidity boiled the smell of oil and grease mixed in with the years' worth of dirt and funk.

I made my way across the lot, squinting and wobbling behind Roni as we passed Sal hollering at a group of customers. "Y'all can let my girls know if you're looking for something in particular. But remember..." He paused before adding a bit of junkyard philosophy: "It ain't junk if it's the fix that takes you home."

Hearing that Sal-ism triggered the silly of the night before. Roni and I looked at each other and, despite the pounding in my head, I burst out laughing.

Inside the cashier trailer, the ancient air conditioner wheezed and strained to cool the air tinged with the smell of Sal's tobacco habit. Roni unlocked the service window, and we began the day.

When we first started working there, Sal called us Sugar and Spice. I thought it was because we look so different. Roni, blond and skinny, me more brown and round. But we balanced each other out in other ways too. Sal says Roni can sweet-talk any old grease monkey, and I keep them honest.

We'd been hired mainly because Sal and Mom grew up together, but we earned our pay. My brother, Paul, had worked there too, as one of the Muscles—the guys who lift, move, and actually handle the parts. This summer he'd stayed at school. Like I planned to do next summer and every year on out.

Our job was to look cute and flirt with the greasy customers while answering the phones and keeping approximate inventory logs and precise records of sales. We handled a lot of cash, especially on days like that one. The separate impound and repo lot gave Sal his steady money, but salvage is way more lucrative than most people think. Seeing as the leading businesses in Dale are Sal's, the tow trucks that bring him his products, river dredging, and the funeral home; misfortune is what keeps Dale's economy running.

My hangover had left me tragically slow and stupid. But somehow, with me sipping Mountain Dew and Roni handling the line of customers through the metal bars, laughing at their jokes and making small talk while calling out their special requests, we managed to make sales, log the new arrivals, and generally get through the next few hours. But during the midday lull, I put my head on the desk and closed my eyes. I said, "I am never drinking again."

Roni laughed. "Oh, yes, you are. I wouldn't be doing my job as your drinking instructor if I didn't insist on taking you to a party. Isn't that the whole point of you learning how to drink? So when you go off to your fancy-pants college you can get drunk and meet rich college boys?"

That wasn't why I was going to college. At least, that

wasn't the main reason. Thanks to Mr. Cauley, my AP chemistry teacher, I'd fallen in love with research and lab work. The sterility of the lab and the need for precision— the direct opposite of the junkyard—comforted me. I had my eye on pharmaceutical work. I liked the idea of helping sick people without having to actually see them.

Ollie rapped on the trailer door. "We need you out here a minute, girls."

Figuring a new hunk of junk had arrived, I forced myself up out of the trailer. As soon as I stepped into the bright sunlight, I saw my surprise. The Muscles had spray-painted stars and flowers all over an '88 Chevy Cavalier. On the windshield, a crooked sign said HAVE FUN IN KOLLEGE, LULU! The hood was propped open with empty bottles and beer cans. I'm pretty sure their ideas about college came from frat-boy movies. But they meant all those recyclables as a cash gift besides.

Laughing helped my hangover.

"You like it, honey?" Ollie threw his arm around my shoulder. "We're just so proud of you and your big...brains."

Randy added, "And big heart. And big smile. And big..."

Sexual harassment is part of the job. It's not like I enjoy it, but in the junkyard, there is a different behavior code than out in the real world. Roni and I knew how to work it in our favor. We had power over those guys, whether they knew it or not. And we knew they'd protect us from anyone who actually tried to mess with us.

"I love it," I said.

"It's perfect," said Roni. "Seeing as Lulu can't actually drive."

All those car freaks looked sad then. They knew I didn't drive but couldn't understand it.

Mom wouldn't let me drive. Of course, she couldn't teach me. Daddy traveled a lot, and Paul had been gone at school. That's why Sal helped Mom with running errands. No way could she handle the stress and risk of me behind the wheel, out of sight. Besides, she didn't trust Mr. Martin, who taught driver's ed. Said she remembered how he drove when they were in school together. Even though not being able to drive in Dale was like living on an island— a hill-filled, desolate island with no chance of rescue— I'd given up the fight. Instead of worrying about getting around town, I'd focused on studying and earning good grades so that I could get out of town completely.

When Sal made his way back to the trailer, he bellowed, "What the hell is going on? Are we having a party on my dollar?"

Roni tossed her blond ponytail and said, "We're admiring Lulu's good-bye present."

Sal squinted at the car, then at me. I didn't think much

of it at the time—my brain was still slow and hiccupy—but I'm pretty sure he flinched. He already knew my plans were about to be trashed. It still makes me mad that Mom told him before she told me. What he said to me was "If you learn to drive, Lulu, I'll get you a real car."

I knew he meant it. Not that it would be anything to show off, but it would run. Sal was always trading and selling cars. But he also knew Mom was the reason I didn't drive.

Then Sal whipped his head around and yelled, "Anyone going to see what just pulled up? Or are we taking the rest of the day off?" He pointed at a tow truck waiting outside the perimeter fence of the impound lot, and stomped off toward the office trailer.

"Mother-of-a-meathead, that man is cranky," said Roni. "He needs to find Mrs. Number Four, and soon." We'd gone through his third divorce with him the previous summer. We knew his many moods. They were all loud.

"Sal's right. I should learn to drive," I said.

"Of course you should," said Roni.

I don't know if I truly had any intention of learning to drive right then. I definitely didn't have the energy for any particular plan, but the seed of the idea was planted. I leaned against my gift car and watched Ollie open the gate for the tow truck.

Sal's is an official state holding site for impounds.

Vehicles get stuck there for months, even years, waiting for trials as evidence for some sort of crime. They can look pretty on the outside while their insides are a mess. They might be stripped to nothing but wires and metal, or could be covered in bloodstains. It's the one part of the lot where smoking is prohibited—some of those cars are so tainted with meth residue, they're literally bombs waiting to ignite.

Roni said, "This job is going to suck without you, Lulu. You know that, right?"

Even though Sal paid us twice what Roni could make anywhere else and threw in bonuses besides, it wasn't something to do alone.

"Buttercup wants Sal to hire her when you leave. I think she wants to meet some Muscles." We watched as Randy, Ollie, and Dawg wrestled a particularly stubborn lift pad on the tow truck.

Randy and Ollie weren't much older than my brother, Paul, but already there was a visible gap from who they'd been in high school. Ollie was still tall and lanky, but his freckles were starting to fold into wrinkles from working outside in the sun and the wind. Randy worried more about what he looked like—Roni and I always teased him when we caught him checking his reflection in windows—but even though he still had his high school swim star's build, he walked like he couldn't quite straighten his back anymore. I could see them heading toward the stereotypical rough-and-ragged look that Dawg wore at thirty. For instance, at that particular moment Dawg's camouflage pants were slipping south in a most clichéd manner.

Roni said, "I don't know if I can stomach walking in on her and Dawg."

I laughed. Not even Buttercup could go for that.

She fanned herself and said, "I'm going back in the cool."

"I'll be there in a minute," I said. "After I log the plates for that car."

That's why I was outside when the next delivery showed up. The Muscles had moved on to other things, so I waited as the truck backed a trailer inside the gate.

I wasn't thinking about the future or destiny or anything the least bit profound as I watched the driver nestle the trailer holding copper tanks and pipes along with wooden boxes into an available spot. I said, "Hang on. I'll get someone to unload that for you."

"Orders say keep it packed up. All the parts need to stay together." He disconnected the trailer and hopped back into his truck.

I peered at the odd collection again. Yelled to him, "What is that, anyway?"

"That's a still, honey. For making moonshine."

There she was. Aunt Jezebel.

3

$\mathcal{I}$ wonder what would have changed if I'd gotten in trouble that first time drinking. The way I was such a good girl, a rule follower, being in trouble might have ended it all. I might never have had another drink. Never gotten my big idea. Would that have changed anything for us? Would it have changed everything? Would we have found each other anyway? I guess it doesn't matter. Since I didn't.

Thoughts of you had turned hazy and faded away, like the rest of that night. Until I saw you on my way to date night with Daddy.

We'd left Mom at home, happily scrubbing the fifty pounds of potatoes Sal had delivered. Sal always found deals in odd places. He'd bring his bonanza by, and Mom would figure out something to make. Sometimes he'd sell or trade her unusual concoctions—but we'd still end up with an abundance of sugar-spiced okra or green bean corn bread. That night we had at least twenty jars of rhubarb-apricot jelly in the pantry. There's probably still some there, even now. But I can't remember what Mom made with all those potatoes.

Back when we first started our dates, Daddy would drive around to the front door and ring the doorbell. He'd thank Mom for letting me go out and let her know our plans—if we were going to have a picnic by the river or get ice cream at Corner Drug or maybe even head down the highway to catch a movie or to play a round of mini golf—and then he'd promise what time we'd be home. It was all supposed to be training for what I should expect on real dates.

Then, on the way, we'd stop at Saint Jude's for reconciliation. Again, part of my training. Daddy says confession is easier if it's already a habit. That way you don't let the bad things build up and spread inside your soul. Plus, associating sins with dating played games in my head. All part of Daddy's plan to keep me chaste, no doubt.

That night, when Daddy pulled into Saint Jude's, I said, "I want to learn to drive." He looked at me, surprised by my sudden request. "I'll be eighteen soon. It's time for me to learn. Past time. Will you teach me?"

"We'll see," he said. "When I get back in town."

"But before I go to school."

He tugged on his mustache and he said, "It might make your mother anxious."

Everything made Mom anxious.

My mother cannot simply walk out our front door. Just the idea of stepping outside turns her into a shaking, wobbly Jell-O mom. She wasn't always that way. She used to drive me to school. She helped in my classrooms. She brought Roni and me to get manicures from Miss Paula on Saturday mornings. Slowly, bit by bit, she changed. I started taking the bus to school. Daddy did all the shopping. Sal helped out when Daddy had to travel.

At home, Mom was peaceful and pleasant. Normal. She cooked surprising concoctions. Too many and too frequently, but definitely delicious. It all changed the second she tried to step out into the world. She didn't even make it to my graduation. We all pretended that she had the stomach flu. Daddy recorded it so she could watch later.

I headed to the confessional alone as Daddy stopped by the church office. He likes to give me room to confess. I'm sure he has his ideas as to what I should mention. I wonder what his biggest worries were back then. Boys, maybe.

He'd never liked me wasting time on boys with no future. He'd warned me not to fall for someone who had no plans to leave town. But that night he didn't have to worry. I hadn't dated anyone since Patrick James ruined my prom. And my dress.

I stepped into the closet-size space of the confessional and breathed in the familiar smell of wood and stone. Even though Father Mick knows all of us and our voices, there's still the old-fashioned screen to hide behind. I knelt on the leather kneeler and made the sign of the cross. "Forgive me, Father, for I have sinned. It's been two weeks since my last confession."

Father Mick's gentle voice came through the screen, "Unburden your heart."

"I've lied to my parents. And I've thought unloving things about my mother."

"Have you invited her to join you at Mass?"

"She can't."

"Then we must come to her. Anything else?"

"I gossiped with my friend. I've had impure thoughts about boys."

Truths used to slip out so easily behind that screen.

Father Mick would be hard to shock. He grew up in Boston, and before he got stuck in this tiny nothing parish, he did missionary work in São Paulo, Brazil. He must get bored with the confessions of this town. I used to think about making something up for him, to keep things interesting. Except then I would have had to confess about lying in confession.

Of course, later, once I actually had something worth confessing, I stopped going.

"Our bodies can bring us joy," said Father Mick. "But they are loud and demanding. Look into your heart and see what God has planned for you. For penance, five Hail Marys and two Our Fathers."

I made the sign of the cross and finished with the Act of Contrition.

He added, "Oh, and to help keep your thoughts off the boys, please weed the graveyard."

"Yes, Father. Thank you."

Drinking hadn't entered my mind as something I needed to confess. Sure, it was breaking the law, since I was underage, and my parents would have been mad, but it didn't feel like a sin against any particular commandment. Yet when I went to scope out the weed situation and found the medicine cup we'd left behind, I looked around to see if anyone had noticed. A little touch of guilt kicking in, even if it was showing up late.

I was following Father Mick's directions when I went out to the graveyard. It's his fault I was there, when all of a sudden you were there too, parking your bike. I hadn't known I'd recognize you so certainly.

You looked at me from under your helmet. Winked and said, "You doing more scientific experiments?"

I blurted out, "I'm sorry about that night. And your helmet."

"It washed out." You tapped it.

"That's the same one?"

"Well, yeah." You took it off, and I saw your buzz cut. "I have to protect my brain cells. They're an endangered species." Your laugh almost made up for your ugly hair.

Buzz cuts remind me of the darkest corners of Dale. The rickety old shacks down by the river. The places where cousins get shot in the living room for eating the last Oreo, the small-minded bigots with hate in their hearts—that's who wears buzz cuts. Moonshiners too, I suppose.

You looked a little mischievous when you asked, "So, how'd you feel the next day?"

I glanced toward the church, making sure Daddy wasn't on his way out. "Probably not as bad as I deserved."

"It's good that you lost so much of the alcohol."

That was absolutely the nicest way to put what I'd done to your helmet.

When Daddy came out of the church, another surprise was that he knew you.

I compared the two of you shaking hands. You in a T-shirt and jeans, Daddy wearing an impeccably pressed shirt and slacks. Daddy's skin a warm brown, yours more golden. You were slightly taller. Daddy was broader, but your muscles filled out your shirt. Both of you practically bald, you by choice. Your grin didn't match your hair or your reputation.

"Mason is renovating the conference room." Daddy threw his arm around my shoulder, Papa Bear–style, and said, "This is my daughter, Luisa."

"We've met," you said.

For a second I worried you'd tell him how. Maybe drinking to the point of puking was no big deal to you. You said, "Lulu is going to help me find a radiator at Sal's."

"Ah, yes," said Daddy. "My daughter knows far more about engines than I do."

When Daddy said good-bye and turned toward the parking lot, I murmured, "Thanks. For not saying anything about the other night."

You reached toward me then. Our eyes met, and I could smell your skin. For a crazy, confusing second, I thought you were going to kiss me. My skin tingled and my mouth watered, even though my head panicked. But what you did was even more surprising. You took one of my curls and wrapped it around your finger. You said, "Do these curls ever make you dizzy?" Then you let it go again, gentle, without pulling at all.

No. But you did.

In the car Daddy said, "Pizza or steak?"

I shook my head, incapable of forming an opinion while my mind stumbled over what you'd done to my hair. I felt surprise. Confusion. Something else too. Something warm and new.

Daddy opted for steak. There are only two real restaurants in town, and they're both owned by Wally Montgomery. That's why the dinner rolls at Monty's Ranch House are made from pizza dough, and the steak-and-fry pizza is one of the specialty items at Wally's Pie Place. I didn't know it then, but Wally also offers shots of moonshine at his bar, under the code name Monty's Revenge. One per customer.

Daddy likes to give people space to mind their own business, so we headed straight out to the patio. He says sitting outside is the California way. We'd stopped visiting Los Angeles, where he'd grown up, when his mama died and my mother turned odd, but he'd always made California sound like something magical, the land of the gold rush, a place where dreams come true.

The night was warm, and the bug zappers buzzed around us as I faced the deep indigo of the Blue Ridge Mountains against the darkening sky in the distance. My eyes had been trained to look beyond those slopes, past the shadows in the valleys, toward a wider, brighter world.

I had no idea my future was teetering on an unfamiliar edge as I ate my chicken steak and sweet potato salad. I felt happy, relaxed. And I felt pretty, thanks to you playing with my hair. I didn't have plans for you—I was too set on leaving. But the way you'd made me feel had me eager to see who I'd meet in San Diego.

When we finished our meals, Daddy wiped his mustache with his napkin and set it beside his plate. He frowned. His forehead furrowed with wrinkles. I reached over and rubbed them. "You have your pug look on, Daddy. What's wrong?"

"Luisa Maria, we must talk." Daddy always sounds formal when he's giving bad news.

I swallowed, suddenly feeling wobbly. I worried he somehow knew I'd gotten drunk. Maybe he'd smelled it on my breath. Or my clothes. Or he'd seen me on the side of the road. I braced myself for his disappointment.

"Your mother would love to have you stay home this fall."

A cold, hard knot formed inside me. "It's not me that she wants home, Daddy. It's you."

We'd had this conversation before. Mom is better when he's home. But he has to travel for work. He can't see what she's like when he isn't there. He doesn't see the contrast. Daddy buys plants in South America and then sells them to greenhouses all over the country. Twenty-some years ago, on a trip to some farms in Virginia, he met Mom. Apparently he kept coming back with more plants. And then, because he'd have to travel no matter where he lived, they decided to raise their kids in the safe mountain town where she'd grown up.

He said, "I took a gamble on a new farmer. It didn't work out. I don't have the money for your school."

I sat back in my chair, completely confused. I tried to make a joke of it. "Are you leaving me between a rock and a hard place?" That's how Daddy always described Dale. It's true, of course, the way it's crammed between two mountains. That's not what he really meant. And that's why his words made no sense.

"I'm sorry," he whispered.

"But..." My dinner sat heavy in my stomach while my head swirled. "There must be something you can do."

He shook his head, eyes on his empty plate.

"What about Paul?"

"This will be his last year. He can't wait."

"I can't wait either, Daddy."

"We can't afford private school, Lulu. Especially not out of state."

"You're the one who told me to pick a Catholic university." My voice was low, close to cracking.

I didn't know what to feel or think or do. I plan things. I make decisions and stick with them. The University of San Diego's biochemistry program was top notch. With state-of-the-art labs. I hadn't even applied to any Virginia schools.

"Daddy," I said louder. "You have to fix this."

I knew eyes from other tables were on me. Ears were listening. But I couldn't stop the words from boiling up and over. "There's nothing for me here. You know that."

He didn't even try to argue.

I threw his own words at him. "The only people who stay in Dale are the ones with no other options."

I read the truth in his eyes: That was me.

I bolted out the door. I didn't want to lose it in Monty's. It'd be all over town by morning that I was having a nervous breakdown.

Dale isn't quite small enough to be incestuous, but close. It's definitely small enough that everyone thinks they know each other's business. They remember when your mother freaks out at your middle school spring festival event and has to be carried out by the paramedics because she's paralyzed with anxiety. You know what it's like to have everyone think they know all about you and your family. To be waiting for you to make the same mistakes.

Back at home, Daddy tried to explain. This wasn't the first time one of his gambles hadn't worked out, but it was the first time I'd felt the ripples.

Mom rubbed my back. "There are things you could do here, Lulu. You could help out at the church and keep working. Sal reminded me you don't even know how to drive yet."

I wanted to say, *Drive? You can't even walk out our front door to check the mail.* I was filled with an all-consuming, dizzying sort of anger. If she wasn't such a Jell-O mom, we might have had other options. We might not even live in Dale at all. But might-have-beens were a waste of worry. And talking about her problem would have broken family code.

Instead I said, "I'm leaving in September."

No more rock. No more hard place. Gone.

4

I stayed up all night researching scholarships and financial aid, but Daddy was right. All the deadlines had passed. Then, in the midst of my searching for the magic solution, an e-mail popped up from USD. A deposit of four hundred dollars was due.

At work I searched the Internet for ideas and stories of young entrepreneurs. I read about a girl who'd raised golden retrievers, and a boy who'd sold some kind of radio circuit boards. One family grew Christmas trees to fund the education of four children. I was only fifteen years too late to start that one. Roni squealed when I found the story about Lullaby Breaker doing a fund-raiser for a girl with leukemia.

She'd developed mad love for Lullaby Breaker ever since she saw them play at Buttercup's birthday party, right before they started their first tour. Back then they were just some local band that Buttercup's cousin Troy played in. I'd missed the party to stay home and study for the SATs, but I'd heard all about Lullaby Breaker ever since. I'd heard "This Feeling" enough times that it didn't sound like music anymore.

Roni said, "Too bad you don't have cancer."

"Too bad you think I'm making a big deal out of nothing."

"Oh, Lulu. I know how much this matters to you—I really do. But I also know you'll figure something out."

Roni didn't get my distress. She planned to stay in Dale forever. She wanted to get married and pop out Bucky's babies, who would grow up and stay here too.

As Ollie came in the trailer to grab a soda from the fridge, bringing with him an overpowering smell of sweat and dirt, Roni said, "Let's buy lottery tickets."

Ollie said, "I want in." Then he belched, making the trailer smell even worse.

"Eww, Ollie," said Roni.

I said, "Buying lottery tickets is throwing money away."

"Can't win if you don't buy a ticket," said Ollie. "If I won the lottery, I'd start a restaurant for peanut butter sandwiches. Peanut butter and mayo, peanut butter and fluff, peanut butter and brown sugar, peanut butter and..."

"Jelly?" I suggested.

He shrugged. "Maybe. I was thinking honey. Point is, I'd invest that money right back into my business, which would then make me even more money."

Ollie has always been my favorite Muscle. He's a dreamer, always making plans, looking ahead, seeing the potential in what most people toss. Kind of like Sal, but with less money. And body hair. That day he made me sad. I couldn't help thinking he was never going to do anything different. He'd always be stuck in the junkyard dreaming his sweet, sticky peanut butter dreams.

Randy and Dawg came in the trailer then too, putting the air quality at grave risk. Randy said, "Hey, Lulu, did Ollie tell you a Malone boy asked about you this morning?"

Too many eyes were suddenly all on me. I said, "Did you help him find a radiator?"

"Is that what you kids call it these days? A ray-dee-aaaay-tor?" Randy can make anything sound dirty.

Roni said, "Does he mean Mason? Why was he asking about you?"

"He said he needs a radiator."

"Didn't buy one," said Dawg.

"That's true." Randy chuckled. "I guess he just wants Lulu's radiator."

Ollie said, "I don't know that you should mix up with a Malone, Lulu."

"I'm not mixed up with him," I said. "But I can not not mix up with whoever I want."

Roni laughed. "Not not mix-upping can be fun." She was always latching on to funny lines.

"I don't trust him," said Randy. "He played dumb when I tried to get him to sell me some moonshine. Said he's not involved with that business any longer."

"But he was?" I asked. I looked at Roni, who shrugged.

You can't live in Dale and not have heard about moonshine. I knew it was a deep and ingrown redneck tradition. Of course I knew it was illegal. Stronger than store-bought liquor. It seemed like every few months there'd be a notice in the paper about an old still getting shut down and dismantled. I didn't have any practical knowledge. Every now and then someone would bring some moonshine to a party, but it felt to me, the nondrinker, like it was simply an excuse to act even stupider than usual.

Ollie said, "All Malones are in the business, one way or another."

"Hoo-boy. A jar of that stuff can lose you a week of your life." Randy smacked his lips.

"That's a good thing?" I asked.

"Depends on the week."

Then Sal charged into the trailer, and all the Muscles scattered. Ollie, on his way out the door, said, "Hey, Lulu, if you have a connection with your not not not whatever you're doing or not doing, I'll trade you a month's worth of peanut butter sandwiches for a jar." He and Randy giggled their way down the stairs.

Sal grabbed his deodorant from the bottom drawer and lifted his shirt, revealing his incredibly hairy stomach in order to spray his pits. There are some visions that can never be erased from your mind, no matter the amount of drink or therapy. He turned to us and said, "You girls did good work with that load-off. Here's a bonus." He handed us each a stack of bills.

"Thanks." I thumbed the money. "Sal, you think I could borrow—"

He cut me off. "I'm happy to give you extra shifts, Lulu, but you're too young to start owing. If you need money, figure out a way to earn it."

I was more surprised by my asking than by his answer.

"You know you'll have a job here as long as you want it."

He meant that nice enough, but for me it sounded like a threat or a curse.

I wasn't sure whether I was relieved or disappointed

that I'd missed your junkyard visit. Especially now that I'd heard you might be wrapped up in the moonshine business.

That's when I checked the inventory for radiators and realized I'd never logged the still's arrival. I'd been so hungover and dazed from the heat, I hadn't followed through on the paperwork. Then the phone started ringing and Sal dumped a ton of files on my desk and, well, I didn't do it that day either. I can hear you saying it's because deep inside, I already knew what I was going to do.

———

Roni came by my house after dinner. "You look awful, Lulu-bird."

She told the truth. I wasn't wearing makeup, and my hair was a tangled mess. I wore cutoff sweatpants with a stained yellow tank top and was eating from a bag of gummy bears for comfort. I looked worse than old Mother Hubbard, who preaches outside the Supermart ever since the Baptists chased her off their lawn.

"Come on, Lulu. I'm taking you out."

I shook my head. "I'm too pathetic."

"That's never bothered you before," she teased. "Besides, we have to go." She danced in place and said, "Lullaby Breaker is playing at Monty's. It's a secret bonus concert to thank the fans who got them started. They didn't even post it on their website." She rummaged through my closet. "Put this on."

The red sundress she'd picked out was cute. Loose enough to hide my gummy-filled gut. "Is Bucky coming?" I wasn't going to be a third wheel.

"He's working. The club pool needed an after-hour cleanup."

I slipped into the dress, put on makeup, and ignored my curls. Sometimes it's better to let my hair be wild. It's like fighting fate, anyway. It's going to do what it wants.

Turned out Lullaby Breaker was playing in the bar part of Monty's restaurant. We heard them as soon as we stepped out of the car, but we couldn't see the band from the doorway, no matter how we turned and peeked around the tramped-up ladies in front of us. Roni leaned to the side. "I wish I could see something other than old people dancing."

One of the ladies gave us a dirty look. I pulled Roni back in line, giggling.

The tattooed bouncer took one look at us and said, "Sorry, girls. Gotta be twenty-one."

Roni pouted. "We promise we won't drink."

Curtis Matthews, one of Paul's friends, peered out the door then. He said, "Hey, aren't you a little Mendez?"

Roni tossed her hair and said, "She's not that little."

His eyes ran all over both of us. "Yeah. I'd say you've grown up real nice."

The bouncer said, "But not enough."

Curtis asked, "Where's your brother been, Lulu? I haven't seen him all summer."

"He stayed at school. He's working in Charlottesville."

"He didn't come home to Mommy?"

Curtis laughed, and the bouncer gave him a high five. I didn't know if that was simple trash talk or if he was actually talking about Mom. Either way, fact was Paul had escaped. The unfairness of it made me grit my teeth and step away from the door.

Out in the parking lot, Roni steamed. "We have to get in there somehow."

"Wouldn't Bucky be mad if you were in a bar without him?"

"He trusts me. We keep each other plenty happy. There's no reason to fool around with anyone else. That's why I know we're ready to get married."

"You aren't even old enough to get into a bar, Roni. What if you get tired of him by the time you can?"

"I'm not like you, Lulu. You're the one who always wants something bigger and better."

She was right, but I wasn't sure why it felt like an insult.

We found the back door, where a pile of wooden pallets

and crates full of empty beer bottles were stored. Roni said, "Let's wait here for someone to open that door and let us in."

"Why would they do that?"

"Well, hopefully it will be some big stud. Named Sven or Oyvind."

"Oyvind?"

She waved my doubts away. "He'll have thick blond hair and gorgeous eyes, and you'll...convince him." She raised her eyebrows suggestively.

"Why me? You're the expert at convincing."

We didn't have anywhere better to be, and we could hear the band pretty well through a small cracked window above our heads, so we sat on the cement step, trying not to notice the stink of stale beer mixed in with something worse from the Dumpster, and listened.

Roni said, "I swear Grungie's voice is so deep it makes my toes curl."

"He's the ugly one, right?"

She frowned disapprovingly while I laughed. "Like Sal says, homely can keep you happy in the dark."

Roni grabbed my arm. "Listen. Do you hear that deep kind of echo? That has to be the wooden box Troy found. I think it's some kind of Peruvian—or maybe African—instrument."

"All I hear is harmonica. Sounds kind of hillbilly to me."

"More like completely new and alternative," Roni defended them. "They're very experimental. I read on their blog that Grungie wants a harp for a new song called 'Angel's Share.'"

"Which one has those ridiculous sideburns? The ones that look like some kind of pet."

"That's Johnny," said Roni. "He's the one who writes all their love songs. 'River Lullaby' is so pretty it makes me cry. I'm going to have it at my wedding." She stomped her foot. "I really wanted to see them play tonight."

"Let's hear you sing." I handed her one of the empty beer bottles from the crate. "Here's your microphone."

Roni shook her head but took the bottle, grinning.

"And I'll play the bottle-rocka." I picked up some pebbles and put them in a second bottle so they'd jingle against the brown glass. "It's an alternative African-Peruvian jingle bell. Very hip. Very big city. Very new style."

She laughed.

I yelled, "One, two, three, hit it!"

"Wait. I actually know this one." She bobbed her head in time and then started singing. Soft at first. Then louder. Pretty soon, she got into it. Me too. I shook my bottle-rocka and danced beside her while she sang. We couldn't hear the band's next song, so she went on to some other song she liked. It was like being in fourth grade again, when we used to pretend we were making music videos. I'd always been her backup. Even though we were major dorks acting even younger than we were, I know that was so much more fun than being in that crowded bar, where we'd have to act cool. Or at least normal. Which we were nowhere near when the door suddenly opened.

Startled, Roni shrieked, long and piercing.

I—as pure reflex—threw my glass instrument. Fortunately, it hit the wall and shattered glass in a million directions, rather than hitting Grungie, the lead singer of Lullaby Breaker.

We ran. Ducking behind Roni's car, I peered through her dusty windows to where the rest of the band had joined Grungie. He pointed in our direction, laughing.

"I can't believe you threw that bottle," she gasped. "Is he all right?" Then she groaned. "I'll never be able to watch them play again."

I'm not sure what came over me then. I felt restless and agitated. Tired of wanting something out of reach. I stood up and walked around her car.

"Lulu," she squealed. "Where are you going?"

"Sorry about that," I called to them, waving. "You scared us."

Grungie laughed, waving his cigarette. "Not the first time I've had a bottle thrown at me."

"See, we were sitting and listening to you play. They won't let us in, since we're not quite twenty-one yet."

They shifted their feet and grinned. They're used to love-crazed girls.

"You need to meet Roni McAllister." I gestured to where Roni hid. "She knows all your songs. In fact, she can sing them as good as you can. Better, maybe."

"I am going to kill you, Lulu," Roni growled, not moving.

Grungie said, "All right. I'm listening."

I stared down at Roni. She glared back, something fierce. "Sing for them, Roni."

"I can't."

"Yes you can. You sing all over the place. And you're good."

"I'll help you out," said Grungie. I still think he's ugly, but he's genuinely sweet too. His voice really is thunder-rumble deep. When Roni joined in, it was obviously not the first time she'd sung along to his voice. There in the parking lot she sang clear and raw, high to his low, but right. Oh so right.

When they finished a verse, he grinned. "Fellows, I think we may have found what we've been looking for."

He moved across the lot and handed her a card. "Call me to try a set."

Roni nodded, clutching that card against her chest.

Someone opened the back door, and they all tossed their cigarettes and moved to head back into the bar. Grungie called back, "Roni McAllister, right?"

"Right!" I yelled, since she was still frozen.

When she thawed, she said, "What the hell is wrong with you, Lulu?" Then, "Mother-of-a-miracle, I sang with Grungie Johnson. I can die now and go to heaven."

"That'd be a waste," I said. "At least try that set before you croak."

Back in her car she was amped up and thrilled. "See how much fun we had tonight? It won't be all bad if you have to stay here. Maybe I'll actually be singing with the band, and you can come watch me."

I couldn't answer with that small space between us. Not where her dreams were spreading out and stretching, while mine were feeling trampled and squashed.

5

*R*oni couldn't wait to tell Bucky about Lullaby Breaker. Since I wasn't ready to go home and ignore my parents, I rode with her to the Country Club. That name makes it sound so much nicer than a community pool and golf course that are only open three months a year. I guess *Country* comes from being surrounded by fields of cows. And *Club* means you have to pay dues. Daddy said he quit paying dues on account of everyone there was jealous of his tan. That had never bothered him while Paul was on the golf team.

Roni squealed wheels into the parking lot and jumped out of the car as soon as she saw Bucky standing on the sidewalk. Was it fate that you were there too, getting on your bike? Or simple coincidence? Is there a difference?

Not that I thought anything like that. Instead, I thought how Randy said you were mixed up with moonshine. I knew you'd been through tragedy and heartbreak over Cindy D'Angelo. You were someone who'd seen and done all kinds of things I didn't know anything about. No wonder you'd let me puke in your helmet.

But you'd also laughed and played with my hair in a most confusing way. Throw in the fact that you knew Daddy and hung out at Saint Jude's, and, well, I simply didn't know what to think. None of it mattered anyway, because I was leaving town. Somehow, some way. Besides, you had horrible hair.

I took the keys out of the ignition, where Roni had left them in her hurry. I got out and watched as you moved your bike like you were ready to leave, until Bucky said, "Put that bike down, Mason. I talked Carly into making us a couple of plates of sustenance."

The night was warm, and the crickets were crazy loud. Above us, the crescent moon peeked over the shadowed hills. We walked past the pool, where the water glowed the softest shimmery kind of blue, and then we scooted around the back of the golf cart garage, heading out to the enormous field of lush grass.

Out on the green, I kicked off my flip-flops and walked barefoot through the damp grass: I wanted to take off like a little kid, to run until I got dizzy and forgot that my life was a mess.

Bucky set his plate on the boulder, and Roni launched into telling him about the bar and Lullaby Breaker. She was jacked up and loopy from it all.

"You were hanging out in a bar parking lot?" asked Bucky around bites of shrimp gumbo.

"We were just messing around." Roni beamed my way. "It was pure luck that the band came out when they did. And that Lulu went insane. Do you think Grungie was serious?"

Bucky could have stopped it all then. Roni was still nervous enough about this idea that if he'd shown any doubt, she would've forgotten all about it. But Bucky said, "Of course he was serious. They'd be crazy not to want you. Hey, Mason, my girl is gonna be famous someday."

Roni turned to you and said, "You know those guys, don't you? Didn't you graduate with Johnny and Troy?"

You gave a funny smile and said, "I was supposed to."

"Oh," said Roni. "Sorry."

"Not your fault."

While I added the fact you were a high school dropout to my confusing observations, Roni said, "I only graduated 'cause of Lulu and Bucky. They're the brainiacs. I have no idea why I hang out with such geeks."

"Is that right?" asked Bucky. "You think I'm a geek, huh?"

All of a sudden they were hanging all over each other, being smoochy and huggy. It was probably even more awkward for you, since I was used to putting up with them.

I turned to you and said, "I heard you came by Sal's." I didn't mention that I also heard your family was in the moonshine business.

"I had to pick up some parts for my boss."

"You didn't get your radiator."

Roni laughed then. "That's right, Mason, we heard you want a raaayy-deee-aaaay-tor."

I ignored her tease. "Did anyone check and see if we have the one you need?"

"Nah. I was on my bike. I knew I couldn't carry it."

"You probably wanted Lulu to help you, right?" Roni moved into Bucky's lap, murmuring about his radiator and overheating.

My face burned hot, even if you didn't know what Roni was talking about. Then their voices lowered until Roni said, "Hey, y'all, we'll be right back," and they disappeared.

I played with her keys, quiet sitting between us. I'd been gauging my distance from you carefully. I didn't want our hands to accidentally brush against each other. Even though we didn't touch, I could feel the heat off your body. Finally I said, "You can go if you want. They'll probably be a while." I silently kicked myself for bringing up what we both knew they were doing in the dark.

You asked, "Can you take Roni's car? Bucky's got his truck."

I shook my head. "I don't know how to drive."

"How is that possible?"

Feeling inadequate always makes me irritated. "It's not that big a deal," I said.

"But don't you work with cars?"

"I know parts and pieces. I just don't know how to make a whole one move. I'm waiting until I'm eighteen to get my license. Which'll be soon."

You were quiet a minute, making me wonder what you were thinking.

"I could give you a lesson," you said. "Since you've got her keys."

Roni and Bucky were nowhere in sight. I was feeling restless and unsettled. Certain my parents would disapprove, I followed you to Roni's car and got in the driver's seat.

Immediately my hands started sweating. "Maybe this is a bad idea."

"No way."

To someone who wants answers and always wants to know she's making the right decision, your certainty is comforting. Soothing.

We sat side by side, a few inches apart. My eyes stayed glued in front of me as you went over the basics of the car, what I needed to keep in mind. I could smell your shampoo or deodorant, something clean, mixed in with your sweat and boy smell too. Our olfactory systems are crucially tied in to memories and comfort and physical attraction. It's science.

I was scientifically aware of you as I turned the key and started the engine.

I put the car in gear and crept forward. Then slammed on the brakes. We both knocked against the seat belts. "Sorry." I started up again.

Even though I blamed my mother for my never having had the chance to learn to drive, I hadn't pushed the issue. Mom's fears might be irrational, but driving was scary stuff. Working at a junkyard provides daily reminders of what happens to cars when they hit other objects. I'd built the whole idea of it up in my mind. My heart pounded as I coaxed Roni's Camaro forward, but at least the view over the dashboard was familiar. I poked along, driving the main stretch of the parking lot, determined not to be like my mother.

"Good," you said. "A little more gas. That's nice. Feel that? Hear the hum of the engine? You need to feel like the car is an extension of you. You're in charge."

Your words don't seem that significant looking at them on the page. Yet the tone in my ear soothed my jangled nerves.

"Look around," you said. As I drove through the parking lot again you said, "Anticipate. As long as you think a little bit ahead, you'll be ready. Slow for the turn. Yes. That's it."

Hypnotic. That's what it was. Your voice was hypnotic.

How else can I explain that I let you talk me out of the parking lot? Past the main buildings and out to Possum Hollow Road? I was driving. On a real road. In the dark. I picked up speed. I went uphill and down. I followed the curves and stayed in my lane. Another car came toward us, its lights shining bright in my eyes, but I stayed on the road. I slowed a little bit, but then you coaxed me back up to a normal speed.

There's not much along that road, only driveways with miles between them. When we passed a sign for the old abandoned quarry you said, "Turn right at the next driveway. We'll turn around and head back."

"I can't." Now that I was moving, it was slowing down and changing directions that scared me. My hands clenched the wheel.

"Let up on the gas." Your voice was steady, but urgent too. "Lulu, if we keep going you're going to run out of road. Hitting Dowdy's Bridge is a bad idea. Now tap the brake, nice and easy."

One minute everything is fine, and the next, it's chaos.

I hit the gas instead of the brake. I panicked and pushed harder. Roni's car zoomed off the pavement and onto the grassy shoulder. A fence loomed in front of us, but you lifted my leg, allowing the car to finally stop. A sleepy cow looked our way, completely unimpressed with the way my heart pounded fast and furious.

You got out of the car to check for damage. Climbing back in, you said, "No harm done."

I hit the steering wheel hard. Then burst out, "I'm never going to get out of this town."

There in the dark, you got slammed with my misery. I told you how desperate I was to get away from Dale. About Daddy losing my college money, and being out of options. I even told you how scared I was of becoming like Mom. I never talk about that. Maybe it was the dark and the way you simply nodded. Or maybe it was because I didn't know you and you didn't know me. Maybe I simply exploded.

"I can't even get in a car and take off," I finished off my rant.

"Maybe there's a reason you're supposed to stick around here."

"That reason is my father's mistake. Now what am I supposed to do?"

"My mama says there's always hope, as long as the moon still shines."

I sat in silence, too absorbed in my negative spiral to respond to your pretty riddle.

"Sometimes," you continued, "best thing you can do is accept you aren't in charge."

I thought you meant my parents. That you were on their side. I was too miserable to see beyond my own reflection in the window.

$\mathcal{I}$ steamed through the next few days. Literally. A heat wave hit, muggy and suffocating. It was too hot to bother waving away the gnats and no-see-ums buzzing in my eyes and ears. Of course I thought about you after that night on the golf course. I wondered if you'd ride your bike in that kind of hot. I hoped you had your helmet on in case you passed out on the side of the road. But even if you had an easy smile and the rhythm of your voice had hypnotic powers, I'd sworn off all Dale boys. You were Mason Malone of infamous rumors. A high school dropout.

I checked and rechecked the Internet for scholarship opportunities but found nothing. Out of curiosity, I also looked up moonshine. It seemed impossible to me that people would pay for something like that in this day and age, yet there was clearly some kind of cult following for the stuff. I found places to buy stills, get recipes, share trade secrets.

Sal came by with a bushel of raspberries the day after Daddy left again. He sat at our kitchen table, adding sugar to Mom's too-sweet tea and laughing too loud. So when Roni suggested we go to Jimbo Queen's field party, I was ready for anything that would get me out of the house.

The party wasn't far from their river-tubing business. Just beyond their pasture, there's plenty of space for kegs and a crowd. You know the place.

It wasn't far to walk from the road where Bucky parked, but it was too dark to see the giant ruts in the field. After I tripped for the third time, Bucky insisted that Roni and I each take one of his arms.

Roni said, "I told you to wear boots, Lulu."

"I don't wear boots," I said. I'd started wearing flip-flops once I got accepted to the University of San Diego, and I wasn't about to stop. I'm superstitious about some things, stubborn about others.

"It's not about fashion," said Roni. "Just wait until you step in a big old cow pie."

I stopped walking. "Am I really going to?"

They both laughed. Bucky said, "You should also wear a helmet."

Roni punched him. "Don't be mean. Lulu is not going to puke tonight."

"I only meant to protect her head in case she falls."

Thinking about you and your helmet, I wondered if you'd be there.

Despite the wide open space, the crowd crammed together between the keg and the speakers blasting music. "They should get a band to play," said Roni.

"Did you ever call Grungie?" I asked her.

"Not yet. What if he didn't mean it? He might have just been scared you were going to throw another bottle at him."

"Have a drink," I said. "That'll get your nerve up."

See what a good student I was?

I didn't expect to like beer, but that yeasty, bubbly taste surprised me. I especially liked that its alcohol content was measurable and finite. That's a dangerous illusion for control freaks.

Buttercup was there with Jimmy, who was on seriously shaky ground. His eyes were red, and he swayed like the scarecrow in *The Wizard of Oz*. I kept waiting for him to topple over. We stood in a circle with Mary Lou, Charlotte, and Tommy. Beau Queen was hanging around, and Patrick James too. I'd already mentally said good-bye to these friends. I'd tossed my mortarboard at graduation and checked out. Now that I didn't know where I was headed, I had even less to say. Buttercup suddenly grabbed at my cup, sending off a spray of beer. "What is Saint Lulu drinking?"

"Well, it was beer," I said. "But now it's gone."

"Get her another!"

"I'm on it," yelled Jimmy. Then, "Anyone got a dollar?"

Patrick James said to me, "You're drinking? You?"

"Yeah. So?" I acted like it was no big deal. The beer helped.

At one point Buttercup yelled, "Shake it, baby. Make me a milk shake."

"Cow dance!" said Roni.

Everyone bent over and shook their hands like they were udders. Of course it's ridiculous, but the beer made it funny too. We made fools of ourselves being all kinds of farm animals. The goat dance meant butting heads against each other's shoulders and backs. The chicken was a strut with lots of neck. During the pig round, Charlotte, Roni, and I snorted, but no way were we going to roll around like the boys and Buttercup did.

"Help me up, Lulu." Patrick James lay on the ground, reaching for me.

I braced my legs and pulled him up. He whispered in my ear, "I'd sure like to kiss you."

It was dark. I was good and buzzed. We'd dated for a few months before things went wrong. So I kissed him. Quick and simple. Then I said, "Now dance like a donkey, you ass."

Then he was hands down on the ground kicking up his back legs, doing those horrid mule kicks we had to do in tenth-grade PE. It was funny enough that I let him kiss me again. I wasn't stingy with kisses back then. They didn't mean much to me.

I hadn't kissed you yet.

All of a sudden, I'm wondering who gave you your first kiss. Mine was playing spin the bottle at Charlotte's boy-girl party in sixth grade. So were my second, third, fourth, and fifth. There was a rut in the carpet in front of me, and the bottle kept getting stuck. Roni hated that I was Bucky's first kiss—he was my number four.

My first real kiss was the last day of eighth grade with Brent Quesenberry behind the gym. I'd adored him all year from across the cafeteria, but that kiss cured me. He smelled of peanut butter and Daddy's Old Spice deodorant, so after a few minutes of him licking my face like a beagle, I stepped away and told him I thought I was moving to Paris over the summer.

Only Roni knows how many boys I've kissed since then. Most of them don't matter. It might sound like pure rationalization and excuses, but kissing a lot of boys was one of my stay-a-virgin techniques. If you keep it light and changing, no one guy expects too much. Except for prom night. Or if you're drunk in a dark field.

I suddenly couldn't shake this picture of myself forever drinking in pastures, playing animal games, and kissing boys I didn't like. I was supposed to be a brilliant researcher, studying the mysteries of the universe, not dodging cow pies and boy tongues. I'd worked so hard to be the good girl, to keep track of my plan. It wasn't fair that it was all being pulled out from under me. The beer flowing through my bloodstream brought all those frustrations up to the surface.

Besides, Patrick James always had kissed way too wet. Now his hands were moving up my sides trying to sneak in for more. I pushed him away. I was buzzed enough to tell the truth. I said, "That's enough. I'm done with you. No more kisses for you. Ever."

He turned nasty and rude. Said, "Forget you, Lulu. You're still too cold for me."

I don't know why being called cold is such an insult. It's not like having standards is a bad thing. But no girl likes being called cold. It's like being called a princess by anybody but her daddy. I poked Patrick James in the chest and said, "That's right. I'm like liquid nitrogen. Better not come near me without your gloves."

Laughing, Bucky pulled me away.

Patrick James said, "I don't even know what the hell she's talking about."

I tried to yell an explanation about the liquid nitrogen, how it's so cold it'll burn skin. But Bucky steered me back to Roni.

"Lulu's gone rogue," he said. "She's making Pat cry."

"Let him cry," I said. "Give me another beer."

"The keg's dry," said Bucky.

"That sucks," I said.

Bucky said, "You know what else sucks? Lulu when she's drinking. Sucks face, that is."

Roni laughed. "Maybe it's time to go."

As we left the field, I thought I saw your shorn head. Impulsively, I darted over and tapped that broad shoulder I thought I recognized. It wasn't you. Close enough that I had to stop and think a second. You've said people used to think you and Seth were twins. That night he had ten or twenty pounds on you, and wore them loose and pouchy. He greeted me with a slow smile.

"Sorry," I said. "I thought you were someone else."

"Yeah?" His eyes traveled over me. "You sure you don't want me?"

Peanut was beside him, wearing his mirrored sunglasses even in the dark. He and their group of friends laughed as I blushed and stepped back, trying to regain my footing.

"What's going on, fellows?" Bucky intervened.

"Just having fun," Seth said. "You interested in something?"

"Nah, man. Gotta get these girls home."

"Is it bedtime already?" Seth's eyes bored into me.

The way you and he look almost alike but also completely different is a mind twist.

Roni sang as we stumbled back to Bucky's truck. Once there, I said, "Roni, I really think you should call Grungie." It felt desperate and crucial that she do this. "It's like what Ollie said. You can't win if you don't buy a ticket. Tell her, Bucky."

"I'm not going to make her call if she doesn't want to."

"I am." I grabbed her phone, where I knew she'd programmed Grungie's number.

"No, Lulu," said Roni. Then, "Yes. Call."

Grungie answered with his deep, throaty voice. "Yeah?"

Roni grabbed the phone. "Hi, Grungie. This is Roni McAllister...."

While she talked, I watched the river between the trees. The river is the one part of Dale that moves. It's a sign of hope and something better in the great beyond. The moon shone on the river, all silvery shimmer, the water rushing on while the moonlight stayed in one place. The moon couldn't let go and roll along with the current.

Roni hung up and stared at me, mouth wide open. "He wants me to sing with them!"

All of a sudden, we'd traded places, me and Roni. She was the river and I was the moon.

Except I had a plan.

7

Roni giggled and hummed as Bucky drove us down the dark road. "We should've made you drink a long time ago, Lulu-bird. You are so fun with a buzz. Beau Queen wanted to talk to you until you had to latch on to Patrick James."

"Bad habit," I said.

"And who was that other guy?" asked Roni.

Bucky said, "Seth Malone. Mason's cousin."

"Really?" She turned around and looked at me. "Did you know that?"

I shook my head, unsure what I thought.

A few miles later I said, "You think Seth would have sold us moonshine?"

"I think he was offering something else," said Bucky. "He deals everything."

I processed that a minute, then said, "I bet people would have bought moonshine if someone was selling it."

"Only idiots."

"Well, there were a lot of idiots there," I said.

"True fact," said Bucky. "Most people are, at least some of the time."

I asked, "What's wrong with moonshine? Why is it illegal anyway? Is it only because it's strong?"

"It's not regulated. You don't know what you're getting," said Bucky. "Might be you're drinking radiator juice or rubbing alcohol."

"But people pay for it?"

"I thought we already established the idiot issue."

"If it's made right, then it's no more dangerous than regular liquor, right?" I persisted.

"What's your point, Lulu? Or are you obsessing for the hell of it?"

"I think we should make and sell moonshine," I said.

Bucky laughed. "And how exactly are we going to do that?"

"Drive by the junkyard," I said. "I want to show you something."

"Ooh, Lulu has a date with Dawg," Roni teased.

Twenty minutes later we were standing outside Sal's by the impound fence, peering in at the confiscated still.

One of the junkyard cats sat on top of the metal cylinder, his glowing eyes staring out at us. "Hi, kitty," said Roni.

"What are we looking at?" asked Bucky.

"That's a still. For making liquor." I took a deep breath, then said, "I think we should take it."

"You are so much drunker than I thought," said Bucky.

"I'm serious. You know I need money. But can either of you say you have plenty?" I went on, in a rush. "I read about it online. Did you know that some moonshiners make hundreds of thousands of dollars in one summer?"

Roni turned around. "Seriously?"

"Yep. And it's made from ordinary stuff. Corn, sugar, yeast. It's like cooking."

"Maybe if you know how to use that thing," said Bucky.

"There are directions on the Internet."

"It's illegal."

"It's not that bad," said Roni. "It's better than making meth."

I'm still surprised how quickly she jumped on my idea.

Maybe her subconscious had tapped into mine. One of our mind-meld moments.

"We could get married, Bucky," said Roni. "We wouldn't have to wait until you're done with college. We could buy a cute little house and..."

"We won't enjoy it much if we're both in jail," said Bucky. "Lulu, I know you think your future has blown all to pieces, but this isn't the answer. This isn't something done on a whim. There's planning to do. Research to be done. You need a business plan." It might sound like he was trying to talk me out of it, but actually, Bucky was luring himself in with the challenge.

"Let's take it," I said. "We don't have to actually do anything with it if we don't want to. We can think about it. Do our research."

"Where would we even put that thing?"

I turned to Roni. "What about your land?"

Roni's grandpa had given her five acres as a graduation present. The lot was on the outer edge of Dale, at the spot where the hills meet the mountain. She'd laughed at the deed, but I'd known it would matter to her someday. She nodded slowly. "That could work. That could actually work."

"Damn, Lulu. You've been thinking about this." I don't know whether Bucky was more impressed or shocked.

He was right, I had been thinking. And the more I'd thought about it, the more I'd decided a thriving moonshine market was a perfect example of what was wrong with Dale. The fact that people could get rich by doing something illegal and dangerous, making something that would most likely only cause more danger and illegal somethings, was the exact kind of negative cycle I had to avoid. I thought I was better than that. I was sure I'd break the cycle and escape.

Roni said, "I don't feel right stealing from Sal."

"We're only borrowing it. Sal won't lose anything. He gets paid for storing it. We'll store it for him off-site. We can always bring it back. Maybe we'll even pay him a cut."

Roni clapped her hands together. "What do you think, Bucky?"

"I think you're both drunk," said Bucky. "That's the problem."

"No," I said. "The problem is that you aren't."

Roni went back to his truck. She slipped her hand under the passenger seat and pulled out a silver flask. She waved it in his face. He stared at her a full minute before he grabbed it and took a swig. He handed it back. "You girls have some too. That way you won't feel it as much when you get shot."

It was way too easy.

Roni had the key on her key chain, since sometimes we open for Sal. Dawg lives on-site in his trailer near the back, but he doesn't run the office or handle the money. She unlocked the gate, then we swung it back, nice and slow to keep it from screeching.

The junkyard looked spooky in the dark. Hulks of cars loomed around us as we crept toward our destiny. A rat scurried across the path in front of me. I squeaked—or maybe it was more of a shriek—and then the cat leaped from the top of the still and pounced. The rat shrieked louder than I had. Roni and I grabbed hands and muffled our half scream–half giggle into each other's shoulders.

The still sat perched on the trailer it came in on. Like it was waiting for us to come along and give it a ride. See what I mean that it was all too easy? No way could we have moved it without the trailer. There was even a pathway for us to wheel it—Roni pulling and Bucky and I pushing from the back, my flip-flops slipping all the while in the soft dirt—right up to Bucky's truck.

Roni said, "It's too obvious something's missing."

Even though I hadn't logged it in the inventory, a hole in the yard would make Sal and the Muscles go looking for whatever wasn't there. We left Bucky messing around with hitching the trailer to his truck, cussing all the while, and crept back into the lot. My skin felt itchy, and my blood rushed around in every direction. "Give me another swig of that stuff."

Roni handed me the flask. "You're so crazy when you drink."

I guess I liked that.

Drunken determination and adrenaline can make up for actual strength. Roni and I pushed three metal barrels into the still's vacated place. If someone went looking for it specifically, it'd be pretty clear the still was missing, but at least the hole wouldn't be screaming for attention.

I'd just *clink*ed the gate shut when Dawg opened his trailer door. A flash of light shone across the yard as he pointed a flashlight our way. He held a shotgun too.

"Shit," said Roni, ducking.

I could hear Bucky panting a few feet to my left. I knew Dawg could see his truck, but I hoped the trailer was low enough to be hidden by the rows of cars in front of the fence.

It was too late for me to hide. I called out, "Hey, Dawg. It's me, Lulu." I moved a few steps to my right, hoping to keep his eyes in a different direction.

"Lulu?" The element of surprise must have been on my side.

"How ya doing tonight?" I stood close to the fence, waving. "I came by to feed the cats."

Roni giggled at my knees.

"They don't need feeding," said Dawg. "They got rats. That's the point of 'em."

"Really? You think that's enough?"

"Keep talking," Bucky murmured from the shadows. "I almost got this."

I called out, "Are you sure rats are good for cats?"

"That's what cats eat."

"Well, I think maybe they need some other food too. What if they eat all the rats? Or what if the rats are dirty or have the plague or, I wonder if..."

"Done," grunted Bucky.

"Well, all right, Dawg. If you're sure those kitties are okay, I'll be on my way. See ya soon." I turned in the opposite direction from the truck. I forced myself to stroll.

A few minutes later I heard Dawg's door shut, but I kept walking. The truck's engine started, and then, a minute later, Bucky and Roni stopped in the road beside me. I jumped in.

"Mother-of-a-heart-attack," said Roni. "I thought you were going to get shot."

"Nah," I said. "Dawg's my honey."

Roni shrieked, "I knew it. You want him, don't you? You're such a Jezebel. I saw you sticking out your boobs for him."

"Poor Jezebel is so misunderstood!" Roni and I melted

into hysterical laughter. It was an old joke going back to when Roni got kicked out of Sunday school in seventh grade. Methodists don't have a sense of humor.

"Stop talking about Lulu's boobs and tell me where the hell I'm going," said Bucky. "I can't exactly drive around with this thing sticking out my ass."

We sat silent. He was right. We'd already used up a fair amount of luck.

"In case you forgot, this is illegal paraphernalia," said Bucky. "Not to mention stolen."

"We're only borrowing it," I insisted.

We drove up the eastern fire road. Roni's grandpa Joe used to take us hiking there. We'd play in the stream and collect rhododendron vines to make fairy crowns.

Roni and I watched Bucky unhitch the trailer, and then we all helped push it off the dirt road and into the shadows. "We'll hide it better in the daylight," said Bucky. "But this is good enough for now."

"You sure you're okay with this?" I asked Roni. "What if your grandpa finds it?"

"He never comes up here anymore. But what if someone else steals it?"

That struck me as hilarious. Bucky laughed too.

"What? This could be Lulu's school money." Roni patted it, sending off muffled echoes.

"Or your house," I said.

"You think I could buy some new boots too?" asked Roni.

Then we dragged a bunch of branches over our hopes for the future.

The next morning we returned to the scene of the crime. At work in the junkyard trailer, I felt tired yet wired, and completely-all-over-jumpy nervous about stealing that still. Every time Sal came near, I caught my breath and avoided looking at Roni. I waited for him to start ranting and raving about the theft. Dawg is a man of few words, so unless he was asked directly, I didn't think he'd bring up the fact he'd seen me.

At one point I said to Roni, "If we can get through today with no one noticing it's missing, then we'll be good. They won't know for sure when it disappeared, and it'll be harder to pin on us."

Sal burst into the trailer as Roni said, "I'm crazy nervous."

"What are you nervous about, Veronica?" he boomed.

"I have my first practice with Lullaby Breaker this afternoon," said Roni. Her quick cover-up was the actual truth. Or maybe that's what she meant all along.

It was a fortunately loud and busy day. The crane swung and the crusher ran for hours. We had a series of deliveries, and the Muscles stayed busy arranging and rearranging the lot. Not one person mentioned the missing still.

The only moment of true weirdness was when Dawg appeared at the service window. I said, "Hey, Dawg," while ignoring Roni's kissing noises behind me.

He grunted and slipped a tattered kitty calendar beneath the bars. Then disappeared.

Roni laughed for at least ten minutes.

Bucky showed up on his way to work. "I see they haven't hauled you criminals off to jail yet."

"Nope," said Roni. "But Dawg gave Lulu a present. She's such a Jezebel."

"So misunderstood," I said automatically.

Bucky asked, "Did Dawg give you the still manual?"

"Do you think there is one?" I asked.

Bucky rolled his eyes. "No, Lulu. I do not think there is a manual for how to break the law."

Roni frowned. "Are you saying we can't do it?"

"Hell no," he said. "I hauled that thing outta here. I'm not dragging it back. It's not like you need to be some kind of genius to make moonshine. We'll figure this out."

I was the one who brought you up. "What do you think about Mason?"

Bucky raised one eyebrow. "I don't spend a lot of time thinking about Mason."

"Randy says Mason's family are some of the best shiners around."

"Shiners? Who are you?" Bucky laughed, and Roni joined him.

I persisted. "Will you ask him to help us?"

Bucky spit in the dirt. Then said, "Maybe. If it comes up. But we gotta watch our mouths about this thing."

Roni said, "We need a code word. So no one else knows what we're talking about."

I sighed. "It won't matter if we can't figure out how to run it."

"Like you'd ever give up that easy." She laughed, then pointed at me, her eyes wide and bright. "Jezebel."

I rolled my eyes. "All right, all right. I confess. Dawg is my boyfriend."

"You girls have ADD," said Bucky.

"No," said Roni. "Well, maybe. But I meant that's the code name. For the you-know-what."

So that's how Aunt Jezebel got her name. So misunderstood.

We didn't even understand how to put her together.

~

Daddy came home for a few days. The tension was thick between us. No chatty family dinners, no mention of daddy-daughter dates. He hadn't magically found my tuition money, so I had nothing to say. I wandered from room to room ignoring him while my mind wandered wildly around my skull. I'd had this great idea about making moonshine and stealing the still and then...I couldn't make the leap to imagine how that would actually happen.

It didn't help that Bucky was working all the time and Roni was caught up in singing with Lullaby Breaker. She might have started out unsure, but Grungie didn't have any doubts. She was in. They even wanted her to sing with them at the Concert on the Green for the Fourth of July. She had two weeks to learn fifteen songs. Of course she knew most of them already.

Then, because it was Sunday, Daddy and I piled in the car and drove to Saint Jude's. The stifling silence made me wish I'd learned how to drive a long time ago. Daddy and Mom should have found someone to teach me. Someone calm, who spoke clear and easy. Someone unflappable. Someone like you.

Sitting in the wooden pew, I tried to listen to Father Mick. But as sweat pooled behind my knees and trickled from my neck to the base of my spine, making my sundress damp and wrinkled, my thoughts meandered out to the woods, where I wanted to be starting a moonshine business. Guilt kept throwing me back in the pew with Daddy.

After Mass, he disappeared to visit over doughnuts in the Saint Mary's Room. I didn't feel up to making polite conversation where talk would inevitably turn to my future plans. Something I used to revel in sharing but was now not worth the air required to speak. So I slipped outside to the graveyard.

It was brutally hot and muggy out there. The kind of steamy day when it's hard to catch a breath. I wandered through the old stones, seeking cool under the dogwoods and maples. I traced the carvings of old tombstones, the coarse edges of the granite headstones comfortingly rough to my fingertips.

Then you were out there with me.

That was the first time I noticed the thin white scar lining your left eyebrow. I resisted the urge to reach out and touch it.

I suppose seeing you that day, that way, well, that's the kind of moment that backs up your talk of meant-to-be.

But I could also argue it was simply me taking advantage of an opportunity.

You said, "I just found out I'm not supposed to work on Sundays."

Standing there with only a few feet of hot, muggy air and a clump of no-see-ums buzzing between us, it was like all these different lobes in my brain were going haywire. I had this vague idea that you could help us with this crazy illegal moonshine plan, but I'd just gone to Mass and was supposed to be feeling pure and holy. Also, there was a distracting place somewhere inside that couldn't stop thinking about the last time I'd been with you, driving in the dark. I remembered the way you smelled inside Roni's car, and I was like an old hound dog wanting to sniff you again to check if my memory was right.

"Will you show me the room you're working on?" I asked.

I followed you down the stairs to the basement of the church. The air in the hallway was a little bit funky, being under the building and earth, surrounded by thick stone walls, but it was also at least twenty degrees cooler.

The room looked dim and shadowy until you flicked on the portable metal light, making the walls glow a soft yellow. A rectangular frame of honey-colored wood lay on the floor beside a pile of tools. The air smelled of new paint. I could smell you beside me too.

You took off your hat then and rubbed your awful hair. I immediately missed your hat. Even though I liked the line of freckles along the edge of your ear.

"These'll be bookcases. Father Mick wants three walls of shelves." You ran your fingers along the wood. "Then I'll make a desk. Maybe a table too."

"You can do that? Make furniture?"

I love your smile. Even though it's crooked. You said, "I'm good with my hands."

With every other boy, that might have been an innuendo. You and your honest way of talking didn't seem to mean a thing except for building furniture.

I turned to look at you, and, I don't know if it was you or me, or both of us, that had moved, but you were suddenly closer than I expected. I tried not to let on the way my heart rate jumped. I stepped back, holding in what I really wanted to ask. I blurted out, "Could you take me driving? If your truck gets fixed, I mean. If you have time. You don't have to. I just want to practice." I eyed the doorway, half-expecting Daddy to suddenly appear. "But you can't tell my father."

You grinned and rubbed your hair. I know now that

means you're nervous. "I could probably borrow my mama's car."

That afternoon we met in the Country Club parking lot. After Daddy dropped me off, we walked next to each other while you rolled your bike beside you. I said, "Are you ever going to come get a radiator so you don't have to ride everywhere?"

"That's not why I ride," you said. But you didn't explain anything more.

I waited outside while you got the keys, so I didn't see that your parents' house is bigger than the front implies. The slightly run-down porch and faded paint job don't line up with the polished hardwood floors and top-of-the-line appliances inside, or the theater room in the back of the house, where eight leather recliners face an enormous screen. It's a moon-mansion. Hidden bits of luxury. They don't want to call attention to any surplus income. Your place, where you live on your own, is bare of any surplus at all. You say the view out the window is all you need. But I didn't see your home until much later.

I will never get into a driver's seat and not think of you.

You coaxed me along the road, going in the opposite direction from the Country Club. Past the place where I drove into the field that first night we rode together. I wasn't sure where we were going until we got there, but I'd been to Prior's Point before.

Getting out of the car, I hoped you didn't see how I wiped my hands on my dress. I think I must have been gritting my teeth because my jaw hurt. I hadn't realized how nervous I was until we stopped.

What I'd always liked about that place were the perfectly flat boulders burrowed into the ground. They look like someone set up tables for a gathering of giants. But you were there for the view. You pulled me up on top of one of the largest boulders. A cool breeze ran over my bare arms. "We gotta go circular," you said. We shifted our feet, rotating inch by inch, taking in all 360 degrees.

Below us, I could see the Country Club nestled between the hills. The brilliant green of the golf course spread out to the brown, uneven fields beyond, those sprinkled with lazy cows. Then, little bits of the buildings in Dale, peeking in and out of the rolling hills. As we kept turning, I saw the blue of the river coming toward us in one place and saying good-bye in another. The highway cut into the landscape as we circled. The cars and semis drove on, not knowing we were there. We were far enough away to be invisible and forgotten.

You said, "Looks pretty, doesn't it?"

I said, "Yep. The farther away we are, the better Dale looks."

You hopped off the boulder and picked up a rock. "I feel like this place only looks forward. The past doesn't matter here." You ran forward a few steps, hurled the rock over the edge, then said, "I used to be pretty messed up, Lulu. Be glad you didn't know me then."

It's true I hadn't known you. But I'd known *of* you. I slid off the boulder and found my own rock to throw. Then said, "Our dents are what shape us."

"Is that from Sal?"

"Of course."

Several rocks later I said, "I went to Cindy's funeral." I had to let you know I knew the past you were trying to forget.

You tossed a rock up and down in your hand. Then asked, "How was it?"

That wasn't a question I'd expected. I thought a minute. Then said, "Sad. But nice. There were hundreds of daisies all over the church." I didn't tell you I'd helped spread them around.

"I missed it," you said, avoiding my eyes. "And I was too drunk to know it."

I threw another rock over the side. "The future is all that matters to me, Mason. I told you, I'm leaving this place behind."

"Yeah? You figured something out?"

"Maybe. Can you keep a secret?"

You were quiet a minute. Then said, "There's no one to tell."

That stopped me mid-throw.

I'd started that afternoon hoping I could convince you to help us make moonshine. I'd imagined smiling at you, tossing my hair, maybe even letting my hand linger on your arm. Then you'd say yes, of course, you'd love to help. But standing among the boulders with you in the wide open space filled with too-bright sunshine, throwing rocks and talking about your dents and looking to the future, I'd realized you were too real to fit in my imagination. I had to talk straight. "Bucky, Roni, and I, we have a still. For making moonshine. Code name Aunt Jezebel."

You listened, looking like you were thinking, so I went on. "She's a good one. I think. But Bucky's worried we're going to blow something up."

"It's possible," you said, leaning against the boulder. "There are all kinds of ways to go wrong."

I picked up the biggest rock I could find. Your eyes lit up at the size of it. I heaved it, but the rock barely made it to the edge. You nudged it down the hill.

"We sure could use some help," I said. "You interested?"

You shook your head. "I'd be more of a liability than a help."

I thought that was a funny thing to say. I'm not sure what I thought you meant. I wasn't thinking things through. I was making it up as I went along. "Take a look at that future," I said, sweeping my hand across the view. "It's full of opportunity. A new tomorrow."

You shook your head, looking somewhere between amused and skeptical.

I had to try a different angle. "If you were to help us out with Aunt Jezebel, I'm sure we could hook you up with any part you need for your truck."

Your almost-smile made me feel like I was on the right track, even if you were still shaking your head. You asked, "What part are you stuck on?"

That was easy. All of it.

I said, "It's in pieces. We're not sure how to put it together." I paused. "I'm thinking we need someone who's good with his hands."

We stood there a minute, a long, hard stare between us, neither of us willing to be the first to look away.

Finally you said, "I guess I could help put her together. But that's it. Just this one thing. I'll help with this one step. Then I'm done."

It wasn't me you couldn't resist. It was the pieces and parts all in a jumble.

"That would be amazing," I said.

"Amazing?" You looked straight at me, squinting, like you were trying to find something. Then you reached out and touched my lips with your finger. So light and quick that maybe I made it up.

I told myself the buoyant, fluttery feeling was relief. Anticipation. Knowing you were going to help made me feel like we had a chance to make this crazy moonshine thing actually work. I didn't know what the future looked like, but it felt within reach.

9

Once you were willing to help, Bucky suddenly had time to take us back to Roni's land, where we'd stashed the still.

All the overgrown green looked the same to me, but Bucky knew how to read it. He had you ride up front while Roni sat with me in the back so you could see where we were headed. And so he could show off his truck for you when he took us off-roading.

Bucky drove crazy up and down those hills once he left the twisty road. I never knew which way the truck would lurch as he drove around trees and boulders and over roots and rocks, and even logs. There was no taking in the view—it was simply a rush of stomach drops, spine jiggles, and full-out body vibrations. A sort of raucous and bruising massage. Even with my seat belt on, every bounceable bit of me bounced. We were thrown every which way and back again.

I have no idea what it looks like from the driver's seat, but off-roading is a mind blur. Adrenaline waves riding peaks and valleys.

Bucky slowed down once he turned on the fire road. Then, even though I didn't see the mound of fallen branches at first, he stopped where the still rested.

After we cleared it off, you peered inside the main tank and tapped the copper sides. "She's shiny clean."

"Is that bad?"

You walked around it again, looking and thinking. "I just don't know why anyone could confiscate it when there's no evidence of use."

"Will it work?" I asked.

"Sure looks like it." You grinned and rubbed your hands together like you couldn't wait to get started.

Bucky wasn't sure yet. "So, Mason, what kind of time commitment are we talking for this endeavor? If we get her set up, then what?"

You held a hand to the air, feeling something I couldn't see. "You'll need a couple of hours to mix and start. Then a few days of this kind of weather to ferment, but with daily stirs. A day or two to actually run the still and package your product. Give it a week to ten days for the first batch. The next'll go faster."

"Will the payoff make it worth it?" I asked.

"I'd guess you might take in two to three for the first run; later you could push it to four, maybe even five."

We were all silent a moment, thinking.

"I can make that during a weekend of overtime," said Bucky.

"Thousand," you said. "You know I meant thousand?"

We got a little giddy then. But even though that sounded like a lot of money, I knew this wasn't any kind of sure thing. When I told you exactly how much I needed to make in the next ten weeks, I needed to know this plan had a just-might-actually-make-it chance.

You didn't say anything at first, thinking over my number, adding things up in your head. Finally you squinted and said, "Selling is hard to predict. She's got a big tank, but it'll all come down to who's buying."

I said, "I think selling will be the easy part."

You shook your head. "Don't expect easy. That's the surest way to slip. You should go for big sales. With real buyers. The little-bit sales can cause the most trouble. You either gotta be completely anonymous or sell to someone who's done something worse."

I heard you. Honest. I'm not sure why it was hard to remember later.

First you taught us about location. It wasn't easy pushing and pulling that heavy trailer up and over roots and rocks, but you knew we needed to be near cold, running water, well hidden and nowhere near any of the property lines. We finally had to leave the trailer and lug the separate parts, along with Bucky's toolbox, up the last hundred feet or so. Aunt Jezebel looked bigger once we got her put together and settled in that spot you liked.

You were so sure. Absolutely in charge. Your confidence made it easy to follow along. Everything about being with you felt easy. We laughed and talked and worked side by side. I didn't feel like I had to put up any walls or put on any acts for you. I was leaving at the end of the summer and you were going to help me. You were haunted by ghosts of the past, but I had something to keep you busy here and now. For today. We simply had a job to do.

At one point, with all of us out of breath and filthy, you said, "Now we'll need a base."

"No, no, no. Now we need to recuperate," said Roni. "Boys, go get that cooler."

"Unbelievable." Bucky shook his head. But you both hiked back to the truck, leaving Roni and me waiting in the shade.

Roni stretched and said, "Mother-of-a-marvel, Lulubird, I'm glad you talked Mason into helping us with this crazy thing."

"Me too," I said. "But you know he's only helping out with this setup. He doesn't want to do anything more."

She frowned. "We need him."

"We can do it," I said, hoping I was right. "Once it's all set up."

"He seems like he loves it," said Roni. "Maybe he'll change his mind."

I knew you had reasons for quitting your family's business. Reasons that were wrapped up in that past you didn't want to look at. But I hadn't told Roni about driving with you, or being up at Prior's Point, or what you'd said about Cindy's funeral. I felt like those were your secrets. They weren't mine to share. Besides, I wasn't sure what we'd been doing throwing all those rocks off the mountain. Nothing had happened between us. Nothing usual, anyway. Nothing I could name or classify.

"He doesn't seem to mind you either, Lulu. Even after what you did to his helmet." She laughed. Then said, "Oh, Lulu, don't mess with Mason's head."

I eyed her, not liking her words. "What is that supposed to mean?"

"It means how you go out with someone and act like you really like him, and then all of a sudden you get bored and done and that's that. Mason's had a hard time. With what happened to Cindy and all."

I focused on wiping my sticky hands against my jeans.

"Don't be mad at me for telling the truth," said Roni. "At least I say what's on my mind. We both know if you weren't going crazy right now you'd never even look his way."

That's what everyone thinks, even now. That I had a passing touch of the crazies.

I said, "I don't plan to mess with his head, Roni. But it's not like everyone wants to settle down and get married, you know."

"That is exactly what I mean." She pointed at me. "You don't think Bucky and I should get married, but you won't tell me straight."

"All right," I said. "I don't think you should get married. I think Bucky should go to college and you should figure out something you want to do too."

She crossed her arms. "Well, it's not up to you."

"I know that, Roni." I shook my head in frustration. "But all of this"—I swept my hand out over Aunt

Jezebel—"this is about making money and me getting out of town. That's it. That's why I'm here. Mason gets it. When we were driving…"

"When you were what?" The hurt sat bare on Roni's face. I don't know what else I expected. We didn't keep secrets from each other. Not back then.

"It wasn't that big a deal," I said, my voice fading into the knowledge I was lying.

She stared at me a minute, then said, "I can't believe you went driving with Mason Malone and didn't think to mention it. You know I tell you everything that happens with me and Bucky."

"There's nothing to tell," I said. "Nothing happened. Not like you mean. Besides, I never asked you to tell me so much."

I hurt her feelings with that.

"Fine," said Roni. "I won't bore you with my life anymore."

So that's what happened with Roni and me when you and Bucky went back to the truck. That's why we were so quiet until you and Bucky decided to chop that poor watermelon with an ax. That smoothed things over. It was too hilarious watching you hack off the ugly giant red and green chunks. They sure were sweet and juicy.

Then we had more work to do. We cleared the low

growth and piled up rocks and logs to use as support and insulation. We took turns digging the pit for the fuel tank so we could help Aunt Jezebel keep a low profile.

Later, Roni and I collapsed in the shade and watched you and Bucky work. The way your sweat-damp shirt hugged your chest and back made Roni's words come to mind. You were definitely mess-tempting.

Finally you threw down the shovel and said, "We'll need to bring out a few more bricks and two-by-fours, but that's all we can do today."

That's when Roni reached out and snatched a bag slipping out of Bucky's back pocket. "What the hell is this?"

With anyone else I might have thought pot, but Bucky is straight-up conservative when it comes to drugs. She went on, indignant. "Don't you know how bad chew is for you? Do I need to show you those pictures of lip cancer again?"

"Oh, come on," Bucky whined. "We're sober as preacher mice. Considering what we're fixing to do up here, it's not time to be picky about a little bit of tobacco. Back me up, Mason."

You laughed. "I'm staying out of this one. I quit that stuff. I quit everything."

"Everything?" Bucky had mischief in his voice. "You quit all vices?"

"Had to."

"Sorry, Lulu," said Bucky. Roni slapped him for me, but I glared at him too.

So there was Bucky making obnoxious innuendos and Roni's words echoing in my ears, and all the while, the way you moved made it hard to stop watching. Knowing you were peeking at me like I was peeking at you made my insides warm and buttery. But Roni was right. I was leaving, and you didn't need to be messed with. I needed to put up a barricade.

I said, "Hey, Bucky, I want to chew some of that tobacco."

"Oh, no," said Bucky. "That's repulsive."

Roni said, "Uh-huh. But if you're going to be repulsive, then so can we."

You tried to warn me what to expect. "Your mouth is going to juice up with saliva. Whatever you do, don't swallow it."

"Is that what those nasty spit bottles are for?"

Bucky laughed. You handed us each a tiny leaf.

"I need more than that," I said. "I can't hardly chew something that small."

"Start with this," you insisted. "Don't worry about chewing. It mostly stays tucked in your lip."

Roni held her clump with her thumb and forefinger. She sniffed it, wrinkled her nose, and said, "You go first, Lulu."

I didn't expect the sting of it. I worked the little bit of leaf tentatively. You were right; my mouth worked overtime. My eyes watered, and I felt instantly dizzy. It never made it to the inside of my lip before I ran cussing and spit the nasty clump in the bushes.

All three of you laughed, most unsympathetically.

I held my queasy stomach. "It's not worth it, Roni."

She looked at Bucky. "Why would you do that to yourself?"

"I never did *that*," he said, still laughing. "Oh, Lulu, where have we gone wrong? You used to be such a good girl. Look at you now. Chewing tobacco and cussing like a cowboy. And that's not even talking about this moonshine plan you've cooked up."

I made a face while Roni said, "Lulu's just having her last bit of country fun before she runs." Then she zoned out for a second, humming to herself.

"Seriously, Mason," said Bucky, refusing to give it up. "You don't hardly know the Lulu we know."

I had no patience for talk like that. Like I had to be something that everyone could count on. I left the three of you sitting on the ground while I circled Aunt Jezebel again, marveling at how all the parts fit together. I asked, "What happens now?"

We all looked to you.

You took off your hat and rubbed your head. "You'll need to get the ingredients. Lots of sugar and cornmeal. Whole corn from the feed store. Be careful, though. Buying up lots of corn can be a red flag for shining." You paused, then said, "The yeast is key."

I said, "I can get yeast. My mother bakes a lot."

You shook your head. "That's not it. Each kind of yeast has its own special purpose. Its own reason for being here on Earth. The kind your mama has is for making bread. There's a different kind of yeast that makes moonshine."

"How do we make the right kind of yeast?"

"Well, God makes it." You laughed. Then looked up and waved toward the trees. "It's all around us. Yeast is a wild thing. Back in the old days, shiners left their pots open waiting for the yeast to move in and get to work."

"That's creepy," said Roni as we all looked up and around the sun-speckled tree branches.

"Nah," you said. "It's beautiful."

I needed actual directions and steps to follow. "Are you saying we should leave the still open?"

"Well. Not actually. I mean, yeast aren't the only critters that'll jump in."

"Ewwww," said Roni.

"Then where do we get it?" I asked.

Bucky said, "Mr. Cauley ordered yeast online for bio labs. But it's expensive, isn't it?"

"Probably," you said. "I've never paid for it."

I felt you tuning out, sitting back, separating yourself from our plan. You'd done what you'd said—and more—and now you were moving on.

It was maddening, knowing you had all the answers but were keeping them tight behind that crooked smile. But I also figured that if you—a high school dropout and ex-waster extraordinaire—knew what to do, I could figure it out too.

I didn't know enough to know what I didn't know.

10

*B*ucky, Roni, and I did the shopping together. Even though our list was simple, your warnings had us a little paranoid. It seemed inconceivable that someone would care about grocery shopping, but we needed a whole lot of ground corn. I guess some moonshiners use only sugar, but you'd said we wouldn't get "money nor respect" if that's what we did.

Waiting for them to pick me up that day, I used Mom's computer in the downstairs guest room she sometimes used as an office. She'd left open a web page where she'd ordered canning supplies for all the various concoctions she'd been making. There, in front of me, were the clear glass jars—ironically, called Mason jars—that some people expected when buying moonshine. It felt like an omen, but one I couldn't read.

I checked my e-mail and saw I'd received another reminder from USD Housing for the nonrefundable deposit. I had more than enough money saved, but *nonrefundable* screamed loud and clear. I was determined to make enough money to leave town, but at the same time, I had no faith that I would. The future, expensive and looming, stretched out in front of me.

Maybe that's why the online price of yeast shocked me. On top of the ridiculous cost for as much as you'd said we'd need, we'd have to pay for all kinds of special shipping and handling after signing a waiver—for which I'd have to lie about being eighteen—stating I understood the yeast might not survive the trip. It was too fragile and temperamental for any guarantee. And, besides, I didn't want to be connected online with something called spirits yeast.

We'd each already chipped in a fair amount of money on this crazy-eyed wild-goose chase of a summertime science experiment. Even though we'd started with a "borrowed" still that had all the major parts, and Bucky could get propane through his father's gas station, we had a lot of expenses going in without knowing if we'd ever get a penny back. We needed little parts like hosing and funnels, and I don't know what else, but you knew. You knew it all. I wasn't going to waste my money on yeast until I learned more from you.

As we headed off to go shopping, I leaned forward from the backseat. "What happened to you?" I asked Bucky, pointing at the big scratch across his cheek.

"That happened on the third, no maybe it was the fourth, climb up that damn hill."

I guess installing the propane tank was a bigger production than Bucky had planned on. But then Roni gave me the best news: "Mason says Aunt Jezebel is finally ready."

A spark lit up inside me.

Knowing Sal always knew where to get the best deals, I'd asked him about buying sugar in bulk. He'd told me how to find Betty's Candy Factory. He even threw in a twenty for me to pick up some fudge and barked, "Make sure you get caramel for your mother."

Did your family buy their sugar from ancient Betty, who carries years of sweets on her bones? I have a hard time imagining any of them strolling through the aisles of fondant and syrups. Can't see how they'd blend in with the women gossiping and sharing recipes. They probably have their own suppliers. I didn't know enough then to wonder about logistics like that.

Roni picked up a bag of cornmeal. "How many of these do we need?"

"More than we're buying here," said Bucky. "You heard Mason. This stuff gets noticed."

"What if we split up and each buy some?" I suggested.

Bucky shook his head. "They already know we're together." Nerves were getting to him. All those aisles of wedding cake paraphernalia probably didn't help either.

So, even though we bought a cartload of sugar—along with two kinds of fudge—we only bought one bag of cornmeal from Betty. Then we spent the rest of the afternoon shopping in at least three Virginia counties.

What started in the spirit of paranoia morphed into plain old silliness. Each store we visited we changed up our act. One store saw the real Bucky, wearing his cowboy hat and with his blond girlfriend hanging on his arm. Another had his curly-haired brunette sister yelling at him. On a dare, two lesbian lovers bought corn at a crowded feed store while holding hands. "They are definitely going to remember us," said Roni once we got back in the truck, laughing.

"Yeah," said Bucky. "But they won't remember what

you bought. That wasn't what they were thinking about; I guarantee it."

Visiting each little town started to feel like a touch of déjà vu. The people in line at the markets looked the same in Narrows as they did in Pulaski. I could have sworn the guy pumping gas in Elliston was the same one working the 7-Eleven in Floyd.

I was so sure of myself that day. I thought I was better than the woman counting her pennies out of a coffee can to pay for her eggs and milk. I doubted the sanity of the man who cornered me talking about his old coon dog who could bark words like *hello* and *more*. When Roni stopped to coo over a couple of drooly kids sucking on sugar sticks, I sat back and felt sorry for their mother, who didn't look much older than us. I was happy to be taking action. Grabbing my future with both hands. Now I realize that's what they were doing too.

We were caught up in being outrageous, so at the last place we went, somewhere near Galax, close to the North Carolina state line, Bucky insisted on bringing both of us inside. I'm not entirely sure what fantasy he was operating off of when he yelled, "Come on, wives, we need to bring food home for the rest of the girls."

"Maybe I'll get some rat poison too," said Roni. "So I can get rid of all them other girls."

Standing in the checkout line, Bucky puffed out his chest and grinned stupidly. He said to the cashier, "My women are making corn bread for the chili cook-off at church."

She looked bored and didn't answer, but all of a sudden the bagger broke into an enormous grin. He said to Roni, "I know you! You're the new singer for Lullaby Breaker."

Roni smiled at him. "Well, yeah. I sure am."

Her adoring, and adorable, fan said, "I can't wait to see you sing on the Fourth. Me and my buddies, we're all driving up for the day."

"Well, thank you so much." Roni leaned forward to read his name tag. "Larry. I'll look for you there. Only another week or so."

He about knocked himself out trying to help us take our purchase out to the truck. He looked more than a little disappointed when Bucky said, "I got it."

Then, while Bucky loaded it in with the other bags, Larry said, "Can you sign my shirt?" He handed Roni a marker from his pocket and bent over so she could sign his shoulder blade.

Back in the truck, Roni said, "Guess I'm going to have to work on my autographs."

Bucky growled, "Now we're documented being here getting this stuff. Don't you ever think?"

"He didn't care what we bought. He only cared about seeing me. You're just being jealous."

I knew she was right. Bucky wasn't really worried. None of us were. The three of us hadn't ever been in real trouble. We didn't understand what the consequences of being caught—or even under suspicion—really meant. Certainly not enough to be truly wary.

Driving home I said, "All we need is the yeast."

"Let's ask Mason," said Bucky. "Meaning Lulu should."

"Why me? You work with him."

"I'm lacking your certain tools of persuasion."

Roni said, "I don't understand why he wouldn't want to do this with us. Besides Lulu's *tools*, it's a chance to make money."

I said, "I think it's too hard for him. He's got bad memories."

Bucky groaned. "Not everything is all about the touchy-feely hoo-ha, Lulu. It's probably just not worth his hassle. This might not even work."

"Yes it will," I said. "It has to. Otherwise we wasted a ton of money today."

The sun flickered through the tree branches like a strobe light, but that wasn't the reason I suddenly felt carsick.

"You know that might be true," said Bucky. "This whole thing is nothing but a maybe."

I couldn't look at it like that. Maybe was too full of room for backing out and changing minds. Maybe is always one step closer to no. Maybe wasn't going to get me out of Dale.

When I got home, I felt sweaty and sticky, as if there was a light layer of sugar film coating my skin. I also felt determined. I went straight to Mom's computer. I logged in and paid my housing deposit. A nonrefundable statement of my intent to get to the University of San Diego somehow, no matter what I had to do.

Then I used Mom's credit card to order Mason jars.

We were so close to getting started. Aunt Jezebel was ready and waiting in the woods. We'd filled rubber storage boxes with all the bags of sugar and corn. The Mason jars had been delivered and hidden in my garage.

But we still needed yeast. Something you knew how to get. So when Roni invited me to one of her band practices, of course I went.

I wanted to see her sing. I was curious about this thing that made her grin and look like she was ready to take off spinning on a moment's notice. It was the way she'd looked when she and Bucky first got together. Since she'd mentioned that you'd been to at least one practice before, I figured you might be there again. With answers.

But Aunt Jezebel wasn't the reason I took so long on my hair and makeup. Moonshine wasn't why I carefully chose my top, shorts, and even my earrings.

Bucky gave me a ride to Grungie's house, the radio blaring that metal crap he loves but Roni can't stand. She'd given us directions and told us to bring a blanket to sit on, but neither of us was ready for the crowd we found. We had to park two blocks over. As we walked along the cracked and bumpy sidewalk, I heard the thump of the bass and drums. Then the guitars and a harmonica. It hit me as we turned the corner. "That's Roni singing!"

As we wove through and around the crowd of chairs and blankets spread across the driveway and dried-up lawn, I felt distinctly out of place. Most people looked older, closer to Paul's age. Yours too, I mean. A couple of coolers were set up and stocked in the back of the yard, and sweet, pungent pot smoke wafted from behind the garage.

Bucky and I squeezed our blanket into a spot in the shade of an elm tree, but then we stood along the driveway so we could see. The band sounded amazing to me, but every now and then Grungie would yell, "Stopstopstop," or, "Not again, you idiots," and they'd all pause to talk and tweak their instruments. Roni did a lot of nodding and pacing. She waved at us between songs, but mostly she stayed wrapped up in the music.

Listening to Grungie's directions was like listening to someone with a thick accent. Not because of the way he talked—it was *what* he said. Musicians have their own language. I only understood about a third of it. Seemed to me like Roni was the star. They were putting extra emphasis on her songs so she'd be ready for the concert on the Fourth, but even in a dirty garage full of old tools, she shone.

I don't know notes or octaves or the difference between sharp and flat, but I know music makes everything *more*. If you're happy, music might make you ecstatic. Simple sad turns into heartbroken. And longing...well, that's what I was feeling that day. Impatient, uncertain, deep-down yearning. Every note and beat made the ache climb a little closer to the surface. It rubbed the wanting into something a little more raw. Longing is halfway to desperation and frustration even without Roni's melancholy take on Lullaby Breaker's "Far from Here."

Then I caught sight of you through the crowd. Even before I saw your face, I recognized the line of your shoulders and the way your T-shirt fit against your arms. You were wearing a red ball cap, and, below the bill, your profile shone sharp and clear to me.

I eyed you from behind my sunglasses. The people surrounding you were, well, rough. Pierced. Ripped-off sleeves. Missing teeth. One guy even had an eye patch. Half the guys wore wife-beater tanks, and, for the women, there were tight camisoles on bodies that spandex couldn't forgive. Some of your friends looked older than my parents, but they were rocking out in their tattooed glory. When you took off your hat...I know it's superficial, but mixed in with that crowd, you looked every bit the redneck shiner Randy said you were.

And yet, when our eyes met across the yard, I felt my blood roar around inside me with the pop of endorphins you sparked. All of a sudden, with a sound track playing in the background, you and the idea of making moonshine mixed together to hit me with an urgent sort of anticipation. For something unknown and beyond my control.

You nodded at me. I started to wave, but then you were hugging some girl with long, straight hair. The rose tattoo above the waistband of her jeans peeked at me. I looked away, feeling heat in my cheeks.

She was a reminder of how little we had in common. Nothing had happened between us. I hardly knew you.

When Buttercup and Jimmy appeared from behind Grungie's house, it was obvious from their red eyes and loose movements they'd been there awhile. Buttercup gave me a big hug, and Jimmy said to Bucky, "Roni looks freaking hot up there. Freaking hot."

Seth and Peanut wandered by too. They knew Jimmy, of course, and Buttercup too. As the guys talked with each other, Buttercup turned to me and said, "Lulu, I could have sworn I saw you driving with Mason Malone last Sunday."

I felt more than saw Seth stop talking, start listening. I couldn't help but look for you across the crowd. You were still talking to that girl.

Buttercup went on, "In a silver sedan, out past the club. Wasn't that you?"

"Maybe yes, maybe no," I said. And turned back toward the band.

She laughed. "Must have been a helluva drive if you can't remember if you were there."

I laughed too, but that laughter was for you. So you'd know what a good time I was having.

"My aunt has a silver Impala," Seth said, looking at me more closely. "You know Mason, huh?"

I shrugged. But he must have caught me looking your way. "Her name is Jessie."

"Who?"

"That girl. With my dumb-ass cousin." He took a long sip of his drink. "He always leaves with her." Then he raised his eyebrows and said, "Want me to bring him over here?"

All I said was "What?" but he threw his arm around me, grinning all the while.

It worked. By the time I'd slipped out from under his arm, you'd moved off your spot on the wall and headed toward us. With Jessie following you. The way her hips moved as she walked made me feel young and naive.

"Hey, Cuz," Seth greeted you, still standing too close to me. "Nice day for a ride."

You shook your head, unsmiling. Jessie's eyes about scraped me as she looked me up and down. I tossed my hair in some kind of primal reaction.

"How ya doing, Jessie?" As Seth leaned in for a hug, I met your eyes behind their backs, but I couldn't read the look on your face.

Then Bucky gave you a sloppy slap on the back, sloshing his drink on my feet. As he and Buttercup talked to Jessie, Seth, and Peanut about the band and whatnot, there was a minute when you and I were the only ones not talking. I turned to you and blurted out, "Thanks for getting Aunt Jezebel ready." Problem was, the band stopped playing right then and my voice rang out too loud.

You frowned, and everyone else looked at me funny.

Then Buttercup laughed and said, "What did you say? Aunt who?"

Bucky laughed and said, "Lulu better take it easy on the funny juice."

I wanted to evaporate on the spot. I felt stupid. Young and awkward, loud and clueless. Nothing like sexy, skinny Jessie.

"I say give her more." Laughing, Seth leaned into me, made me stumble.

As I tried to regain my balance, you said, "Be careful with this one, Seth. She's jailbait."

Then, before I got over my shock, you left with Jessie. Just the way Seth said you would.

Jailbait?

Maybe I could have understood if you'd warned Seth about me puking. But calling me jailbait? You obviously thought I was young and immature. Apparently you also thought I was loose and easy. Like I'd do something with Seth. I was insulted to my very core. No one thought of me like that. I'd always been the good girl. The ice princess.

Seth winked at me and said, "Told you. I know my cousin." Then he and Peanut moved on. I let Buttercup pour me an icy-cold drink with a burn, which was unfortunately delicious in the hot sun.

At some point an unsteady Bucky plopped down beside me. I said, "Mason called me jailbait."

He laughed.

"It's not funny. I'm mad. I'm not talking to him."

"Good. 'Cause he's not here. Have another drink."

After the band put away their instruments and most of the fans left, Roni finally joined us where we sat, sloshed and stupid, in the grass. "Y'all should come meet everyone."

"There's my girl," Bucky yelled. "Star of the show."

Roni squinted at him. "Are you drunk?"

I said, "Mason left with a skank, Roni. She had a tattoo on her wazoo." I was sure you were wrapping your whole self in her long hair and kissing all her hidden tattoos.

"You're sloppy too?" She glared at both of us. Then said, "Stay here and be quiet while I get my stuff." Roni's worlds had collided.

"What does she mean *stay*? Doesn't she know I'm not no dog?" Bucky yelled after her, "I'm not no dog!"

"Shhh," I said, and giggled.

As we stumbled to Bucky's truck, Roni scolded us. "I can't believe you two. Why'd you have to get so trashed? Lulu, you're supposed to be the responsible one."

"You said I'm more fun when I drink."

"Bucky, were you keeping an eye on Lulu? You know how she gets."

"What does that mean?" I complained.

"Babysitting is women's work," said Bucky. "I am definitely not a woman. I'm not a dog and I'm not a woman." It's good that Bucky rarely drinks.

At his truck he made a halfhearted fuss about driving, but it didn't last.

"Sorry if we embarrassed you," I said from the back.

"It's all right. Everyone else drinks there too. I just feel like I have to be on my best behavior. I'm afraid they'll kick me out."

"But you're better than any of them."

"Damn straight," Bucky agreed. "You don't need them."

"Yes, I do, Bucky. I do need them." Roni reached out and brushed hair from his eyes. She looked back at me and said, "For the first time ever, I have something I'm good at."

Roni was my best part of living in Dale, the only thing that had made high school bearable. She was my best everything, most all my life. I see now that I wasn't the best for her. She always compared herself to me, and the things I thought she should be better at. That wasn't good for her soul. At least heartache inspires songs.

After I got out of the truck at my house, she handed me a piece of gum through the window. "Chew this and get straight to bed. I don't want you getting grounded."

I tiptoed inside, chomping on Roni's gum. I heard

voices, an unfamiliar giggle. At first I thought Paul had come home for a surprise visit and brought a girl with him. But then I realized it was Mom giggling. I peeked in the living room. I stood in the doorway absorbing the scene. Mom had her feet curled beneath her on the couch; two wineglasses sat on the coffee table between her and Sal, who sat across the room in Daddy's recliner.

"Hey there, Lulu, darling."

"Hey," I said, sticking to my spot.

"Hello, Luisa," said my junkyard boss with no shoes on. His hairy bare feet looked obscene and embarrassing.

My buzz made me bold as I said, "When does Daddy get back in town?"

Mom said smoothly to Sal, "Lulu is still a daddy's girl."

"Well, she sure looks more like him than you," said Sal.

It's true, of course. Mom is so tiny she makes my average look Amazon. Where she's thin, I curve. Her short blond hair is fine and the straightest kind of hair there is, while my dark brown curls go everywhere. But when six-year-old me had a crisis of identity and wanted to look like her, I remember Mom saying she'd ordered me this way to show how much she loved Daddy. She said I've got my daddy marked all over me. But she didn't say that to Sal.

12

*T*he next day, sober but fighting a hangover, I still couldn't believe you'd called me jailbait. You had some nerve, especially since you apparently had a girlfriend. Or at least, someone who you always left with. On top of what had happened with you, whatever I'd walked in on with Mom and Sal sure made me restless too.

I didn't want to be mad. I wanted to get over the burning irritation I couldn't seem to shake. It didn't matter that you had a girlfriend. One who was pretty but edgy and lean, nothing like me. It made things simpler. Cut down on things to wonder about.

The only thing that mattered was that I start working

with Aunt Jezebel. I still needed you to tell me where I could get yeast.

I went for a walk. I kept off Main Street, making my way along the edge of town, following the back roads lined with the alternating patchwork of fences made of wood and stone and barbed wire. It was hot enough that dogs stayed in the shade rather than bothering with me as I marched by, the flapping of my flip-flops adding rhythm to the cicadas' screechy song. I figured the sweat streaming along my sides and running down my neck was a purification process, purging my body of alcohol.

I decided to purge my soul as well. I arrived at Saint Jude's, sweaty and dusty. I headed straight for the restroom, where I cleaned up with paper towels. I know Father Mick isn't supposed to be concerned with worldly details, but that confessional is a cozy space. Personal hygiene was the least I could do.

I stepped into the hallway and collided, hard, with you. I stepped back, blinking and readjusting my space. It wasn't fair how impossibly happy you looked to see me, because—even then, breathing in the warm and spicy smell of your skin with the feel of your arm under my hand for balance, and no matter what my head said I logically had the right to feel—the fact was, I was mad at you.

"I was just thinking about you, Lulu."

"Oh yeah?" I narrowed my eyes. "Well, stop."

"Stop what?" You cocked your head at me. "Stop thinking?"

"I know what you think of me," I said, glaring. "And I don't like it." I spun around and charged outside.

You followed me out to the graveyard. "Are you mad at me?"

"Of course I'm mad," I said, my voice more shrill than I liked. "You called me a slut."

You blinked. Stepped backward. Rubbed your ugly hair. Then finally said, "I did?" You were someone who'd done too many things he didn't remember.

"You called me jailbait."

"You're saying that's the same as calling you a..." You shook your head. "Why would you think that's what I meant?"

"You thought I was actually going to go somewhere and do something with Seth? You had to warn him about me? Really? That's how you see me?"

You stared at me. It was hard to breathe in the heat after having had a brief respite in the dim, cool church. The air was thick and muggy, and I was choking on my frustration.

"Lulu, you don't have a clue how I see you."

You stopped me with that.

Father Mick opened the door then and said, "Luisa,

did you need me?" As I crossed the stone path back to the church, he called to you, "Thanks for the good work today, Mason."

I'm not going to tell you what I said to Father Mick in reconciliation that day. I'm not sure I know. There was a lot of incoherent babbling about Mom and Sal and going to school and stealing versus borrowing and crossing lines. Father Mick talked about forgiveness and patience. Trust. At one point he said, "If you need help, remember to ask," which made me impatient all over again. But he wouldn't let me leave until I calmed down. I was in there long enough you had plenty of time to run away, but you didn't.

"I'm sorry," you said the second I stepped outside.

"Me too." I handed you one of the mints Father Mick had given me on my way out the door. We sat on the stone bench and sucked our candies together.

"I didn't mean what you thought, Lulu. I was ragging on Seth. Not you. Of course not you. He knew it." The muscles along your jaw pulsed. "I know you want to make money, but don't get mixed up with him."

"I'm not," I said. I hadn't asked Seth to get your attention by hanging on me, but I didn't want to tell you that was what he'd been doing either. You leaving with Jessie made it clear that had been an embarrassing waste of time.

You rubbed your hair, looking down at the ground.

"Seth is a slightly better version of who I used to be." Then you looked me in the eye when you finished what you had to say. "I'm an alcoholic."

I couldn't wrap my head around your words. Alcoholics are old. Smelly and messy. They aren't cute boys with irresistible, crooked smiles.

"I'm in recovery. I've been sober for two years, four months, thirteen days." You went on. "I used to be trashed all the time. But if I have a drink—even one little drink—I can't stop. If I can't stop, I'll die. It's pretty simple. Most of the time, I remember that. But some places, some people, are triggers, setting me off. Make me act like the jerk I used to be."

I wondered about Jessie, who you'd left with. If she was part of who you used to be, or who you were now. Either way, I had some ideas as to how she might have helped distract you. Since I didn't have the right to ask, I said, "I wasn't drinking." Then added, "Well, I did later. But not with Seth. I never used to drink."

"I did. A lot." You gave me half a smile. "I'm not telling you not to drink, Lulu. I just wanted you to know. Since we keep running into each other."

You made it sound like pure coincidence. Like I hadn't worked to find you at Lullaby Breaker's practice. Like I hadn't had any ulterior motives that day I asked you to take me driving. Like you had no idea how impatient I was to start making moonshine.

But then you said, "How's Aunt Jezebel?"

I shrugged rather than answer.

"Got everything you need?"

You looked so eager, like you actually wanted to know.

"We can't find yeast," I said. "It's expensive and hard to order. Do you know somewhere around here?"

You were quick to offer. "I can get you yeast."

You probably felt guilty. Wanting to atone for your words. Maybe I should have said no. I could have saved you a lot of heartache if I'd turned and walked away. Forgotten my wild idea. But of course I said yes. At least I added "please."

You say it was meant to be that we ran into each other that day, and that you'd borrowed Bucky's truck to bring wood to Saint Jude's. It was all so we could make that trip to see Jake.

You started the engine, then sat, thinking. "I'm going to need some liquor."

"I thought you don't drink," I said.

"Jake does," you said, as if that meant anything.

I reached under my seat, pulled out the flask I remembered from the night we took Aunt Jezebel. I opened it, and the smell made my eyes water. Yours too.

Easy makes a good sell for meant-to-be.

The river runs rough and rugged north of the Queens' Tube Trailer Spot. All along the riverbank, peeking out from behind trees and bushes, little shacks and lean-tos pop up like mushrooms. Made of mismatched boards and tin and old tires, most are built to last through deer season, or to serve as summertime fishing spots. Some, like the shack you parked beside, seem to have always been there, ever since the river started flowing. They're part of the mud and rocks along the shore.

I climbed out after you, looking at the precarious tilt of the shack. The propane tank peeking out from behind looked like it had taken a wrong turn—it seemed far too new and too big to be there. "Ready?" you asked.

I don't think anything could have made me ready for Jake.

You knocked on the lopsided door and called, "Jake? It's Mason."

I heard a shuffling noise from within, and then the door creaked open. A figure—a man, I mean, but it was hard to be certain at first—stood wobbling in the doorway. His face was a smear of scars. Different shades of skin creased and overlapped in a dizzying crisscross of old hurts.

When he said, "What are you doing here?" I saw his mouth had no teeth. No bottom lip either. Then his blood-shot eyes focused on me. He said, "Hello, Beauty."

"This is Lulu, Jake. Can we come in?"

I followed you into that small, dark room, keeping my breaths shallow, trying to avoid the murky something in the air. Ahead of us, Jake dragged his useless left leg over the wooden pallet floor. I eyed the ceiling, where the metal sheet fastened with wire had newspaper and straw stuffed into the corners and gaps.

Sunlight streamed in through the slatted walls and the one window that overlooked the river. I stood there, looking out, with my arms crossed in front of me, keeping my hands close and clean. Behind me Jake said, "Only the river knows where it wanders," making me think of Sal's wisdoms.

"Have you been eating, Jake?" You peered around the stacks and piles of things.

He said, "Soup?" His overstuffed chair creaked as he set himself into it.

You picked up an open can from the floor by his chair. "Is this it?" You sniffed it and made a face. "Ugh. That's not soup, Jake." You opened the front door and dumped whatever it was in the dirt. Then you searched among the piles. "Let me make you something."

"I'm not hungry," he said. "I'm thirsty."

"You gotta eat something." You peeked in his one cabinet. "Peanut butter on crackers sound good?"

"Give it to Beauty."

"All right. I'll make sure Lulu eats some too."

You placed a couple of crackers smeared with peanut butter on a plate next to him. True to your word, you handed me a cracker too, and kept one for yourself. "C'mon, Jake, let's eat."

I forced myself to take a bite even though my stomach was turning flips. You met my eyes over the crackers, raised your eyebrows, and smiled.

He said, "I told you. I'm thirsty."

You sighed. Then handed him Bucky's flask. He pressed it close to his chest with one shaking hand as the other unscrewed the top. I could smell the alcohol, even over all the mildew and earthy dirt smells, some of which had to be Jake himself.

He lifted it and sipped. Closed his eyes and breathed deeply.

You reached out and took the flask back. He clawed at it, made a guttural retching noise. "Goddamnit, boy, hand that over."

"I will." Knowing Jake was fresh out of patience you hurried on. "But first I need a bit of the baby."

I felt queasy by then. It was the smell of that place, but also the uncertainty. Jake and his shack were so unlike anything I'd ever seen, I wouldn't have been the least bit surprised if you'd gone and lopped off some bit of a real live baby.

126

He growled, "I thought you didn't have use for Baby no more. Thought you turned your back on her."

"I know, Jake. But I'll take care of her."

"You gonna feed her right?" Jake wheezed around each word.

"Yep. I'm even gonna bring her out to the woods."

"That'd be nice. Real nice." He rubbed his scarred hands together. "She likes the woods."

"I sure know it."

He turned to me. "Beauty, will you love Baby too?"

I said yes, hoping I had the right answer. I must have because Jake got up and shuffled across the room. I looked to you, but you were watching him. I couldn't see what was hidden behind the dingy bit of fabric he'd pulled aside, so I took a few steps to the right. Jake turned around—faster than I would have guessed he could—and said, "You stay right there. We don't like a crowd."

I froze in place.

"It's okay, Jake. Lulu's just excited."

Excited was not how I would have described my panicky, nauseated feeling, but I wasn't about to argue. I stood silent and still.

Jake bent over and pulled open a door. I heard a seal released, realized there was a small refrigerator hidden within the jumble of old boxes and furniture. I guess that's what the propane tank was for. He set an enormous jar on the table beside him, but the way he stood with his back to me made it impossible to see what he was doing. The floor trembled as I heard sounds of scraping and tapping. When he'd finished, having pulled the old sheet back over his work space, he shuffled to us, cradling a brown glass jug in both hands.

You took it from him, then handed him the flask of liquor.

We sat there a few more minutes, but it was clear we'd faded away from Jake. He only had eyes for the drink.

As we got up to leave, you said, "I'll be back sometime soon, Jake. I'll let you know how she does. Try to eat some crackers."

As you closed the door I heard Jake say, "Welcome home." I don't know if he was talking to the liquor or you.

Outside, I breathed, deep and desperate for fresh air. You led me to the water, where you sat on the bottom of a turned-over metal rowboat, still cradling the jug Jake had given you. I stood at the water's edge, watching the river run. The sun hid behind the clouds, leaving the day hazy and subdued.

I asked, "Who is he?"

"Friend of the family. Taught me to fish. He used to be the best shiner in three states. Now I'm not sure he can eat anymore. Alcohol does that eventually."

"Why'd you give him liquor? Doesn't that make it worse?"

You shook your head. "He's too far gone. His body needs it. If he suddenly up and quit, he'd die. It's gonna kill him either way."

"What happened to his face?"

"He fell into a barrel of hot mash during a fight. Everyone was drunk, Jake most of all. But being drunk is also what helped him survive. He didn't hardly feel his skin peel off."

"That's...awful." Words were too inadequate.

We were both quiet a minute. Now that I'd met Jake, you being an alcoholic meant something more than I'd first thought. But it was him too. The idea that he might have once upon a time been like you. He'd been young and strong. He'd had lips. Maybe someone had kissed them.

"What's in that jug, Mason? What is *Baby*?"

"This is the yeast, Lulu. Baby is the key. This is where the moonshine starts."

That wasn't the yeast I knew. "I thought yeast was dry and grainy."

"Not when it's ready to work." Your eyes shone bright. "You're talking sleepy yeast. Baby is awake and hungry. But she's not just any yeast. This here is the same batch of yeast my daddy and his daddy and his before him used in every batch my family ever brewed."

Yeast is a live thing. It has DNA. Each strain has its

129

own personality. It eats and breathes and grows. Take some out and more grows back. Baby, the Malone family yeast, had been Jake's roommate for years. Whenever a Malone needed a fresh start, they'd come see Jake and take a bit of the baby.

"I guess I better help you get the mash started," you said. "You heard Jake. I gotta take care of Baby."

It was like you truly didn't see Jake and that shack—and Baby—like I did. You didn't see the dark and dingy shadows that made me hesitate.

"Why'd you quit your family's business, Mason?"

You kicked at the sandy mud. "They quit me. They don't trust me ever since I got sober. My family is thick with functioning alcoholics. Me, I couldn't function. I'm the weak link."

I didn't understand the meaning of your words. Not really. But I recognized the feelings I heard in your voice. I got that your family didn't fit your skin. Like me with mine.

I kicked off my flip-flops and stepped into the water. The cold of it made me gasp. Turned my toes numb in seconds. You stepped in beside me. We stood there in the shallows, letting the river rush by.

I was in way over my head. And you were getting pulled under.

13

We left early in the morning the day we mixed the mash, all four of us piled into Bucky's truck. Baby was on the backseat with us while the bags of sugar and cornmeal sat packed inside plastic boxes stowed in the bed of the truck. Your bike was back there too, since you don't like to feel like you might get stranded somewhere. Having an escape plan helps you feel like staying sober is within your control. I didn't have to be an alcoholic to understand that.

Bucky said, "I'm so glad to be getting this crap out of my truck. Feels like I've been driving the Betty Crocker-mobile." He drove too fast heading into the hills; we all felt the same kind of eager. Even you.

I snuck peeks at you as we rode along with the music blaring. Little glimpses, seeing you in parts. The freckles lining the edge of your ear. The shape of your nose in profile. The little white scar by your eyebrow. Your hands, rough and callused, tapping along with the music. Your mouth. Which broke into a lazy, crooked smile every time your eyes caught mine.

When Roni had asked Bucky, he didn't seem to know much about Jessie. He didn't think she was your girlfriend, at least not in any formal sense of the word. Even if she wasn't an ordinary, regular, whatever to you, I knew better than to mess where she'd laid a claim. I'd never gotten in a full-out fistfight, not like the one Buttercup had in the cafeteria freshman year, but I'd been threatened. There's a particular blond cheerleader I wouldn't want to meet in a dark alley, even now. I knew the jealousy of Dale girls didn't listen to reasonable explanations about favors and secret projects in the woods.

So, sitting in the back with you, I was careful not to touch. But I looked.

Bucky parked on the opposite end of Roni's land, so we hiked through the woods hauling everything. Roni and I carried a plastic box between us, while you and Bucky each slung one up on your shoulder. Bucky is taller and looks stronger than you in some ways, but you had him beat with grace. You loped through the woods like you belonged there.

I know the woods are beautiful in the thick of summer, lush and bursting with fresh growth. I'm sure the sky was a brilliant blue. But I didn't notice any of that. I only had my eye on getting to Aunt Jezebel, my copper hope.

It couldn't have been easy, all that work you and Bucky had done to finish the setup. The propane tank sat inside its ditch, and the pipes leading out were nestled beneath the tubs and barrels.

"This looks like a mad-scientist laboratory." I peered in, checking it out. "We can be like Frankenstein."

You laughed, and Bucky said, "Figures you'd want to make yourself a man, Lulu. One special-ordered and perfect. To do whatever you say."

"Ooh, make me one of those too, Lulu-bird," said Roni. "Mine's too mouthy."

Bucky turned to you. "How do we start?"

You gave us the tour, beginning with the vat where the mash gets mixed and cooked to prepare for fermenting. Then you narrated us through the steps for an actual run— from the starter tank to the condensing worm on to the collection barrel—where we'd get our moonshine whiskey, as long as the temperature was right. Pipes connected all the different parts, bringing propane in one way and sending alcohol out the other.

Listening to your clear and patient explanation reminded me of Mr. Cauley and AP chemistry. No one would guess you didn't graduate from high school. I know you think that bothers me. It definitely bothers Daddy. But I've seen the gifts you have with making and building and fixing. I know the way you can look at something and understand intuitively its inner gears and workings. There's all kinds of smart and not. I'm proof of that.

I was itching to get started. Not only because it meant I'd be that much closer to making money but also because you made it sound fascinating. Like I'd been missing out.

You showed us the cutoff valve for the fire. "You gotta keep dirt and the shovel close by for random flames. But it's the cap that's most likely to cause problems."

You had us each practice using the metal crook you'd made from an old pipe to lift the cap. "Inside this tank will be like molten lava. Even the fumes are like gasoline. The seal has got to be tight. No kindas, sortas, or almosts. Otherwise this bit of metal will pop like a bomb."

"Oh, man, I want to see that," said Bucky.

We laughed, but the nerves were back working in my stomach. Jake's scars haunted me. And the more you taught us, the more I realized we needed you to stick around and see us through.

"Give me logistics," said Bucky. "Day by day."

"We can't do it all today?" Roni asked.

"Today we mix and boil the mash," you said. "Then it needs time to work. To ferment."

"That's Baby's job, right?" I asked.

You grinned. "Baby's got a sweet tooth."

Bucky rolled his eyes. "Whatever. What do we need to actually do?"

"Someone will need to stir it every day, but that's it. In a few days, the liquor'll be ready to run. That's when Auntie needs a lot of company."

Roni said, "What if I have practice?"

"We can take shifts," I said.

You said, "It's better to have at least two people here."

Bucky said, "Unless it's Roni and Lulu. Then we probably need three or four."

"Don't be such a chauvinist," I said. "Roni and I are perfectly capable."

"I'm not," said Roni.

"Two girls alone in the woods? Seriously, Lulu?"

"It'll be like we're camping," I said.

"Camping is a good decoy," you said. "If you set up

over that way, then you'll have an excuse to be out here if someone wanders through."

"Is that what your family does?" asked Bucky.

You shook your head and frowned. "Nah. They work indoors. An old warehouse. Being out here in the woods, this is serious old school." Your eyes lit up with your smile.

"So that means you're gonna be here, right? As payback for my nice graduation flask you gave away. Seriously. You're not going to leave me alone with these two, are you, Mason?" Bucky clapped a hand on your shoulder, but you slid away from him, went back to talking procedures.

By the time we fed Baby, mixing her in with the cornmeal, sugar, and water, not one of us could swear innocence if we were to lay a hand on the Bible in a court of law. Although you'd say we were simply letting nature take its course.

Maybe that's what was happening with us too. Nothing but nature.

Remember that vine we swung on, launching ourselves down the hill? When Bucky fell flat on his butt, you laughed so hard you caught the hiccups. Roni sang about honeysuckle something until you offered to pay her a dollar to change tunes. She took you up on it too. We all laughed so much that day. I'm not sure why Bucky and Roni decided to tell every let's-embarrass-Lulu story they could think of. Of course the puking in your helmet had to be rehashed. But the absolute worst moment was when Roni said, "One thing I know for sure, is if Lulu had been drinking her way through high school like the rest of us, there's no way she'd still be a virgin." It got about a hundred degrees hotter, and I couldn't even look at you.

As we tried to wash up in the stream I said, "I feel sticky," and showed you my grubby hands.

"You have something on your face." You leaned in to wipe my chin, then said, "Oops," because your hands were worse than mine.

"We need more than this nothing bit of creek," said Bucky.

None of us were ready to let go of that day yet. About twenty minutes later we pulled into the dirt parking lot of the Queens' Tube Trailer Spot. It's a brilliant simplicity of a business to rent out inner tubes and then charge double for a ride back up the road.

Roni had a swimsuit stashed in Bucky's truck, but even if she'd had an extra, her tiny top wouldn't do the job for me. So while you and Bucky went to get the tubes, I pulled Roni behind the bushes, along with Bucky's knife. "Stand guard," I commanded. I slipped off my jeans, and then, wearing only a T-shirt and my underwear, I went to work cutting the legs off. The fabric was thick and I trembled from nerves, but with Roni holding it taut, I hacked away. It's some kind of miracle I didn't hack into her too. Midway into the second leg you came to check on us. It was like it never occurred to you we might be behind the bush for privacy.

"Y'all ready? Bucky's…" Your voice trailed off as you realized I wasn't wearing any pants.

I know my face must have turned wild shades of red as I pulled down my T-shirt, awkwardly, because of the knife in my hand. Not that my shirt was long enough to cover everything anyway.

You whipped back around, and Roni burst out laughing. "What's the big deal, Mason? It's the same amount of skin as you'd see with a swimsuit."

Sure didn't feel that way.

Even if you had some kind of girlfriend and we were almost done with our some kind of business arrangement, I felt shy around you in your shorts and no shirt as I came out from behind the bushes. Besides you getting a sneak peek at my behind, after all day in the dark woods, the sun felt too bright. My ragtag outfit of cutoff jeans and a T-shirt tied in the back was nothing to make you look twice. At least I'd worn a pretty bra, since it showed as soon as I got wet.

I couldn't help but notice the lines and windy ridges of your muscles. Of course you were in shape—all that biking and hauling and working with your body all day every day—but I hadn't seen the results so definitely. You even made Bucky look soft.

I stepped into the river's edge, taking a minute to get used to the cool of the water, feeling unsteady on the pebbly ground. Bucky crashed through the water past me, sending out a gush of spray and waves rolling across the surface and over us. I shrieked in reflex. After that it was easy to dive in.

I sat in the hole with my back pressed against one side of the inner tube and my legs dangling over the other. The river moved quickly; it must have been a high-water day. We aimed to stick together, but the river is in charge of steering. We rolled and flowed and every now and then bumped into each other. I was pretty sure at least one of the times you crashed into me was on purpose.

We neared the beach where we usually hang out way too soon. Sometimes we get a ride from the Queens' van and make another run, but none of us felt like getting out of the water yet. You pointed downriver and said, "Aren't y'all going to ride the Bottoms?"

"Excuse me?" said Roni. "Are you sure that's sanitary?"

We knew the place you meant. I'd gone as far as the rocks that mark the start, but I'd never had the nerve to ride the actual rapids.

Roni said, "I don't know. I had my sights set on warm sand sleepy time." She turned to me. "What do you think, Lulu?" She probably expected me to back her up for beach time, but your smile persuaded me to follow.

We rode our tubes to the ridge of rocks crowded with people waiting their turn. Standing inside my tube, I planted my feet between the rocks.

You talked over the din. "After the ride, bear right and come back around. You don't want to hit the Wormhole." I knew what you meant. Mom had warned me about that chute-style rapid ever since my first trip to the river.

You set your tube in the frothy, white water and jumped on. Raced along the surface—and dropped—plunging into a hollow. With a whoosh of speed you popped out, completely airborne for several feet before crashing back to the river's surface. I laughed at the look on your face.

Bucky didn't go quite as far when he popped out, but his obvious shock was truly hilarious. When you both came back to the start, Bucky said, "Let's go, Roni."

"I don't know," she said. "Just watching the water swirl makes my tummy feel funny."

I helped you hold the tube while Roni climbed on Bucky's lap, and then we let them go, into the vacuum. Roni's shriek must have traveled all the way upriver to the dam in Elmsworth.

Roni yelled from the water below, "You've got to try it, Lulu."

I was scared to do something so obviously out of control. Old habits die hard, you know. But I was a shiner now. I took risks, lived on the edge. Except I had to do it alone. Didn't matter that you'd already seen me without any pants, I wasn't about to climb in your lap the way Roni had with Bucky.

You held my inner tube in the churning water. I was distantly aware that other people were waiting and watching, but you seemed completely focused on me. I couldn't help but notice the way your shorts hung low on your hips. Adrenaline coursed through me as the water rocked my tube, trying to wrestle it out of your hands. I grabbed your wrists. "I'm scared."

"Do you believe you have a purpose to be here on Earth?"

"What?" I laughed at your unexpected question.

"Do you have plans and goals and dreams?"

It felt like you were teasing me, but I nodded.

"I know you want to see Aunt Jezebel in action. Have faith you'll make it through."

My heart raced almost as fast as the water around me.

You leaned in close. Your voice rumbled against my ear. "I'm not letting go. Not until you say."

"How do I make sure I go the right way? How do I steer?"

"You don't. You let go. You trust."

I watched the tremendous force of the water racing down over the rocks. "Okay."

"You'll have to let go of my arms."

I laughed a little. And rolled away with the water.

Into the rush and the roar. Fast. Faster. I popped in the air, trying to grab on to something that wasn't there, reaching, stretching, holding on to nothing, not sure how to breathe, if I could breathe, if I'd ever breathe again, and then *splash!* Back down into the calmer waters. It was over before I'd figured out if I liked it.

I immediately wanted to do it again. And again. And again.

When we took a break to warm up on the sunny rocks, I was spent and giggly from adrenaline overload.

All the time we'd been there, different groups had come and gone along those rapids. Some people, like us, rode a bunch of times. Others went once and then either headed to shore or kept going the way you'd warned us against. I didn't pay much attention to any of them until a long-haired guy stood dripping next to us. He said to Roni, "Could you settle a bet?"

Bucky moved closer to her, eyeing him.

142

"Are you the new lead singer for Lullaby Breaker?"

"Nope."

His face fell. "Damn."

She flipped her wet hair around. "But I am their new accompanist."

"That means you sing, right?" His face lit up. He turned to his friends. "Told y'all."

Then one of them said, "Shit. Is that you, Malone?" He squinted and laughed. "I thought you were either dead or in jail."

You simply said, "Not at the moment."

That's the thing about Dale. You are what you are, what everyone thinks you are. Forever. You weren't who you'd been any more than I was who I'd always been. You and I, each in our own way, were in the midst of a metamorphosis. Caught in the change, not all one way or the other. Right then I saw how his words made you fade.

Roni said, "Stick a fork in me, I'm done. Take me to shore, Bucky."

Bucky stood to follow her, but you headed toward the rapids again. Without a word you launched yourself off the edge.

I didn't see you at first, down at the bottom. I didn't worry, though. Each ride had left me needing to re-acquaint myself with up and down once I hit the open river. When I finally spotted you, I paddled in your direction even though you were farther away than usual.

My inner tube bumped along the rolling water. Then I suddenly got caught in a stronger current pulling me downstream.

"Paddle this way," you yelled.

The water was too strong. My inner tube raced along faster than it had all day. In the direction of the Wormhole.

Your inner tube popped up and sailed downstream without you. My heart raced even faster then. You'd let go on purpose so you could swim to me. You grabbed hold of my tube and pulled me toward the shore. "Kick, Lulu."

I kicked and paddled, fear giving me strength.

We finally managed to get to where we could stand and stay firm against the current. I gasped for breath, my inner tube knocking against the rough water. You stood downstream, blocking me from slipping away again.

Panting, I asked, "Is the Wormhole really that bad?"

"Not worth the risk."

"What about all your faith in hopes and dreams? What about trust?"

"Still gotta weigh the odds. Can't use faith as an excuse for reckless stupidity." You eyed me, unsmiling. "It's not too late to back out of what we started today. You haven't done anything illegal. Not yet."

"You think I should give up?" I searched your eyes.

"What if people look at you the way that guy looked at me? What if you really do spend time in jail? And when you get out, everyone thinks that's all you're ever going to do, all you'll ever be?"

For me, staying in Dale already felt like its own kind of jail.

"We can't do this without you, Mason."

You didn't argue.

I said, "Maybe you need this too. You can make some money. Enough to do something new. You could leave Dale. Start over."

You led me and my tube toward the shore. Just before we stepped out of the water and onto the sand you looked back at me. "Wherever I go, I'll still be me."

That's a good thing.

Then you said yes. You'd ride along with us.

14

For the next day or two, Aunt Jezebel bubbled and brewed in the woods. At some point you and Bucky made a quick visit and stirred the mess we'd started, then turned around and left her and Baby to work a little longer. I was curious but didn't insist on tagging along. Now that you were a part of the plan, I believed it might actually happen, even if I wasn't there.

Then it was the Fourth of July and Roni's big day for her debut performance with Lullaby Breaker. The Fourth on the Green has always been a highlight of the summer. The Green—a memorial for the soldiers who died during the Civil War—hosts a celebration of our country's original act of independence. The people of Dale don't find it at odds to celebrate America's birthday in the same place they honor the men who tried to break away from her.

Different bands—playing country, rock, bluegrass, and old Appalachian tunes on rough and simple instruments—were going to be performing all day, but Lullaby Breaker was the main attraction. Even though they were all from Dale, they'd toured the state and had actual, real-live groupies from the greater outside world. Some had started showing up a few days earlier. Roni and I had actually gotten stuck in five minutes of traffic on our way to work.

RVs and tents full of good-natured fans set up in the fields behind Church Row—where the Protestants hang tight together on the opposite side of town from Saint Jude's. Between the laughter and the music and the bonfires and the clotheslines hung from tree to tree, it looked like a mash-up revival and refugee camp.

Getting ready at her house that morning, Roni was a squirmy mess of nerves. "Do I try to look elegant or sassy? Big hair or sleek?" I helped her curl her hair, but she immediately washed it out and blew it straight again.

"And what the hell do I wear? Why'd you ever make me join the band anyway?"

"What are the guys wearing?" I asked.

"Blue and true, whatever the hell that means." She bolted for the bathroom and threw up.

I got her a Sprite and met her at the bathroom door. "Nerves much?"

She finally settled on jeans and a tight red T-shirt with a silver star—the outfit she'd planned all along—and wore her hair straight. Her silver cowboy boots finished the outfit with a little bit of flash. When Bucky pulled up in front to take her downtown, I called after her, "Don't forget your Sharpie."

She laughed and waved out the window of the truck.

～

I worked the Saint Jude's bake-sale booth that afternoon. Mom and her middle-of-the-night baking had provided most of the stockpile. Sal had been coming by every day to sample her wares, and he'd brought all her sweet treats down to the Green that morning. Her mini-pies disappeared immediately, and people bought her brownies by the plateful.

When my shift ended, there was still time before Lullaby Breaker would take the stage. I wandered the Green with Buttercup and Charlotte, passing the booths of homemade crafts—multicolored quilts, cornhusk dolls, wooden toys that you could make if you wanted—but mostly we were seeing and being seen. That was what the Fourth was really about.

I saw Jessie sitting on a wall laughing and was glad you weren't there too. Not that I didn't want to see you. I just didn't want to see you with her.

I wonder if we'd ever passed each other during other Fourth of Julys. Did you ever run wild with the other kids? Used to be once we'd blown our money on the games and goodies, we'd retreat to the trees to play tag, war, or sardines. But you had your first drink when you were eleven, and by twelve you were getting good and drunk a couple of times a month. At age thirteen you were drinking every day. Right? Isn't that what you said? You must not have the same memories as me. What can you remember at all?

As the sun dipped lower, a big group of us waited by the stage. I saw people I knew from school that I hadn't thought of all summer. Randy and Ollie were there too, looking cleaned up and wearing matching T-shirts that said RONI LIKES MY JUNK. Jimmy and Patrick James passed around spiked Gatorade bottles, but I wasn't tempted to drink. There were way too many eyes of the town watching, and I was buzzed enough with the idea of hearing Roni sing. But I did think how we could turn something like this into a business opportunity. A couple more days and we'd have something to sell.

I said to Bucky, "How are Roni's nerves?"

He shook his head. "Why's she doing this if it makes her so upset?"

I think the nerves must be part of the thrill. Because once Roni came out onstage, it was obvious she was where she belonged. Her voice belted out clear and strong. She moved across the stage smooth and sexy, but like she had no idea she was anything special.

Roni had said that the hardest thing about performing is waiting for the crowd to get involved. So when I saw Bucky standing with his hands in his pockets, I grabbed his arm and made him dance. We all danced together. The whole crazy, happy mob.

Then I saw you.

There ought to be a word for that moment when two people find each other across a crowd. It's that moment our eyes meet, the jolt of happy seeing your crooked smile directed at me. Everything else grows fuzzy while you come into sharper view. It's the way my mouth waters and my insides get warm and jumpy. My fingers want you to be within touching distance. Vision and anticipation coming together. I'll call it visicipation. That's what hit me.

I moved to you. "Hey," I said.

"Hey."

"Are you waiting for someone?" I meant Jessie, of course. You shook your head. "Just here to see Roni sing."

I grabbed your arm. "Come dance." I pulled you into the mob of my friends, forcing you to join the swarm.

There's something about country music that encourages stepping in close, no matter the tempo. As the notes and rhythms wrapped around us, I tuned myself to you. Your arm was something solid to hold on to. As easy as rolling along the river, we flowed away from everyone else. With our eyes locked on each other, I could hardly breathe.

Breathing is overrated.

When the band finished, they slipped off the stage and were lost from view as a pack of men moved in to retrieve the instruments and equipment and we all cheered, long and loud. You and I moved into the shadow of the stage. The echo of notes filled my ears, and my body swayed in time to phantom tunes.

Roni appeared, her face shiny and smeared with makeup.

"You were amazing." I hugged her. "Ugh. I can't believe how much you sweat up there."

"I know. It's as good as sex."

Then she was swallowed in a crush of congratulations and hugs and gushes. Janis, her mom, gave her flowers, looking more than half lit. I wonder if she's what you'd call a functioning alcoholic. It would explain a lot of Roni's childhood.

I turned to you, but you were looking at your phone. "Hey, Lu. I gotta go."

"Aren't you going to watch the fireworks?" After dancing, my mind had moved on to wondering about sitting with you in the dark. I wasn't sure what I wanted to happen, but I was willing to experiment.

Your eyebrows pinched together. "I have to meet someone."

Seth had warned me that you always left with Jessie. I forced back a wave of jealousy. "Okay. See you." I turned to follow the Roni love-throng.

You must have heard something in my voice, because you moved in close and whispered, "It's about Aunt Jezebel."

"What? With who? I'm coming."

"You can't."

"Why not? I have a right to know what's going on."

"I'm talking to a buyer. He won't meet with someone he doesn't know. This could mean real money."

I watched you walk away, but it was only a moment before I followed.

At first it was easy. I hung back in the crowd, watching your short hair moving through the swarm of insignificant people, away from the Green and on to Main Street.

Once you turned the corner at the barbershop and headed behind the row of businesses, I didn't have a place to hide. I stood at the wall and peeked to see which way you would turn at the end of the alley. My heart thumped and my hands sweated against the bricks as I felt the adrenaline charge of being a spy girl on a mission.

Too bad I wasn't any good at it. You saw me. I ran down the alley to join you in that employee parking lot behind the buildings. "You have to get out of here, Lu."

"This is my deal too."

You got a text. "Dammit. He's almost here."

Crazy kicked in with a vengeance. I scrambled into the back of a parked Chevy pickup and lay down. I said, "I'll hide here and listen."

You peered over the back with a wild look of exasperation, but there wasn't time to argue. I heard a voice, thick with the hills, say, "Long time no see."

You greeted him. I could tell you were shaking hands, moving him away from my hiding place. I pressed my body against the cool metal and into the musty smells, ignoring the dirt collected in the crevice by the tailgate while the two of you chatted about the weather and fishing and raccoons big enough to steal babies. I remembered how much I'd always hated playing hide-and-seek. The looking, the panicky worry I'd never find anyone. And waiting to be found was lonely and terrifying. It was one game I didn't mind losing. That night in the truck bed, the stakes were a whole lot higher as I waited, praying Hail Marys until the line *at the hour of our death* took on too much emphasis.

You said, "I appreciate you meeting with me."

"I'll let you talk," he said. "For old times' sake."

"I'm making our virgin run this week. It's all new hardware. Good ingredients."

"I gotta ask," he said. "You mixed up in that other stuff?" There was a pause, then he went on. "A little taste of moonshine is our God-given right. Ain't no reason the government should get in the way of a man and his drink. But that chemical shit, well, that's wrong. I don't want no mixing in that."

"We see eye to eye on that one."

"You might be the only one in your family."

There was a catch in your voice as you said, "This is me, stepping out on my own."

"Then you got nerve, boy." He chuckled. "I might could use a new source. I'm about fed up with that moron in Harrisonburg."

"Sure would appreciate you giving me a chance."

That's when my phone went off. I pressed closer against the truck, trying to stop it, but the vibration against the metal made a strangled buzzy-humming noise. I knew it was Roni wondering where we were.

I heard footsteps and prayed the two of you were moving on, but then a catch and lift in your voice made me realize someone else was there too, and walking toward my hiding place. A second later I saw a man with a beard pass by, and without any hesitation, he opened the driver's door and got in the Chevy. He must have been in a hurry, because I didn't even roll over before he started the engine. The beat of music inside his cab reverberated out.

I could have choked on my spit except a heart attack was going to kill me first.

I heard you say, "Whoa, I saw someone. In the bed there." You banged hard on the side of the truck, which stopped its backward motion. I took the chance you'd offered and sat up.

The driver rolled down the window and said, "What the hell?"

"Looks like you have some extra cargo. She must have passed out back there."

"Lord Jesus," said the driver. "Unbelievable."

Our client was already gone when the first boom of a firework crashed in the sky above us, setting off a silver spray. I climbed out, holding tight to your hand. As I hit the pavement, you scooped your arm around me. I leaned into you out of relief, then played along, stumbling and slurring. My recent drunken moments helped my acting skills.

You said, "I'll take care of her," and led me away from the truck and its grateful driver.

I staggered beside you as bursts of colors turned the sky rosy, then green. I looked up at you, and we laughed that hysterical laughter that comes with close calls.

It was even better than sitting in the dark.

Once the fireworks were over, we made our way to Bucky's truck.

You said, "That was crazy, Lulu. I never should have let you do that."

"Let me? You can't take my credit. That was all me." I stopped walking. "Mason, I need to know everything about this moonshine business. I want to go with you to stir the mash."

So, by the time an exhausted Roni and quiet Bucky showed up and you took off on your bike, we had a plan to meet the next day.

You'd left on your own, no sign of Jessie.

Driving home, Roni turned around to face me. "Grungie asked me to go to Richmond with the band."

"What's in Richmond?"

"They have a big-time gig there. In a real concert hall."

Bucky said, "I told you. You aren't going to Richmond with a bunch of guys, Roni."

"You come too. You can be my roadie." She ran her fingers along his arm.

"I have to work."

"You don't even know when it is!"

"And there's Aunt Jezebel," said Bucky.

"I can't believe that's more important than my singing."

"It's for our future," said Bucky. "You know that."

Roni moved away from him. "You know what you need to do for our future."

When Bucky stopped his truck in front of her house, Roni jumped out with me, arms full of flowers, boots, and her bag. "Thanks for the ride, Bucky. Glad you had time to do that for me."

"Get back in here, Roni."

"I'm too tired to fight right now. Whenever you can fit me in your schedule, I'll be there."

His truck peeled off down the street.

"You okay?" I took her bag she was about to drop.

"Hell, no. He pisses me off."

Inside, she stuffed her flowers into a jar of water and grabbed us a couple of sodas—Janis was still out—and then I followed her down the basement stairs. Roni gulped down her drink, then turned to me, grinning. "That felt good tonight." She let out a huge belch—she knows how to project more than her singing. "Yep, real good." We laughed, but then she growled, "There is no way I'm missing playing in Richmond."

Roni stripped off her clothes and pulled on a giant

T-shirt. She slipped under the sheet. "Do you think Bucky thinks I'm too stupid to marry?"

"Of course not. He loves you."

"I know he does," said Roni. "But sometimes I think he wishes I was smart like you."

"You're crazy," I said. "And you're smart too."

"I'm not like you and Bucky, and we all know it. If you try to tell me I am, then I'll never trust you again. Damn, Lulu, I'm honestly okay with it." She closed her eyes for a minute, then opened them again. "Maybe Bucky worries our babies won't be smart enough."

"That's stupid, Roni. Not you."

"Forget it. Tell me about Mason." She rolled on her side and said, "Watching you two dance reminded me of how Bucky and I used to be."

When I closed my eyes that night, I saw bursts of color against a dark sky.

15

You picked me up after my shift at the junkyard, driving a surprise. I circled your little green truck, giving it the ten-point check Sal taught me. I've always loved Ford Rangers. They aren't so full of themselves as the 250 Bucky drives. "How'd you get it running? Did you get Ollie and Randy to help?"

"I always knew how to fix it." You sounded offended. "I just didn't."

"Isn't your bed kind of shallow?"

"Good eyes. How about you get in?"

On the way out to Aunt Jezebel you explained how your truck was a bootlegger mobile. It had been painted at least three different colors before this particular shade of green. You'd designed the secret compartments. The shallow bed was due to a storage area, divvied up into eight separate holding tanks. Each one the right size to hold a gallon. The seats lifted up for more storage. You even had a metal safe box under the driver's seat.

"My last delivery, for my family, didn't go so well," you said. "I left my truck, full of moonshine, parked on Dowdy's Bridge. Then I disappeared."

"Where'd you go?"

You were quiet a minute, then shrugged. "I ended up at rehab."

I wasn't sure whether to laugh or just listen. You looked like you weren't sure either.

"When I got back, Seth had parked my truck outside my house." You thrummed the steering wheel with your thumbs. "He'd taken the entire engine apart. Left each and every piece scattered across the ground. Told me when I got the truck put back together, then I could come back to work."

"Why would he do that?"

"At first I thought he was just messing with me. Or being a..." You shook your head. You were shy about cussing in front of me then. "But I also think he knew I'd need something to do."

"You didn't fix it?"

"All but the radiator," you said. "By the time I got to that point I'd ridden a lot of miles on my bike and it was clear I wasn't going back with the business."

Except now your truck was fixed.

Once we reached Roni's land, clouds brewed on the horizon. "Looks like we might get a thunderstorm," I said as we hiked through the woods. "Will that matter?"

"Some say thunder rolling makes the liquor smooth."

Near the top of the hill you said, "It's about ready. I can smell it."

To me, the corn turning smelled rich and sweet. Not bad or good, exactly. But demanding and relentless. When you opened the lid, the odor overwhelmed the woods. You staggered backward. At first I thought you'd been burnt, or bitten. Maybe that's what it felt like.

Hands on your knees, bent over, you gasped. "It's turning. That smell. It's..." Your voice didn't sound like you.

"I'll close it," I said, already moving toward the copper tank.

"Add more sugar." Your voice came out short and choppy. It was scary to see you, who always radiated your own brand of vibrant energy, looking so pale.

Standing by the holding tank, I followed your curt instructions. The ugly, soupy mash swallowed the sugar with a gurgle and burp. I stirred it and then placed the cap on, making sure the clasps were sealed tight.

You stumbled a ways down the hill. I followed, uncertain. You said, "I didn't know it would hit me that way." You wiped the sweat off your face and took a deep breath.

"What happened?"

"That smell. The alcohol is there. It's almost ready to run. The knowing it's there, raw and on the edge, that's worse than having an open bottle of whiskey on the table." Wild-eyed, you went on. "I know how to walk away from the bottle. But that growing smell... I haven't been near that since I quit. It ambushed me."

I didn't understand. I don't know if I ever will, not completely.

"I'm such a damn drunk. I want to stick my face in and eat myself to death." I heard disgust and shame in your words. "Deep inside me, there's this ache that never goes away. Sometimes I think I'd rip my skin off if it would help get that liquor inside me."

You looked like you were ready to bolt or crumple.

I could have given you space. If I'd walked away, you wouldn't have been surprised. But I'd been with Mom when she got stranded at the mailbox. I'd found her cowering in her car after hours of trying to will herself back in the house. There'd been too many times I'd tried to convince her she could step outside, simply to get a breath of fresh air. I knew shaking. I'd seen hands wringing. Eyes wide with fear and anger.

"Hey," I said, soft and low. "It's okay." I murmured easy nothings and rubbed your back.

Once the clouds let loose and rain poured down, drops of water pattering against the thick, leafy roof, finding their way to us, I finally felt your muscles relax and your breathing turn steady. Summer rain has its own scent. In the woods it blends with the smell of dirt, old wood, and new growth. The rain cleared the air of mash and let you breathe.

We slipped and slid down the wet hill. I tried to cover up the urgency I felt by chatting about the woods and jumping in puddles and my dead cat, Sherlock, who I still missed—anything so I wouldn't have to think about the darkness nipping at your heels. When we stood by your truck, face-to-face, too wet to notice the rain, you said, "You saved me."

I didn't want you to need saving.

Maybe that's why I invited you home with me that day. To get you back on solid ground. I found you one of Daddy's shirts that was too wide and too short but would do while yours dried. I let Mom feed you her raspberry chicken and cornflake casserole, which is so much better than it sounds.

Later we sat on my front step breathing in the after-rain air and talking. As the dark settled in, lightning bugs danced around us. Watching the little flicks of yellow light, I told you about the time Roni and I tried to have a séance in my tree house until we got scared and knocked over the candles, almost setting it on fire. You told me funny stories about growing up in the valley, like the time you brought a bobcat kitten home. And how you'd drag a juicy meat bone up and down and over the ground for miles, setting up an obstacle course for your hound dog, Boo.

"How'd you get that scar?" I asked. "The one by your eyebrow."

Rubbing the little white line, you told me, "One night while I was working the family still, a cougar attacked me. I fought him off with a broken bottle, but first he got me with one claw." Suddenly you laughed. "Nah. I fell out of my bunk bed when I was five. My mama stitched me up in the kitchen. It feels like there's twine buried there."

I reached out and felt that you were right.

We talked for a long time about our families. You told me about growing up with a pack of much older brothers; how all four of you slept in one room so the other bedroom could be your wrestling arena. You and Seth used to be inseparable, but now he couldn't seem to forgive you for going to rehab. I told you about Mom before she got stuck. How she used to take me up on the roof so I could count clouds and see the sunset without all the trees in the way.

"She's given up," I said. "She's not even trying to get better."

"Maybe it's not her time yet," you said.

I shrugged. "I can't be like her. I have to get out of here."

That was also the first time you talked about believing in a higher power. "Do you believe in meant-to-bes, Lulu? Like today. I didn't know I'd react like that. But God knew. So he sent you with me."

I grew up with church being center. I prayed the Rosary, lit candles, went to Mass and reconciliation, but I wasn't used to talking about God like that. So certain of his intent. I swallowed back the obvious: It was my fault you were there in the first place. Not God's. Instead I explained how growing up as one of only a handful of Catholics in town had made me feel a weird mix of better and worse, like religion was a competition. The only way to win was to follow the rules.

You also told me stories about drinking. Slow and bare bones at first, then adding a little more, bit by bit. Sometimes letting things out makes them lighter to carry. You told me how Father Mick made you feel welcome when you met him after an AA meeting at the church. How you and Jessie call each other for support. She has a boyfriend and a little girl with red hair. When you leave together, it's to keep each other from drinking. "She's like a sister to me," you said. "Except sober."

So there wasn't Jessie, or any other girl, sitting with us on that step. Just what I'd hoped.

We'd gravitated closer together by then. Our legs stopped their brushes and settled in, warm and tight against each other. My heart thumped from the simple touch, the way you smelled, close beside me. But even with you warm and solid at my side, an invisible veil of remembering you on the hill slipped between us. Made me turn my head away from your gaze, kept me from looking at your lips.

Instead, I told you how I couldn't wait to get to California. How I was going to do research and develop cures for unusual diseases with weird names. Or for people with issues like my mother. I wasn't sure exactly what I'd do, but I'd have options. I'd get to decide what mattered most. Whatever it was, I'd be able to do something that made the world better. Not just swap out one rusty part for another.

You stood up, clasped your hands together above your head. Then turned to me, let me peek inside at what you'd caught. A lightning bug, looking dim, ordinary, ugly, crawled across your fingers. You let it go, and then it shone bright.

"We're going to get you your money, Lu."

Didn't you hate that I still wanted to make moonshine? Even after seeing you struggling, I still had my own desperate need to make my plan work.

You said, "I didn't think I could do this moonshine thing. Ever since I got sober, I've been on autopilot. Everything rigid, everything the same. It was the only way to make it through the day. That's why I didn't put my truck back together."

You turned to me, caught my eyes so I couldn't hide from yours. "Lu, you're helping me see I'm tougher than I thought. I can do this."

Ethanol is poison. But we drink it anyway. It causes trouble enough, but its lethal cousin methanol ferments alongside it. It has to be separated, drained, and thrown away. Methanol will most likely kill you. If it doesn't, it'll leave you brain damaged, blind, or paralyzed. And then you wish it had.

To get the ethanol, you have to work around the methanol.

To get out of town, I had to drag you through the muck.

16

My impatience bubbled up, agitated, restless and ready, like Aunt Jezebel's bittersweet mash. But finally, the waiting was over. It was time to make moonshine.

We'd decided to camp for two nights—before and after the run—to be sure we'd have enough time. The timing was hard to predict.

"Each run's a little different," you'd said. "Things'll happen we can't guess."

That didn't keep me from trying to anticipate every possible outcome. Getting caught. Arrested. Fires. Ending up with scars like Jake's. You breaking down again. Or drinking whatever we brewed.

You and me...

That was the hardest to guess. On top of the obvious anxiety and stress over the actual running of the still, I was spending two nights in the woods with you. You, who didn't have a girlfriend after all.

Roni and Bucky had, of course, made up from their fight on the Fourth. Roni was going to Richmond with the band, and next time Bucky would try to go too. So, they'd be all over each other, and that would leave you and me, to be...

The great unknown.

It still amazes me how little resistance I met. Mom trusted me then. My disappointment over school was a tender topic. I was a bruise she didn't want to push too hard against. There was no sign of the mother she used to be. The one who'd checked and double-checked every plan. The one who called parents to confirm they'd supervise the parties I wanted to attend. Who expected me to make the right choices.

When I told Mom where we were going, she simply said, "Camping? Where will you sleep?"

It wasn't that she worried I was up to something illegal. She didn't even seem to consider that boys might be included. For someone who can't step onto her front porch without breaking into a cold sweat, the idea of sleeping in the woods was inconceivable.

"I'll be in a tent. Remember, I was a Girl Scout." Never mind that our troop's idea of camping was eating microwaved s'mores in Charlotte's living room. Mom made me call Daddy to double-check the plan.

"Hello, Luisa," he said. "Good to hear from you."

"Hello, Father," I said, just as formally. I was still punishing him.

"Since when do you enjoy the great outdoors?"

"If I'm not going to college, I need to get working on my redneck skills. I might take up opossum hunting next." I didn't say anything about making moonshine, but I thought it.

In a small and steady voice he said, "I know you're angry, Lulu. I appreciate you making the best of the situation. Have fun and be safe. How's your mother?"

"Talk to her yourself." I handed over the phone.

When Roni and I arrived, you and Bucky helped haul our gear and the jars up to Aunt Jezebel. You were both so giddy and wired you needed something to do. As you bounced up the trail beside me, there was no sign of that broken boy I'd seen.

Right before we reached the last part of the trail, we all caught the whiff at the same time.

"Whooo-eee, what is that?" Bucky asked.

Roni said, "Mother-of-a-stink-bomb, that is awful."

They weren't talking about the fermenting corn smell. We must have made some skunk mad with all our traipsing through the woods. The funk of his stench was enough to make our eyes water. I was thrilled. Now maybe Aunt Jezebel's smell wouldn't have any power over you.

After your breakdown, I'd read about alcoholism on the Internet. Tried to figure out what it meant. I wanted to make sure you didn't have a relapse. I wanted to control your temptations. But that's not something someone else can hold for you, is it?

Tucking our noses into our shirts whenever the stink got too bad, we checked each part of the still to make sure, yet again, that everything was in place. I had a clipboard with my notes and a diagram to check off each step of the plan. I caught your smirk as you looked it over.

"I want to keep track of what we do. So we know what works."

"You don't think I know what I'm doing, do you?" you teased.

"I think *I* don't know what you're doing. That's a completely different issue."

You took the clipboard from me. You erased and fixed the part I'd drawn backward. When you turned to show me, we were face-to-face, eye to eye. A sudden heat rushed through me. You moved to recheck the alignment of the pipes, and I turned and fussed with something, pretending I hadn't just wanted to kiss you.

As much as I'd stressed and fretted over what might happen with you, I was sure *something* would. I'd felt the heat passing between us. I was sure it wasn't only my heart that raced when we were close together.

Bucky brought up sleeping arrangements after we'd moved downwind of Aunt Jezebel. "I can't help but notice we only have two tents."

"Girls in one and boys in the other," I said.

"Wrong answer," said Bucky. "No offense, Mason."

You said, way too quickly, "I was planning on sleeping under the stars."

"That's not what you call Lulu, is it? Stars?"

Roni laughed. It took me a minute to get it, but then I concentrated on not looking your way.

Eating outside makes everything more delicious. I'd brought Mom's coconut-chicken sticks to share, and your strawberries were the sweetest I had all summer. We cooked Bucky's corn, husks and all, right in the fire. Roni's lemon bars pushed me over the edge to stuffed silly. Then we laughed and joked around the hypnotic flames of the cozy campfire.

After Roni started playing her ukulele, I asked her, "Are you nervous about going to Richmond?"

"I don't like the idea of staying in a hotel by myself, but I'm excited to sing on a real stage."

You said, "Roni, you've changed my mind about country music. It's not nearly as bad as I thought."

"Thanks. I think." She laughed. "What kind of music do you like, Mason?"

"I had to give up listening to metal," you said.

I knew that was because of what you called triggers. The associations that made you want to drink. You said, "This old guy named Beethoven plays some pretty decent tunes."

Bucky said, "I'm sure glad the old folks' home let you out for a night."

Even though he was joking, your age truly was an issue. Not so much the number, but the way those extra years had been spent. Drinking. Getting into real trouble. The things you'd done, the girls you'd been with. Cindy, and other girls too, even if Jessie wasn't one of them. There were issues sitting between us at that campfire, but I knew issues and boundaries might be hard to see in the dark.

Roni said softly, "I'm mostly just glad to have something to do when Bucky and Lulu leave me." She leaned into the arm Bucky wrapped around her. I knew they wouldn't last by the fire much longer. Then I'd be left with you.

There were still way too many hours of the night ahead of us that I didn't know how to navigate. I said, "Let's all go for a walk. We can look for stars. And the moon. I think seeing the moon would be good luck. For tomorrow. A moon before moonshine." My nerves made me babble.

"I'm only going two places," said Roni. "To bed and to sleep."

I'd never felt quite so wide awake as I did when Bucky followed her into the tent. Every nerve in my body was on high alert. I got up and poked the fire. Brushed off the rocks. Straightened the pile of wood. Kept busy moving and rearranging. Fiddling and putzing for no particular reason. Except to avoid looking at you.

"I think the fire is low enough to leave it," you said. "It's pretty damp out here. Let's look for your good luck moon."

We each brought a flashlight, but you led the way, walking too fast to be friendly. I shined my light at the ground, trying to keep your footsteps visible. We walked toward Aunt Jezebel, but closer to the stream. The trees grew so thick it was hard to see anything above us, but you moved as though you knew where you were going.

When we reached the place where the stream pools into an eddy, the sky revealed itself, wide and open, sprinkled with stars all around. But no moon.

"It must not be up yet," you said. "We could wait and see if she shows."

Your face was hidden in the shadows, but my eyes followed the outer line of you—your broad shoulders, arms, the stance of your legs. I thought about you shaking from the smell of fermentation. I squatted and poked a stick into the dark, unsettled swirls. "Is this going to be too hard for you, Mason? You sure you want to stick around tomorrow?"

I thought you were avoiding my question when you said, "I looked up San Diego. It's by the ocean, right?"

I nodded.

"I saw the ocean once. When I was about six. My father took me with him when he had to make a delivery down in South Carolina. He set me up on the beach to wait while he did his deal. Told me not to go in the water any higher than my knees."

Six years old and left by yourself on the beach. That's a hard thing to picture.

"So I'm standing in the water, letting the waves roll up over my feet, when a gust of wind blows off my hat. It flies into the deep water before I can do anything about it. I'm just a dumb kid, so I start crying."

For the record, you were a kid, period. A kid alone on the beach.

"I know my hat is as good as gone and I'm worrying what my daddy's going to do to me for losing it, when all of a sudden this big wave crashes over me, gets me completely soaked. But it brings me my hat, washed up on the dry sand.

"I was sure it was some kind of magic. Or God himself. Because all I knew was the river, and if you drop something in it, then you better start running downstream. The ocean, even though it's huge and terrifying, and there's no way to follow the water all the way out, the waves come back. It gives you a fighting chance."

I quit poking the mud with my stick and stood up.

"I already lost my future once, Lu. But ever since you came along with your crazy plan, I feel like I might get something back."

Just above the treetops behind you, the moon, enough to hang a wish on, peeked out. I pointed. "The moon's here."

"Our good luck."

"Or at least a fighting chance," I said.

Back at the campsite, there was an awkward moment of saying good night. You looked for a spot to put your sleeping bag. "Mind if I lie on the edge of your tent?"

We lay down on opposite sides of the nylon wall, me

inside the tent and you out with the moon and the stars. I listened to your rustles as you settled in.

"Good night, Mason."

"Yes it is, Lu." Your voice was so close, yet not.

I heard you roll over. I could see the shape of your back and shoulders pressed against the tent. I felt the pressure and warmth of you beside me. My thigh was already there, but I leaned ever so slightly into you. You pressed back.

"Hey, Lu?"

"Yeah?" That touching without really touching made it hard to breathe.

"You think you can tell me something from school?"

"Like what?"

"Doesn't matter. School always put me to sleep."

If I was Roni, I could have sung you a lullaby; but I don't sing. I don't tell stories either. Instead I said, "One, hydrogen. Two, helium. Three, lithium. Four, beryllium..."

The periodic table is a steady list of things to build with. Little bits and pieces of the universe, all in a row.

17

*T*woke to birds gone wild, like I was in the jungle. I never knew there could be so many different sounds and songs.

As I crawled out of the tent, you greeted me with a generous gaze, almost enough to make me forget I looked a mess, then turned back to the coffee you were brewing over the fire. The early morning air felt thin during that line between night and morning. The thrill of what lay ahead sent shivers along my skin.

I called into the other tent. "Wake up, sunshines."

Roni grunted and Bucky cursed.

Adrenaline waves coursed through me—probably

through all of us—as we ate a quick breakfast of Mom's apple empanadas and your strong coffee. Maybe it was the caffeine, but you were jumpy, revved up, several beats ahead of the rest of us.

Aunt Jezebel sat waiting beneath the white-gray sky. Remnants of the skunk scent lingered, but the brew smelled rich and funky. There was no escaping it.

Roni said, "I can't tell if that smell is making me hungry or sick."

I watched you for any sign of the wreck I'd seen the day we turned the mash. But you smiled with clear eyes. Anticipation reverberated off your skin. "We have to caulk the joints," you said. "Any leaking vapors will catch fire in a flash."

The gluey mixture of flour and water seemed awfully primitive, but you swore it was best. "It's got better give and take than any chemical mixture. Even the pros come back to nature for this."

You made deliberate, methodical checks of all the joints, pointing out where I should add the paste. Then you went back and rechecked my work, sometimes slapping on more gunk.

We'd already cleared all the dried leaves and twigs from the fuel connection area, but the bucket of sand sat ready in case of fire. I relaxed into your compulsive checks.

"What happened to your neck, Mason?" I pointed to the line of red bumps.

"Lonely mosquitoes snuggled up with me last night."

Did that help when I coated those bites with our paste? Did we invent a new treatment? You didn't complain about those bites after that, but you're not one to fuss.

When you looked to the brew tank, I caught a second of hesitation. If I'd blinked or turned away, I might have missed it. "Hey," I said. You looked at me almost like you'd forgotten I was there. "Let me help. Tell us what to do."

You raised your eyebrows. "I think we're ready."

As the four of us circled together I realized there weren't any other anyones anywhere I'd rather be with.

You said, "So far, what's going on up here is all organic. We haven't done anything illegal yet. We could sit back and let that mash turn to vinegar. It's not until we start running the still that we've crossed a line."

"You, maybe. The rest of us stole a still," said Bucky.

"We're only borrowing it," I said lamely.

"Last chance to step out," you said. Of course we all shook our heads.

Roni said, "We need some kind of ceremonial start. Let's hold hands."

I was between you and Bucky with Roni across. Her two blond braids hung down over her shoulders.

Bucky farted, long and loud. He said, "What? You have something else in mind?" Then, "All right, all right. Auntie J, please be generous and don't blow your top."

Roni said, "I think we should have a real prayer. Lulu?"

I froze up. All those prayers I'd memorized for catechism didn't seem to fit. Then you said something that sounded exactly right: "Dear God, you truly are the higher power. We humbly ask you to help us to stay safe and sane today. Help us be successful so that we might be able to go out in your beautiful world to do the good you expect."

"Amen," we all responded.

I'm glad we divvied up the starting steps. Roni turned on the gas, and I lit the flame. You and Bucky managed the tank. We were in this together.

Our giddy giggling eventually settled down, since it took hours of watching and fussing and tending to coax Aunt Jezebel's mash to the right temperature. I'd helped Mom in the kitchen enough to know it can be a split second from barely hot to stuck fast in the pan.

At one point you cooked sausages over the propane flame. You told us, "One time my uncle Sampson used a poison ivy stick to cook like this. Couldn't figure out why he had hemorrhoids at both ends."

Ew and ouch.

You told us funny stories about your family's moon-shining, and even though I think it's practically child abuse, I could see the hints of golden memories you kept. Your good and bad were mixed together so completely that it was almost impossible to tell one from the other.

Maybe that's what I'm looking for right now. A way to measure what's good and what's bad. Maybe it's as simple as holding on to the silver and gold while letting the ash blow away.

I thought I heard a tremble in your voice when you said, "Bucky, lean in there by the faucet and check the smell."

"Wooo-hoo, sweet baby Jesus." He wiped his eyes and said, "I think I'm drunk off the fumes." He giggled a little maniacally.

You and Bucky heaved buckets of icy river water near the holding tub and set up siphons to keep the liquor cold so it could condense and the flavor would come out smooth, like what you'd called liquid silver. I watched the muscles of your back and arms working as you moved up and down, from spot to spot, checking on each and every facet of Aunt Jezebel.

All of a sudden she let off a metallic boom. I jumped back, Roni shrieked, and Bucky spilled coffee down his front. "What the..."

"That's a sweet fine sound," you called out over the

deafening thuds. "If a still thumps in the woods and no agents are around to hear it, does it make a sound?"

"It's too early for philosophy," yelled Bucky over her bangs and crashes.

"Who cares about a sound—it's making moonshine!"

As suddenly as she started, Aunt Jezebel was done with her complaints.

"Here we go."

In a flurry of movement, you and Bucky moved in, ready to collect.

The release spot let out a gush, steam puffing loose all the while. Aunt Jezebel settled into a rhythmic rumble with the sound of liquid hushing along the pipes. As the steam hit the condensing worm, the sound turned fluid. She settled into a steady flow—one step higher than drips.

"This here's pure poison," you said. The scary chemical smell made it easy to believe. We couldn't simply dump it on the ground for how flammable it was. We put it in its jar labeled HEADS, marked with a skull and crossbones.

After a bit, the smell shifted and mellowed. Or maybe my smell receptors had been dulled to drunk. I checked you for any sign of meltdown, but I didn't see any hesitation.

You called this part the hearts, the best of the batch.

At one point Bucky asked, "Are we rookies holding you back at all?"

"It's definitely different working with people who are sober and intelligent. But it's also weird to think about it so much." You probably meant my charts and diagrams.

The last bit—the less potent tails—was visibly more cloudy and oily. You said we could use it to start our next batch; it would add flavor and richness to the mash. I heard *next batch*, as in we'd do this again.

By the time we were running the hearts for the second time, you seemed to be feeling a timing urgency. You said, "We can't run under the noon sun." All your advice was two parts practical to one part superstition. Who's to say what's what if it works?

As Aunt Jezebel finally slowed and creaked to a stop, we turned off the heat.

You stood on top of an empty Coke can, balanced on one foot, wearing a big, dopey grin. Then you bent over, and tapped the side of the can beneath you. It instantly collapsed into a thin aluminum pancake.

"And that," you said, "is what'll happen to Aunt Jezebel if you don't open her up and let her cool. Her tank might implode."

So many problems we might have had without you.

After we cut the alcohol with spring water, Roni and I

devised a jar-handling system: Hand a jar, fill a jar, set the jar, lid the jar. You showed us how to check the bead. Roni couldn't get over the idea that an air bubble could show the alcoholic proof.

"It's because of its density," I tried to explain.

Moonshining is pure chemistry, but Roni didn't care about the why. She just liked tipping the jars to check the bubble-beads. Finally, we spread out the swarm of jars in the shade.

"Now if we were pros," you said, "we'd let this age for a better flavor. But our buyers can do that. If they care."

I picked up one of the jars. The moonshine was impossibly clear. Except for the weight, I might have thought it was empty. This invisible something was my ticket out of town.

When I held it to the sunlight, the whole thing shone.

After cleaning the gunk out of the tank, we headed back to the campsite for lunch and a break. Besides my sore muscles and a nasty bruise on my shin, my skin itched and felt laced with tiny scratches. I know it doesn't make sense, but even my hair hurt. Being that physically tired, where every inch of me, inside and out, ached—but mixed in with the thrill of what we'd accomplished—worked a little bit like drinking. Made me feel silly and light. Even though it was hard to move. "We did it," I said as we sat around the charred remains of our fire.

"Hell, yeah," said Bucky.

You leaned forward in your chair and said, "Roni and Lulu, you are by far the most pleasant looking—and smelling—shiners I've ever worked with."

Roni said, "That's not true anymore. It's a good thing we all stink enough to not care."

"Speak for yourself," said Bucky. "Some of us are smart enough to sit downwind."

You said, "I think we did real well today. The first batch is always the hardest."

"When do we start a new batch?" I had to ask.

Roni groaned. "Mother-of-a-chain-saw, I'm going to kill Lulu right here and now."

"Isn't that the plan? This isn't enough," I said. To you, in particular, "Is it?"

"If you want to sell more, then yeah, you need to make more mash."

"We should have brought more sugar and cornmeal," I said.

"We need to make some money first," said Bucky. "So we can afford more ingredients."

"One other thing," you said, and then paused. "Someone needs to taste it."

Silence.

Eventually Bucky said, "Is it safe?"

You frowned, your face an unfamiliar collection of lines and edges. "We can't sell it if it's not. Someone's gotta make sure it's good."

"Be my guest," said Bucky.

"He can't," I said.

Roni said, "I don't want to either. I don't even like the smell of it."

"Who usually has the first taste?" I asked.

"That's not usually a problem," you snapped.

I guess most moonshiners aren't afraid of what they're making. Liking it too much is a more common problem. You'd set up the rule we shouldn't drink on the job, and we'd listened to you. None of us wanted to be the guinea pig or canary or dead drunk. As in actually dead.

You stood up, started pacing. At first I thought you'd stepped on something when I heard that crack. Then it was obvious it came from the thick woods around us. You froze. Put a finger to your lips and raised your other hand to silence us. Squatting, you pulled a gun from the ankle holster under your jeans.

You were wearing a gun.

A real gun.

Had been all day. Maybe every day.

You pulled it out so quick and easy—it wasn't your first time.

My heart thumped in my ears almost as loud as Aunt Jezebel getting ready to work. When I couldn't see whatever you were looking for in the trees, I locked my eyes on you. At the junkyard we see shotguns. What Sal calls the *Don't Make Me Shoot You* of guns. All threat, no accuracy. A smaller gun, like a pistol, requires aim and intent. It's itching to fire. Yours made you look unfamiliar. Your furrowed forehead shone with beads of sweat; your lips pursed together as you pointed it toward the bushes.

At the same moment, we all saw what had broken the stick. A deer, now frozen, stood about twenty feet away. Roni begged, "Don't shoot it, Mason."

You lowered the gun but looked wary.

I couldn't stay quiet any longer. "Who did you think was out there? Why do you even have that thing?"

You looked at the gun in your hand, then back at me.

"Don't you know it's the people who have guns that end up shot?"

"Oh, honey." Roni laughed. "Here we go."

Bucky said, "Mason, you might as well quit right now. Lulu's senior debate topic was gun control. You get her going, she'll never stop."

I never got much support for my ideas. Not in a place like Dale, where everyone and their mother has some kind of gun; but that didn't keep me from saying what I thought if I got the chance. Right then I was simply too pumped up and too exhausted to stop. "What or who would you be okay with shooting?"

Bucky said, "Give it up, Lulu. Nothing happened. It's over."

"Guns only cause trouble." The adrenaline rush kept me running my mouth without my brain attached. "It's so...so...stupid. And redneck."

"That's right," you said, your voice steady. "That's me."

Your eyes were already gone.

"I...I didn't mean you, Mason. I meant the gun."

I fought back hot, surprising tears as you disappeared over the hill without looking back.

"I didn't mean him," I said. "He can't think I did. Can he?"

Roni shrugged.

Bucky said, "Mason doesn't see that gun like you do, Lulu. I'm sure he held a shotgun before he ever held a pencil. It's part of the household. You got spoons and forks and cook pans and, oh yeah, the ammo is right there next to the toilet paper."

While Bucky worked on getting the fire going again, Roni and I went to the stream to wash up. I waded in, splashing cool water over my sticky skin. I wished I could also wash away what I'd said to you. At the same time, I still didn't trust guns. Here was one more reminder of the gaps we had between us.

Back at the campsite, Bucky was in a mood. He threw a log on the fire with a crash, sending sparks out of the ring.

"Don't burn down my land, Bucky," said Roni.

He pursed his lips. Pointed at me and said, "Looks like you're in charge again, Ms. Mendez. Now that you ran the know-how off the job."

I couldn't blame him for blaming me. I blamed myself. I'd known you were barely on board with this plan. And now I'd gone and pushed you off.

The sun was low, and we'd pulled out some hot dogs and potatoes for dinner by the time you made your way up the hill. Did you know not one of us expected you to return?

"You go for a ride?" asked Bucky.

"Down by the river."

"How many miles do you think you ride in a week?"

You said, "I don't think of it that way. I just ride until I'm tired."

That's yet another way we're different. If I took up riding—which in itself is unlikely—it would be all about the miles. Something measurable and finite. Goals to meet and pass.

Roni, determined to make things smooth again, chatted

about all kinds of something and another. I was too unsettled to chime in until she said, "Mason thinks we should build a house up here."

"Oh yeah?" said Bucky.

"Wouldn't that be something to tell the kids?" She laughed. "Junior, your bed is right where your aunt Jezebel used to stay."

I said, "You should see the furniture Mason's making for Saint Jude's."

"Is that right?" Roni turned her attention on you.

"I love building things."

For some reason the pause after your words made annoying tears prick at my eyes again. I gave myself a stern, silent lecture about not looking at your lips or your hands or your eyes or pretty much any part of you.

Eating gave us something to do and talk about. Then, afterward you stood up and said some sort of magic gibberish. You opened your hands over the fire. An enormous roar and whoosh raised the flames three feet.

"Whoa!"

The heads—the part of the run that's too toxic and flammable to pour on the ground—made for reckless fun with the fire. What is it that we love about making a fire burn wild? Pushing it to burn higher and hotter. I'd seen gas fires at Sal's. The damage that kind of heat can do to the metal shell of a car is humbling. Those flames that night seemed to be just as strong and hot. I knew the potential for destruction. And yet they're also mesmerizing. Energizing. Again and again we laughed and screamed at the way the fire danced and leaped, thirsty for more fuel.

Finally, we all hit a wall of exhaustion. Bucky and Roni left for their tent, and you looked ready to fall asleep in your chair.

I said, "I'm sorry about today. With the gun."

You said, soft and sweet, "Me too."

"But, Mason. Who were you worried about?" You'd talked to us about ABC agents and arrests and red flags, but I didn't think you'd point a gun at anyone wearing a badge.

"Other shiners. They're the first to know when there's a new still."

"Why do they care?"

"Competition. Tradition. General meanness."

"What would they do if they caught us?"

You frowned in the dim light of the coals. "You ever see *Deliverance*?"

I'm glad I hadn't then. I didn't know what to be scared of. Not exactly. I think you were kidding, mostly.

"Remember how I told you I might be a liability?"

"We can't do this without you, Mason."

You didn't disagree. You just said, "Some people wouldn't be too happy about me helping out rival shiners."

I laughed a little. Because I was nervous, but also to think we could be seen as actual competition. "Mason, I think you should sleep in the tent tonight. Unless you think the mosquitoes will miss you too much."

"You can't sleep out here either," you said, clarifying my invitation.

You were asleep before I even arranged my blankets. I lay in the dark, where I smelled your skin mixed in with the smell of smoke.

I didn't have to put up any boundaries because you weren't even knocking at the wall.

18

*T*didn't sleep well that night. My body ached in unfamiliar spots. My mind raced, replaying all the steps of working Aunt Jezebel. I heard noises from the woods beyond the tent wall. Within the tent, I heard you. Breathing, shifting, being there, next to me. Once the tent glowed with early morning, I gave up and watched you sleep.

Your eyes moved behind your lids. You looked peaceful. Younger. It wasn't hard to picture that little boy losing his hat on the beach.

An achy, restless wanting feeling bubbled up in me. It was too much and too early in the morning. I needed space to get my head set. I slipped out of my blankets and unzipped the tent.

Then I saw your gun lying beside you.

My heart rate quickened. I don't know if I was mad or scared that you'd brought that thing in the tent with us. I couldn't hang on to either feeling. You could have hidden it from me. I never would have known it was there. I knew you'd left it out in the spirit of open honesty. That's something I admire because it's so hard for me to be that way.

You slept on. Tentatively, I reached for the gun. It was cold and heavy against the palm of my hand. I turned it over. Found the spot where it fit.

On my knees, I wrapped both hands around the metal handle and tried the position I'd seen TV cops use.

"Lulu," you said, startling me out of the roar in my ears. "I couldn't leave it outside."

I lowered the gun. "It's okay, Mason. It's only a tool."

I meant it too. I'd put my trust in you to help us. I looked to you as the expert. Danger laced everything we were doing. I didn't have the right to doubt you about this one thing I knew nothing about.

"Yeah?" Your eyes searched mine. You stopped me when I tried to hand it to you. "Put it on the ground," you said.

I did, between us.

"That's the safest way to pass a gun. In case it's loaded.

Which this one isn't." You picked it up, opened the chamber to show me the empty space. "You always want to check that."

"Show me how to use it."

You sat up, rubbed your eyes. "Nah. You don't need to know that."

I wasn't sure enough to insist. Now that you were awake, I needed to get out of the tent. Being so close to you first thing in the morning had me off balance.

We didn't hang around that morning. You and Bucky had cleared our camping spot by the time Roni and I brushed our teeth. The stone fire ring was scattered and the ashes covered with dirt. Except for a few broken branches, someone would be hard pressed to notice we'd been there.

I didn't like leaving our treasure stashed under a leafy shelter, but there were too many jars to hide until we knew for sure where it was going to end up.

We still needed someone to sample it, so I filled a few water bottles with the liquor. I marked them xx, for two runs through the still, the way you said the old shiners did. That's also the sign for poison, but I prayed it wasn't.

I was the last one down the hill to where the three of you had parked. Roni had left for practice and Bucky was already in his truck. He called out the window, "It'll be a hoot if we actually make some money off this thing."

"Yep," you said. "We'll see."

Then I was left with you. My heart wasn't sure it could handle being so close to you without the buffer of Roni and Bucky. Not having any other choice, I climbed in your truck beside you. I watched you put the gun in the metal box under your seat. You started up the engine and eased forward. Soon it was clear we were stuck in the soft clay dirt.

We got out and checked the situation. You took off your hat, rubbed your hair, and said, "You drive, Lulu. I'll push."

You shoveled gravel around the wheels, and I got in the driver's seat. I hadn't driven your truck before, but I put the key in the ignition. Adjusted the seat, checked the mirrors. I started the engine, got the window down, and waited for instructions.

"Move along, nice and easy."

I pressed gently on the gas. The wheels whirred and hummed. "A little more gas," you called.

I felt the bump as the truck edged over the ridge. I concentrated on pushing the gas, not too fast and not too slow. But I didn't pay attention to the tree on my right.

"Head left!" you yelled. I was already hearing the screech of metal on tree by the time you yelled, "Left! Other left. Leftleftleftleft. Stop!"

I was wedged in so tight with that tree I could see the grain and texture of the bark pressed against the glass of the passenger window.

"Sorrysorrysorrysorry," I said, getting out of the truck.

"Hmmm" was all you said.

You circled around, checking each view of the damage. Then you sighed.

That sound hit me dead wrong.

"Mason, are you in or out?"

You met my eyes but didn't answer.

"I need to know."

You said, "I can't make any deliveries like this. The truck will stand out too much. I can't be noticed."

It didn't matter if you were right. Not in that moment.

"Are you going to take off running anytime something goes wrong?" My cheeks burned hot and my eyes blinked too fast. "Because, as you can see, things go wrong sometimes. I'm going to make mistakes. I'll screw things up."

You rubbed your hair and kicked the ground.

"We want your help, Mason. But I need to know you're in it all the way."

You started a smile, then stopped when you realized I wasn't going to let this go. "It's no big deal, Lu. It's just a beater truck." You reached to move a curl off my face.

That intimate move, the gentle way your finger brushed my cheek as you gazed at me, completely set me off. I exploded. Like a shot of moonshine in an open flame.

"Why do you act like that, Mason? Why do you touch

my hair and my face and why do you smile so sweet and, and, and..." I knew I was losing it, but was too exhausted for damage control. "What are you playing at?"

I took a deep breath and threw my heart at you. "Do you like me, Mason? I don't mean as business partners or friends or anything like that. I mean, do you *like* me? Do you want..."

The way you looked at me loosened me from the inside out.

You finally kissed me.

Long and sweet and deep.

I never knew kisses could feel like that. The trembling in your arms told me something had hit you too. I wrapped my arms around your neck, found your hair was almost long enough to take ahold of. Your hands felt strong and warm against my back. Tentative touches and tastes shifted closer, firmer. We opened up to each other, grew more certain in our kisses.

I could have rationalized that it was exhaustion letting my guard down, or the new reckless me I'd been trying on for size, or any million psychobabble reasons for the way I pressed against you, not caring about my usual rules and guidelines. You say it was finding our place in fate.

Finally, pausing to catch our breath, we looked into each other's eyes. "Wow," you said.

Exactly.

Then we laughed. That was good too.

Even filthy and tired and standing on the edge of the road where I'd smashed in the side of your truck, kissing you felt right and melty and perfect. All over.

After a while, when my knees were shaky and my middle had completely turned to liquid, I said, "We have to do something about your truck."

You nodded, keeping your eyes locked with mine. "Guess so."

I laughed. "Really."

You decided to drive backward instead of forward to dislodge your truck from the tree. You jostled it, inching and edging bit by bit, avoiding the softer spots where we'd started. Finally the truck screeched free. The passenger door was bent into a tree shape. The bark had even left an imprint in the paint. I knew where to fix it.

I didn't think about Cindy as we drove your banged-up, smashed-in truck to Sal's. I didn't think about much of anything except kissing you and the way I felt in your arms. Later, away from the spell of you and your lips, I did. Cindy drove into a tree too. That's how she died. I couldn't help but wonder…were you thinking of her when you were kissing me?

That morning, grimy and tired, but humming and tingling from kisses, I directed you to the back of the junkyard, close to Dawg's trailer. He stood inside the metal fence, watching us. I climbed out to talk to him. "We need some spot work done. Quick and quiet. Without Sal being bothered."

He eyed me, then your truck, then you. Sometimes it's like I can see Dawg's thoughts behind his eyes. It's like a bolt fitting into a nut, being tightened, turn by turn. Finally, he said, "Okay."

A few minutes later you'd parked behind the Dawg-house. I scanned the yard for Sal. He might not have minded the Muscles' helping me, but he would have had questions I didn't feel up to answering. He'd for sure tell my mother anything he saw.

"What's this I hear about a damsel in distress?" Ollie appeared around the corner of the trailer. Then, "Whoa. Who hit you?" I like to think he'd be equally concerned if I was the one hurt, but seeing your mangled truck seemed to truly make him falter.

"I kinda sorta hit a tree," I said.

Ollie shook his head, making *tsk-tsk* sounds. "There ought to be laws against trees running wild across the road."

"Can you fix it?" I asked.

"Course I can fix it."

"Real fast?"

"Do you want it done right or do you want it done fast?"

"Fast," you and I said together. And caught each other's eyes. You grabbed my hand. That meant so much to me.

Coming back into the real world had me feeling uncertain of the rules. I didn't know if those kisses were something to keep secret and out of sight. But the way you gazed at me made me warm and mushy inside, all over again.

Right now, this minute...I miss your touch.

Back then I felt Ollie staring at us. We were that obvious, already.

I said to him, "So, you gonna help us or just think about it?"

They had that dented door off in minutes. Of course Ollie had to narrate his fix step by step as if I'd ever try this on my own. You listened politely, even though you could have done most of the work yourself if you'd had the right tools. Seemed like the hardest part was taking the outer sheet off the frame, but he looked most serious when he used that rubber hammer on the backside. Midway across he said, "Lulu, you need to find Randy and tell him where we are so he doesn't get pissed or ask Sal."

I turned to you, but Ollie said, "Leave Malone here. I need his help."

Because of you and your kisses, all those scavenged rejects of old cars looked shiny and bright to me that day. By the time Randy and I made our way back to the improvised body shop, Ollie had dragged out the dent puller. He made his way across the door, suctioning the metal back into place, little by little. When he was done, only tiny ripples pocked the metal like old acne scars. My mistake was almost erased.

Wouldn't it be nice to have one of those for life?

"We could get it better if we had more time," said Ollie.

"No. It looks great," I said. "I promise I'll pay you guys. Soon." Yet another debt.

"Nah," he said. "We're good. Dawg made a withdrawal."

I looked to Dawg in confusion. He held up one of our water bottles marked with the poison sign.

"Wait, Dawg," I said, too late. Before I could choke out any kind of warning, Dawg opened the bottle and gulped a big swallow. He smacked his lips.

I covered my eyes. Then, when he didn't fall to the ground, I peeked. It hadn't killed him. If any of the poison had trickled in, it would have knocked him out immediately. Otherwise, we didn't have to worry. Aunt Jezebel was clean and we'd used all natural ingredients.

We paid them on the spot, one bottle each.

I thought that's why Ollie asked you to stay. So he could try to weasel some moonshine from you. But you said he was threatening you about being nice to me. Asking your intentions and warning you to be careful with my heart.

I thought that was a ridiculous thing for him to say. My heart was tough. Undentable.

19

At home, everything was the same. Daddy was gone. Mom baked all hours of the night. Sal kept her stocked with new ingredients and kept her company in the kitchen.

Nothing was the same for me. The same way Aunt Jezebel and Baby had transformed the innocent sugar and corn, I was changed too. Kissing you set off a serious chemical reaction. Me plus you equals heat. Feelings bubbled up and over. You were where I wanted to be.

It could have been awkward and weird waiting to see how you'd act the next time we got together—I had no idea when that would be—except I found you sitting on my front step the next morning when Roni drove up to take me to work.

"How long do I have to wait before I call you?"

I laughed. "You don't have to wait."

"I didn't want to be pushy."

I held out the piece of Mom's freshly baked cobbler. You leaned in as if to take it, but instead you kissed the spot on my neck near my ear, sending delicious shivers along my skin.

Roni honked her horn.

We saw each other whenever, wherever we could. Remember the stolen kisses behind the backhoe when you rode all the way out to the junkyard on your lunch hour? We both felt wrong kissing in the room at Saint Jude's, but the graveyard was a different matter. I'd found something that could, at least temporarily, distract me from thoughts of money and moonshine.

You.

Kisses.

We exchanged hundreds, maybe thousands, of kisses, each one making me want another.

One night, sitting on my front steps, I asked, "Why didn't you kiss me sooner? Didn't you want to?"

"Of course I wanted to," you said, showing me what you meant.

"When did you first want to?"

"When did we first meet?"

I laughed. "I know you didn't want to kiss me that night. Not when I was hurling in your helmet."

Looking more serious, you said, "I really don't know. I can't remember a time when I didn't want to. But I'm used to…fighting my wants."

I got that. Believed in it. But I also believed in fighting for what I want.

You also took me driving. You had your truck now for us to use, and me driving into the tree must have reminded you I needed practice. As I drove on those back roads I asked, "So when will we make our first sale?"

"Soon," you said. And, "Stay to the right."

"Is it that guy from the Fourth? When do we meet him?"

"On the road, Lu. Eyes on the road." Then you said, "We're figuring that out. He's got lots of rules as to how this'll go."

I didn't know what kinds of rules there might be. I only knew I felt impatient. Worried that all our work and investment would go to waste. My days and nights were full of you, but they were slipping away, too fast. Each day gone was another day closer to my deadline marked in red on the kitty calendar. Just under two months. Fifty-one days.

During one drive you showed me the gravel road that leads to your family's business. We couldn't see the old warehouse building from where we drove, but I felt it tug at you, turning you quiet.

We drove down to the river to visit Jake, bringing him sandwich fixings and one of Mom's apple-peach pies. His shack looked even more precariously perched on the hillside than I remembered. I asked, "If Baby is so important to your family, why do they keep it here? Shouldn't the yeast be somewhere safer?"

"We can't keep it on-site," you said. "It's too risky. What with the odds of fire or explosion. Or drunken dumbness."

I got that, but I also couldn't help but feel like Jake's shack must look different through your eyes.

"And it's a way to keep him in the business. He's earned his place. It's a matter of respect."

Jake didn't answer your knock. Holding the grocery sack, you turned to me and said, "Wait here a minute."

I heard you behind his lopsided door, moving around, talking low to him. After sounds of shifting steps and moving something heavy you called, "Come on in, Lu."

Jake looked even worse than his shack. He slumped in his chair, his piercing eyes the only parts of his gaunt face that moved. He croaked, "Hello, Beauty."

"Hey, Jake."

You handed him a tiny bit of bread.

"I'm thirsty," he said, stubbornly.

"You're in luck. I have a fresh brew," you said. "Baby's done good work."

You had to help him with the first sip. His hands shook too badly as he tried to lift the bottle to his mouth. Then he grabbed on and took another swig by himself. He sat up a few inches, smiled his scary, lipless grimace, and said, "There's real corn in there."

"A course." You laughed. "We made it the right way. Up in the woods."

He bobbed his head up and down. It was a wonder his skinny neck could hold the weight. "Tell me. Tell me all about it."

It was like you were telling him a bedtime story. Your voice, velvety smooth and lulling, described the hill where we set up Aunt Jezebel; the way the stream ran close by. All the things we mixed together, each step we took. Jake nodded and chuckled and sipped his bottle.

"And of course we stayed out of the noon sun," you said.

"It'll burn it," Jake said. "Damn sun'll burn it every time. She's jealous of the moon."

"We could use your help, Jake," you said. "We're trying to make some serious money."

I think the idea of selling thrilled him as much as the bottle settled his nerves. He grinned and smacked his jaw open and shut. "Have you called Charlie Ellis? That's the thirstiest son-of-a-bitch I ever knowed."

"You know how I might get ahold of him?"

Jake chattered awhile giving us names. I thought you were humoring a sick old man with your questions. But you knew he had connections. He knew who'd want to buy some fresh moonshine. He finally pointed you toward the old leather notebook tied with twine he had hidden beneath the barrel in the corner.

When you stood up to leave, I did too. Jake was dozing off by then, the bottle still in his hand. You gently put the cap back on, then we crept toward the door. As the sunshine hit my face, Jake croaked one last bit of advice: "Watch out for the devil."

That warning didn't mean much to me. The devil gets plenty of blame in Dale. The higher up the hills or deeper into the river valley, the more he's mentioned. He's feared and reviled, but definitely respected.

I didn't know that you and Jake knew him personally.

As I drove away, you said, "Guess I better find out what Seth has been up to."

Keeping my eyes on the road, I asked, "Why's that?"

"Jake always called Seth the devil." You laughed a little.

I didn't ask why or what that meant. I've never been one to turn stones over to see what lurks beneath. But I did hear the tinge of missing in your voice.

You dropped it. Turned back into my sweet, silly driving instructor. Sloughed off the dim dark of Jake's shack.

Instead, you took me parking.

I mean, you actually taught me to park. You said, "You can't take off if you won't be able to stop when you get where you want to be."

The high school parking lot already seemed smaller, dingy and faded, something I'd left behind. The football team was practicing, reminding me that fall lurked beyond the horizon. Fall, when I'd be off to California.

That was the crazy, confusing thing. We were making money so I could leave. All the days that had brought us together had been working for something that was going to pull us apart. Aunt Jezebel had come through. Jake had approved the taste. You had customers to call. If all our plans and hopes worked out, I'd be gone.

For the moment, I wanted to slow down and enjoy the ride.

20

A couple of days later Bucky stopped by Sal's near the end of my shift.

I was sitting in the loader with Randy getting a lesson on maneuvering the big yellow machine. Driving it was remarkably simple. Only the size of it made it something to take seriously. When Bucky drove up, I backed in, parking beside the Dawghouse.

"Not bad, Lulu," said Randy. "We'll make you a Muscle yet."

Bucky was there to pick up a part for his father, but also, he was lost with Roni off to Richmond with Lullaby

Breaker. I was thrilled not to have to ride home with Sal, who was bringing a load of rhubarb to my mother.

Bucky said, "Mason wanted me to tell you he'll be back in a few days."

"Back? From where?"

"He's selling Aunt Jezebel's baked goods."

"You sure? He didn't tell me."

"Yeah. We decided that you might make it more complicated than it needs to be."

"What does that mean?"

"You know exactly what that means. Plus Mason's paranoid. He told me to tell you not to call or text in case someone traces it."

I looked at my phone that I'd already pulled out, about to do just that.

I was so excited that you were making a delivery I could almost forgive you for not telling me about it yourself. It made me desperate to do something to help. The only idea I had was to make more mash, but we needed cash for the ingredients. Impulsively, I hunted down Ollie and asked if we could make some kind of deal.

Either Dawg didn't drink his payment for helping us fix your truck or he was immune to its effects, but Ollie and Randy had been pretty close to useless around the junkyard while they'd recovered. They didn't see it as a bad thing. So, while you were off making your delivery, I sold Ollie the rest of my cooler's worth of those poison-marked bottles for enough money to buy more cornmeal and sugar. You'd already showed us how we could reuse Baby a few times.

I think Bucky and I did a pretty good job mixing the mash. We're both particular enough that we checked and rechecked each other every step of the way, bickering the whole time. I wished you were there to guide us, but Bucky was the one to say it. While we waited for the mixture to boil he said, "It's a good thing you and Mason finally got to it, huh?"

I hated that he'd made me blush.

"It's been ridiculous watching the two of you in heat all summer."

"You're so gross, Bucky."

He laughed. "Only because you're repressed, Lulu. Sex is a natural bodily function. You're going to do it eventually. And I guarantee you'll wonder why you waited."

I concentrated on stirring the mash. He was only saying what I'd always believed. That sex—and love—is a matter of biology. Instinct.

You'd made it feel like something more.

We hadn't done much beyond kissing. Heated hours of kissing, but for someone measuring progress, there hadn't been any quantifiable change. All clothes stayed on. Curious hands had roamed the landscapes of each other, but there'd only been quick, furtive slips beneath to reach hot skin. The way I ached inside whenever you held me close felt like something so different than hard science.

When Bucky dropped me off at my house that night, I told him something I hadn't told anyone else. "I got my roommate assignment. Her name is Ashley Jones."

"And?"

"She's from someplace near San Diego called Rancho Santa Fe. I thought it sounded like a farm. I Googled it, and her neighborhood is filled with mansions. She's so rich it's crazy."

"Is she hot?"

"You'd like her. She's blond and skinny. What about you? You set for school?"

"I don't know if I'm going."

"You're kidding, right?" It wasn't fair that I had to work so hard for something he could have so easily. "You have a full scholarship, Bucky."

"Not everything is about money."

"Roni'll wait for you," I said. "She's crazy about you."

"Of course she is. Who wouldn't be?" He laughed. Then shrugged. "I like it here."

"What if you're doing the same exact thing in ten years?"

"I don't see anything wrong with that."

That's what I had to guard against. Biology. My hormones working to betray me. I was not going to let my prehistoric instincts trick me into thinking it might be okay to stay in Dale.

After he drove off, I hid the leftover mash ingredients around back, then came in through the garage.

I heard Mom's whimpering before I saw her huddled at the bottom of the basement stairs.

"I heard something," she said. "But I couldn't find the light switch."

"It's right here." I flicked it on, revealing my mother quivering in pink pajamas.

We sat there, arms around each other, until Mom's breathing calmed. Even then we had to scoot our bottoms up, one step at a time. Finally, at the top of the stairs, Mom stood on shaky legs as I walked her to bed. I tucked her in. Brought her a glass of water. Kissed her good night.

Then I posted a bunch of photos online. Picked some from prom and Roni's eighteenth birthday that looked like I was having a wild time. Made myself into a new funloving, free-flying party girl. I told Ashley Jones I couldn't wait to meet her in September.

21

I felt anxious while you were gone. I worried you'd been arrested. Or taken hostage. I wondered if you'd filched our liquor and drunk yourself into oblivion. You hadn't called or texted me one single time. At first I didn't call you because Bucky said you didn't want me to, but after the second day I wasn't about to call you first. You obviously didn't miss me like I missed you.

Roni came back from Richmond with a whole new look. She'd gotten her hair cut supershort. Her makeup was bolder and always on. She radiated a new confidence, even sitting in the trailer at Sal's. "They loved us," she said about the concert. "I never felt such a rush." All the

Muscles crowded around her, acting ridiculous for her attention. Randy pulled up the latest Lullaby Breaker video online, and they all cheered as if they were at her show.

Once we were alone in the trailer she said, "Being in Richmond made me realize different places have different tempos. Like songs. Richmond is faster and louder than Dale."

I nodded and rotated back and forth on my stool.

"I guess what I'm saying is, I finally get it. Dale just isn't your speed, is it?"

Tempo was a good way to explain it. Dale seemed anemic to me. Slow and sleepy, or even sluggish, like there's something caught in the fuel line.

Roni looked out the window. "Grungie wants the band to go on tour. He has a few gigs lined up in North Carolina. Don't laugh....He even wants to go to Nashville."

"I'm not laughing. You guys are good. And they're better with you."

"Grungie says he's getting more calls ever since I joined."

"When do you go?"

"I haven't asked Bucky yet."

"You need to do what's best for you, Roni."

"Bucky's what's best for me." She sounded certain. So sure.

"If he's off at school, why would he care if you're playing with the band?"

"He doesn't like me being with all those guys."

"I thought he trusted you."

She sighed. "You don't get love at all, do you, Lulu?"

I felt defective when she said things like that. Because she was right.

Roni said, "I think Mason feels left out that you and Bucky mixed mash without him."

"You saw Mason?" I swear my insides fluttered.

"He and Bucky stopped by my house on their way to work."

The flutters turned into a hard lump. I checked my phone again. Nothing.

Feeling irritated and closed in, I said, "I'm going to unload those baby things Clara-Jane brought by. I'll see if there's anything worth selling."

Out in the This-n-That section—the collection of miscellaneous household things for crafters and hoarders—the gnats adored me, collecting in my curls and dive-bombing my eyes and nose. I was looking for space and quiet. Machine grunts and metal clangs don't count as real noise. I'd already set out some wire baskets and an old-fashioned high chair when I looked up and saw you.

I hadn't expected you to show up at Sal's. I definitely

didn't expect the surge of happy that flowed through every inch of me seeing you ride in on your bike. I clutched a box of empty baby food jars so I wouldn't throw myself into your arms.

"Hey," you said. "I'm back."

"I see that." I put the box down, smoothed its top for something to do with my hands.

"Whatcha got there?"

"Junk. Seeing as you're in a junkyard."

You leaned your bike against the chain-link fence. "Can we take a walk, Lu?"

I shook my head. "I'm on the clock." Sal probably wouldn't have noticed or even cared especially, but I wasn't about to give in to your casual invitation. I'd been stewing and worrying about you, and now here you were, perfect and gorgeous and smiling.

"I guess I should have called first. But I forgot your number."

I shook my head at your lame nonsense, even if you did look a little embarrassed.

"I took your number out of my phone. In case something happened. I didn't want you incriminated. I forgot I'm no good at remembering phone numbers." You scrunched your nose in a way that was unfairly adorable. You bent over and picked up one of the baby food jars.

"You think this little guy'll grow up to be a moonshine jar someday?"

Baby moonshine. It was your idea, even if you didn't know it.

Right then I said, "I gotta get back to work. Call me sometime. Oh, wait. You can't."

"Something wrong, Lu?" Your voice sounded so inappropriately amused. You moved closer, your crooked smile all for me. "I've been about crawling out of my skin to get over here and see you. Are you saying you want me to leave?"

I forced my hands to stay behind my back. "What am I supposed to think? You didn't tell me you were leaving. Then you don't even call. I heard from Roni you were back. Roni, who could have given you my number, for instance. Or Bucky. Or a million other ways you could have found it."

"I didn't think of doing any of those things. I guess I was too busy thinking about seeing you." You moved in next to me, only inches away, but still not touching me. You smelled so good it made me homesick for your arms.

No other boy had ever made me so unsteady, so unsure of how things were supposed to go. Trying to cover up the way you melted me, I said, "I'd think you'd treat a business partner better."

You lifted my hair, allowing a cool breeze to hit my

sweaty neck. "That's what you're mad about, Lu? That I'm not a good business partner?"

"What if you'd run off with all our hard work in the back of your truck?"

"You'd track me down." Your eyes never left mine.

"What if you were hurt? How would we know you needed help? Haven't you heard of the buddy system?"

"Does that mean I'm your buddy?" Your voice was teasing, your lips so close.

Finally I caved. "I thought you were my boyfriend." I kissed you then. I didn't even care if anyone was watching from across the junkyard.

With your fingers through my belt loops, you grinned goofy at me. "I like hearing that."

"Good." I played with your shirt.

"Check my back pocket."

I reached around you, pulled out a thick wad of bills. "Oh my..."

"You done being mad now?"

I ruffled the bills, too many to count right there. "I can't believe it worked."

You laughed.

I'd missed your laugh. I realized leaving wasn't going to be as smooth and easy as it would have been a month earlier.

I glanced at the cashier trailer, but the dark windows and the bars made it impossible to see if anyone was looking out. I stuffed the money back in your pocket. "If Sal sees this, he won't let you leave until you spend it. But, Mason. You can't up and disappear again."

You tilted your head and said, "I didn't know anyone cared if I made it back."

I cared too much.

Everything about us getting together was mixed up and confusing. Backward. We'd gotten so close before we ever kissed, and then kissed like crazy, but we still hadn't gone on a real date. I'd already missed you before I'd left. It was like eating an ice cream sundae upside down and we were making our way down to the sweetest tastes of chocolate and cream.

But.

I had to stay focused on leaving. Daddy had been gone for a longer stretch than usual. Ever since I'd found Mom whimpering in the dark, Sal had been helping out more than I liked. Having him around our house was a loud reminder that I needed to make more money.

We'd split up the huge wad of cash you'd brought back from your sale up in northern Virginia, leaving seed money for supplies and expenses in our community pouch held by Roni, who we all trusted best. I'd immediately sent my share to USD.

I still had a long ways to go, but if we could make that same amount each week—which would mean running Aunt Jezebel as fast as she could go—I'd have enough by mid-August. That'd even give me a two-week cushion to finalize plans and pack and maybe even have a bit of summer vacation. But that didn't leave a lot of room for mistakes along the way. I didn't realize then just how good that first sale was. Good enough that now, looking back, I wonder if you took your cut.

Fact was, we had to make more moonshine. The mash Bucky and I had made while you were gone was ready. Getting back to our spot in the woods felt like a homecoming. Aunt Jezebel's copper sides had blackened and she was starting to show green spots from being outside, but she was beautiful to me.

As we walked around her, I thought you were simply taking in the smells, the birds and chipmunks talking, the way the sunlight flickered through the branches above the mossy ground. I held your hand as I breathed in green and dirt and sunshine and you.

You suddenly let go of me and knelt in the leaves. "Someone's been here." You showed me the limp bit of twine. "I put this up last time Bucky and I were here. Someone broke it."

"I bet that deer came back," I said. "The one you almost shot."

"Deer step higher than people."

"Who would be up here? No one else has the right to be on Roni's land."

"You really think everyone follows the rules, don't you, Lu?"

"Well, they should."

Never mind that we were breaking all kinds of rules.

That run went a little bit rougher than our charmed first time, but it was all right in the end. Bucky burned his forearm early on, and then there was that moment things got backed up and you had to jiggle something free. Mostly it was a job and we did it.

We—all four of us—were a little subdued that day. I was caught up in my usual muddle of impatience. You were probably thinking about that string and wondering who might have been there and why. Bucky and Roni must have been thinking about their fight the night before even though we didn't know anything about that at the time.

Roni steered clear of Aunt Jezebel altogether. Instead,

she raked leaves and pulled weeds. When she started rear-ranging rocks to make a wall, Bucky said, "Quit playing house, Roni, and help get these bottles ready."

She threw a rock at him and took off toward the stream. Bucky stomped off to follow her, leaving you and me to finish and clean up.

As we scrubbed Aunt Jezebel's insides with lemon juice I asked, "Who do you think was up here, Mason? Are we going to get arrested?"

I love the way you take your time to say what you mean. After you finished wiping her down and closing her back up, you said, "I don't think we have to worry about the law. They'd have to have a reason to snoop around private property. It's easier to catch a sale."

"Who else would be here?"

"Might have been a poacher. Or a lookie-loo. Some people make a hobby of finding stills." Your hair was long enough now that it looked a little mussed when you bothered it. You being nervous made me nervous too.

"But that's not who you're worried about."

"Word's out that I've been asking around for sales, Lu. Never know how far those echoes travel."

"What should we do?"

"Wait and see. Pray if it makes you feel better."

I wonder if you knew I wasn't praying so much

anymore. I was still going through the motions, going to church, saying grace before meals, praying the Rosary with Mom. But I'd given up on God getting me what I needed. It was up to me to make it happen. You were helping. But I could only count on me.

"Mason, do you have your gun with you?"

"Maybe." You looked wary.

"Teach me how to shoot."

"Why?"

"I want to know how. In case I ever need to."

"It's my thinking that I make sure you don't have to."

"It's not like I'm going to get a gun, but it'd be a shame if something came up and I needed to know how but no one had ever taught me."

You were quiet a minute. Then said, "I guess I could." Then added, in a gentle, firm voice, "Only because all those facts and fears you spouted off—those are about people who don't know what they're doing."

You led me away from Aunt Jezebel, closer to where we'd camped. You pulled the pistol from your ankle holster and handed it to me.

I turned its surprising weight over in my hands.

"You have to check if it's loaded, Lu. You always have to check." The urgency in your voice made me feel scared and protected in the same breath.

Once you'd removed the magazine and emptied the chamber, you let me turn the weapon over in my hands, had me look at it from every direction. I practiced pointing it. You stepped behind me. "Let yourself stumble." You pushed my back, making me step forward to figure out it was my right leg that needed to go in front. You faced me again, placed your hands on my shoulders, then my hips. "Keep your head straight, that's where your aim'll go. Now brace yourself." You pushed at me, testing my stance. "Good. Nice and steady."

You showed me how to load the gun. Made me do it on my own a couple of times. Finally satisfied, you stepped behind me and said, "Lift her." I lifted my arms straight in front of me, holding it in my right hand with my left one supporting the hold. You stood solid and warm as you wrapped yourself around me. The stubble from your cheek rubbed mine as you helped me hold the gun. "Cradle it like you'll never let go."

Your heart beat against my back, we breathed together in perfect time. Then you stepped away. "Take the safety off."

I did, easily.

"Pull the trigger."

"You sure?" Sweat trickled along my neck and down my sides.

"Nope. Put her down a minute."

I wiped my left hand off on my jeans, transferred the gun to it, and wiped the other hand. "Okay. I'm ready."

"Take a minute."

"I'm all right. I want to do this."

You stepped back, out of my line of vision.

The sound was deafening. Literally. My hand tingled and throbbed. Adrenaline coursed through me; my heart danced wildly in my chest. I took a couple more shots before Bucky and Roni came running.

Roni said, "Mother-of-a-gangster, what the hell are you doing, Lulu?"

"What are you staring at?" I asked Bucky, ignoring the heat in my cheeks.

"I have no idea," he said. "No idea at all."

I didn't either.

~

It was Roni's idea to hide the bottles of moonshine in my silly gift car parked outside the cashier trailer. It was too much hassle to haul them back and forth to Aunt Jezebel when the goal was to sell it all as soon as possible.

We labeled the boxes of bottles BOOKS, ensuring the Muscles would have no interest, and stuffed them in the backseat and trunk once you jimmied off the lock. It was like I was packing up for school.

You, who believes in meant-to-be—what do you think about the way I didn't have to go looking for customers? They came to me.

One day, when Sal was working off-site, a man came to the cashier window and mumbled, "I'd like some of your, uh, special."

At first I wondered if he was slow, or a pervert who'd need me to sic Dawg on him—we've seen both. He said, "Ollie sent me. Said you had some poison. To drink."

I got his meaning. But was too surprised to answer. Roni stepped up to the window and said, "We might be able to connect you with our contractor who handles rat control. Leave us your name and number. We'll get back to you."

"Shit, honey. I don't care about rats. I just want some moonshine."

Roni almost growled, "Shut it. What do you think this is?"

He stepped back from the window mumbling curses. "Ollie said..."

I whispered, "We could make a sale."

She shook her head. "Sometimes you are too naive to believe."

Once he left the yard, Roni paged Ollie. When he and Randy showed up at our trailer, she got right to the point.

"Where do you get off telling your loser friends that Lulu is a moonshine dealer?"

"I don't think Lulu's a dealer. I think she's making time with one."

I said, "Mason is not any kind of anything dealer. That was my cooler. Mine. Not his."

Randy said, "So you are the dealer." He turned to Ollie. "Told you."

"You don't have to put it like that."

Ollie held his hands up. "I'm not looking to get anyone in trouble. I thought I was helping some friends with mutual goals in mind."

Roni kicked him out of the trailer.

"Might want to think about it," Randy called back over his shoulder. "We got a lot of loser friends."

I said, "If someone's a friend of Ollie and Randy, it's probably all right."

"Do you actually want to get arrested?"

"If we sell our own brand of rat poison, it's not really our fault if someone uses it for something else. Is it illegal to sell rat poison?" It probably is, but that wasn't my point.

"What if Sal finds out?" Roni crossed her arms over her chest and tapped her foot. "You need this job as much as I do, Lulu. What if we can't sell enough for you to go to school? Don't you want to keep working here? It's a better job than anything else you could get."

I didn't, and yet I'd have to.

It was such a circle of a puzzle. If I sold the moonshine on Sal's property, I might lose my job. If I sold enough I wouldn't need that job. If I didn't sell, I could keep my job, but I didn't want it. Hard to know which way to play.

A little later, Roni sighed. Then said, "Thing is, I don't want to work here if you're not here, Lulu. Not anymore."

So we pulled out the empty baby food jars. They weren't anything Sal cared about. We washed them out and dressed them up with our dead rat logo. We kept our xx sign as the dead eyes, then added whiskers, a pointy nose, ears, and a long skinny rat tail that wrapped around the jar. It was a silly design that tickled us. Pretty soon we had the cutest little baby moonshine jars anyone had ever seen. Somehow those little jars of pseudo–rat poison didn't seem big enough to take seriously.

Roni said, "Well, all right. Let's rid the world of rats."

What's that saying you have? If you kill one rat, three more move in to celebrate? Yep.

Wally's Pie Place was crowded and booming with music that night we went out with Roni and Bucky. It was strange to have a first real date after so much time together, but nice to get fixed up for you. To not have twigs in my hair and sludge on my skin. You might not mind when I'm a mess, but I could tell you liked how I looked that night. You looked good too with your pressed shirt and smooth-shaven face.

I was feeling giddy and light. We'd sold a bunch of rat poison jars, and you and Bucky had made another batch of moonshine that morning. You'd assured me the new mash was started and Baby was doing her thing. All according to plan.

I felt your hand on my back as I waded through the crowd of middle school kids playing video games in the front lobby. Once we hit the main part of the restaurant and people from school waved from their tables, you let me go. Bucky, who knows everyone, and Roni, who was on her way to being famous, stopped to talk along the way, but I headed straight for the back booth.

It felt unfamiliarly ordinary to be sitting under a roof and at a real table. You concentrated on the menu while I said, "What kind of pizza do you like?" And "Have you tried the honeyed wings?" Then, "Do you like this song?" Conversation didn't flow easily. Finally we sat in silence within the noisy restaurant. There was too much space between us in the booth.

"It's crowded in here," I said. "Maybe you should scoot closer to me, leave room for someone else."

You looked at me funny. "What will your friends think about you being with me?"

"Which friends?"

"You're the one who rushed us back here."

I know it was weird to be back in the real world, but I couldn't believe you'd think I was hiding you. "I quit worrying what people think about me a long time ago,

Mason." That was one of the best parts of knowing I was leaving. I kissed you then, for way too long to be polite in public.

Roni plopped down on the opposite side of the booth. "Well, everyone'll know about you two after tonight. Some of the biggest mouths in Dale are here."

I laughed. "Did you tell them it's only our first date?"

"First date, huh?" Bucky eyed us across the table, then asked you, "Did you pick Lulu up?"

"He sure did."

"Did you meet her daddy?"

I said, "He's out of town. But Mason already knows him from Saint Jude's."

"Doesn't matter what he thinks he knows. If Mason's your date, you know your daddy's gonna suddenly look at him from a whole new point of view."

"Is he that bad?" you asked.

"Worse."

"True fact," said Roni. "He made Connor Martin almost pee his pants."

That might be true. But that's Connor's problem, not Daddy's.

"Well," said Bucky. "I think it's my duty to serve as Mr. Mendez's ambassador and ask a few questions." He grinned evilly and handed you a napkin. "Did you know you're wearing the same shade of lipstick as my one and only precious daughter?"

I blushed a little to see the rosy smudges around your mouth from mine, but I wasn't about to let Bucky know.

You wiped your mouth and said, "I wanted to color-coordinate."

"Uh-huh. Well, make sure you don't wear matching underwear." Bucky pointed suddenly. "You weren't just thinking about my daughter's underthings now, were you? Because you wouldn't think about the Virgin Mary's lingerie, would you? I'm getting the feeling you are, boy. What is wrong with you, having thoughts like that? Is your condition treatable?"

He had Roni and me laughing while you tried to keep a straight face.

Bucky went on. "Are you going to do something with your life, Mason? Ten years from now, will my daughter be proud to have spent time in your company?"

Sad but true, Daddy really does ask that one.

"Enough, Bucky," said Roni. "You're making me nervous. I can't even imagine how poor Mason is feeling."

"Don't say I didn't warn you," said Bucky. "You better invest in some really good deodorant. He smells fear."

I linked my arm with yours, wrapped my foot around your ankle.

The waiter appeared then. You and Bucky knew him. I felt him checking me out, and I wondered what he thought about us being together. Did he think I was too young for you? Pretty enough? I cared more what your friends thought than my own.

After we ordered our steak-and-fry pizza Bucky said, "So, Lulu, you think you're going to start eating weird tofu-pesto-spinach pizzas once you're in California?"

I laughed but didn't feel like talking about California right then.

"I guess if you never come back, it doesn't really matter what you eat. Not to us, anyway."

"Shut up, Bucky," said Roni. "You keep this up, they'll never go out with us again."

"That's what she told me. She's never coming back. Isn't that right, Lulu?"

That's what I'd said. I'd even said it to you. It wasn't that I'd changed my mind; it simply didn't fit in there that night. I would have kicked Bucky under the table if I thought it would have knocked that smirk off his face.

"Sorry I forgot his muzzle," said Roni. "He gets cranky when he's hungry." She leaned across the table and said, "Y'all, I have big, big news."

I checked her finger but didn't find a diamond.

"The Queens are having another field party, and

Lullaby Breaker is going to play." She beamed and then said her real news: "We're even playing two songs that I wrote."

"Wow." I turned to Bucky. "That's amazing, don't you think?"

"Mmm," he said, more subdued.

Something occurred to me. "Let's sell moonshine at the party. Remember how they ran out of beer? We could probably clear a run's worth."

"No way, Lu," you said. "That's too much face time. Selling to people who know our names. We have to make big out-of-town sales."

"Do we have any more of those lined up?"

Before you could answer, a man stopped by the table. Swayed with his buzz, holding a beer in one hand. He said, loud and slow, "I know you."

At first I assumed he was another rabid Lullaby Breaker fan. But instead of looking at Roni, he leaned over the table toward me. In a voice meant to be a whisper, but way too loud, he said, "You got me laid."

You hopped up from the bench—looking incredibly hot, because I'm shallow and like when my boyfriend acts tough—and said, "Apologize for that mouth."

He laughed and shoulder-nudged you. "Lighten up,

son. I don't mean no disrespect. She sold me a magic potion. Works like a charm on the ladies."

Roni said, "Do you mean the rat poison, sir?"

I exaggerated a gasp. "You didn't actually give that to someone, did you? We can't be responsible if you're going to misuse our product."

He cocked his head, uncertain. "Poison?" Then he busted out laughing. "You're yanking me. I know what I had."

You looked ready to pop him. On general principle for being rude and crude. I reached up and grabbed your hand. "Sit down, Mason."

"Maybe you'll get lucky and she'll drink her own potion." He laughed again and disappeared into the crowd.

"Mother-of-a-creeper," said Roni. "That poor girl, whoever she is. Probably doesn't know what hit her."

I hadn't thought of what we were selling that way. That our moonshine might make people do things they wouldn't normally do.

"What was that about?" you asked.

Roni and I looked at each other.

Bucky said, "Didn't you know the girls have been selling more than auto parts down at Sal's? How do you think Roni could afford these nice new boots she's wearing?"

He leaned back in the booth, with his arms crossed. "Has Lulu been keeping secrets?"

I tried to explain. "Only a few bottles. To friends of Ollie and Randy. All the money is going to the group. Ask Roni. She's got it all."

You said, with an edge, "This isn't about money. It's about being smart. I told you, homegrown sales get messy."

"We've got to sell it somehow."

"Give me a chance. It takes time."

I didn't have time. The days were getting crossed off of my kitty calendar way faster than the money was adding up. "I want to come with you whenever you go again," I said. "In case something goes wrong."

Bucky laughed. "What are you going to do, Lulu? You got some secret superhero skills we don't know about?"

"I could call for help."

"Who are you going to call?"

He had a point. We were on our own.

Alone.

We couldn't call the police or our parents or Sal or anyone at all. There was no backup. No rescue party. No one in the whole wide world could know what we'd been up to.

The four of us had to stick together because there wasn't anyone else.

Later, we strolled out of Wally's moving slow and lazy, a few feet behind Roni and Bucky. I took your hand, wishing that I didn't feel quite so full of pizza, but glad we had matching garlic breath. I wanted to finish up our first date making you forget about being annoyed with my side sales.

A voice broke through the dark, "I saw your truck."

You stopped. Looked across the parking lot to where Seth stood waiting. Dropped my hand.

Seth said, "Peanut said you sold it, that it wasn't you parked here. But I knew you wouldn't do that. Not without telling me."

When he settled his eyes on me, I said, "Hi, Seth. Good to see you again."

"I wish that meant something," he said, with an off-kilter smile that glowed in the parking lot light. "Unfortunately, you must have pretty low standards for good, seeing as you're hanging out with this ugly thing." He moved in close enough that I could smell his metallic breath.

I backed up a step.

Seth said, "Whoa! Shoo, fly, shoo."

"Take it easy," you said.

"Of course. Nothing but easy." He laughed too loud and too long. "Oh, come on. You know what I mean. Skip to my Lu, my darling."

"Oh, that's funny." Roni sang out, "Fly's in the buttermilk, shoo, fly, shoo." She's always been good at the art of deflection.

"That's it!" Seth spun around. "Exactly. But seriously." He turned back to me. "Shoo, fly, shoo. I need to talk to my cousin here."

"Don't talk to her like that." Your voice sounded sharp. Then, "Talk to me tomorrow. I gotta get Lulu home."

"That's the problem with dating babies, Cuz. They gotta go home to Mama. That's all right. I'll come with."

"Not happening," you said.

All of a sudden, a shot of venom laced his words. "You owe me, Mason. You know you do. I'm happy to skip little Lulu along, but one way or another we're talking."

You and he faced off. I wasn't sure how I'd ever confused the two of you. Not now that I knew every splash of freckle and crinkle around your eyes, the exact way you grinned and listened and eyed the world. Your strength was for lifting, his for weighing down.

You said to me, "Give me a minute."

I stood with Bucky and Roni as you walked him across the parking lot, talking low.

Roni said, "What does Seth want?"

"Hard to say," said Bucky. "He's flying on something. Couldn't you see it in his eyes?"

242

A hard lump sat in my stomach as I watched Seth climb in your truck, right into the seat I thought was mine.

You came back, said, "Bucky, can you get Lulu home?" Then, to me, "I'll call you later."

"You sure you have my number?" I tried to tease.

You gave me a quick kiss on the cheek and then you left.

Feeling a deep and annoying disappointment, I climbed in the backseat of Bucky's truck. Through the window, I watched you pull out, wheels screaming in the night.

You never told me what happened with Seth that night. I didn't ask either. The way I didn't tell you every time Mom turned to a quivering Jell-O mess, you didn't have to tell me the details for me to know your burden wasn't an easy one to carry.

24

Roni had been itching to go night swimming all summer. It was one of those things we did every year—something we had to do at least once before I headed off to college. Usually we went to the tiny pool in her grandpa's trailer park, but when you and Bucky had to work late at the Country Club, she and I showed up with bikinis under our clothes and mischief in mind.

We didn't expect any hesitation. You and Bucky looked at each other. Raised eyebrows, grunted and grimaced. Roni and I have a much more perfected mind-meld.

"You don't want to swim with us?" Roni asked. "Seriously? You have other plans?"

"Maybe we can meet you later?" You looked hopeful.

Roni crossed her arms and glared.

"Whaddya think, Mason?" Bucky said. "Shall we bring 'em along?"

"Yes," I said, because it didn't matter where.

But yes. Of course yes. We absolutely wanted to go on a secret moonlight delivery.

You'd made a deal with a friend of Jake's. "He wants a silent deal," you said.

"Which is why y'all weren't invited," said Bucky. "Seeing as neither of you understands silence."

You were supposed to drop ten one-gallon milk jugs in the woods beyond Betty's Candy Factory. Our client would show up later, pick up the liquor, and head on his way. No face-to-face contact, no money directly changing hands. It was the kind of deal made when there's no trust on either side.

"It's not uncommon," you assured us. "It's safer. For all of us. That's why we'll make even more than usual. They're paying for the convenience."

"When do we get our money?" I asked.

"He'll leave it at the gas station," Bucky said. "In the locked drop box."

"What if your dad gets it?"

"Lulu, do you really think we're idiots? That we can't think of something like that?"

"Sorry," I said. "But?"

Bucky groaned. "It's a specially marked envelope. My dad won't touch it."

Roni squealed. "Are you using one of my envelopes?" Apparently Roni left Bucky sexy love notes at work. Bucky's dad knew better than to mess with the pink-hearted envelopes.

We drove into the valley, with Roni singing and all of us silly and wild. We were ahead of my weekly sales goal, had more bottles on hand and ready to sell, Baby was working the mash with Aunt Jezebel, and the stars sparkled bright in the sky. Everything was perfect.

The four of us unloaded the jugs and stashed them beneath the plastic tarp in less than fifteen minutes.

"All right," you said. "Let's get out of here."

"That's it?" I said. "We could wait and spy from behind those bushes."

"Nope," you said, scooping your arm around me. "That's a violation of the terms. We have to leave. Immediately. In fact, we need to return to the club as soon as possible."

"For an alibi?"

246

"And important studies." You tugged at the stretchy cord hiding beneath my hair. "I need to investigate what that red strap leads to."

After parking down the Country Club driveway where Roni had left her car, we crept back to the pool, whisper-giggling. At the locked gate Bucky turned to you. "Can you get us in?"

I thought maybe you had a key, since you worked on maintenance and repair. Instead you shimmied up over the top of the fence. Dropped down and opened the gate.

The night was warm and the water cool. The full moon was almost too bright. Definitely enough light that I felt shivers when you first saw me in my bikini.

The cement deck felt bigger without the usual crowds. Every sound echoed. Every splash and giggle bounced back at us. At first we tiptoed and whispered, but the same way we adjusted to the water temperature, we relaxed into the night. You put Bucky to shame on the diving board. I don't know where you learned to flip like that.

Bucky couldn't stand you beating him at something, so he challenged you to distance leaps off the side of the pool. Then, while you two tried vertical reaches for the flags over the lap lanes, Roni and I hung our calves over the edge and lay back in the water like we used to do when we still had underwater tea parties and dreamed of being mermaids.

I asked, "You decide about the band tour yet?"

"Nah. Maybe after the Queens' party I'll know better."

That's when you and Bucky couldn't stand that we weren't watching your tricks. The two of you leaped over us.

After squealing and splashing and wrestling, Roni and Bucky anchored themselves to the stairs of the shallow water while you and I drifted in the deep end. At some point they disappeared the way they always do.

You and I talked about silly nothings. Flirting, ducking, dipping under, then up again. Moving in and out of each other's reach. Even with all that chatter, I had trouble focusing on much of anything except the warmth of your skin when we touched. After a long, deep kiss, feeling dangerously out of breath, I pulled away.

You looked surprised, but didn't try to hold me back as I climbed out of the water. I lay facedown on the warm cement, trying to calm my trembling. That wasn't shivering. Not from the cold. That was because of you.

I'd had the virtue of chastity drummed into my head all my life. Or at least ever since my breasts popped out. The advice of Mrs. Young, my catechism teacher, on dating had been "When you're with someone special, leave room for the Holy Spirit in between." And "If you're tempted to go too far, ask Jesus to come sit beside you for a while."

That's a hard image to shake. Basically, the threat of hell and disappointing my parents had kept me saying no. Fear worked.

You had a way of making me brave.

It scared me.

You leaned against the wall, arms resting on the edge. "You all right?"

"Mmm-hmm."

"You gonna stay out there?"

"Yep."

We were silent, the dark night between us. Then you turned back to the pool. "I'm going to take a lap."

While you swam in a burst of flurry and noise, I shivered alone in the dark. I knew me saying no and needing to cool things down was going to put a bump between us. I still had about six weeks left in Dale, and we still needed to work together, but now things were going to change. We'd argue. I'd avoid being alone with you. You'd get irritated and frustrated and make awkward comments to make me feel guilty. I'd been to this place too many times to pretend it could go any other way.

Back at the wall you said, "Hey, Lu?"

I didn't answer.

"We're not going to do anything you don't want to do."

"You're not mad?"

"That'd be impossible."

I knew that wasn't true. I'd been called prude, frigid, ice princess, prick-tease, and worse. After prom, Patrick James wore gloves to school and told everyone he'd gotten frostbite from me.

You said, "I've never done this before."

"Done what?"

Your voice had turned husky. "All of this. Any of this. Being with you."

Of course you had.

"Not sober. I started drinking before I cared about girls. Then I was always drunk or stoned. Always. Once I finally got sober, I couldn't deal with anything more than surviving. There hasn't been anyone else. Not like this."

I slipped back in the water and wrapped my arms around you. We had to work together to stay afloat.

Cool water, warm night, hot skin beneath the surface. Moon shining all around.

Later, closer to early morning, with my lips feeling deliciously tender and my neck tingling from tiny scrapes of your whiskers, I snuck into my dark house. I was surprised to hear Mom's voice coming from the guest room.

I dreaded coming home each night. Hoped I wouldn't find Mom broken down in the dark. After that last bad night I'd called Daddy, but since I caught him as he was about to board a plane for Brazil, I didn't even bother telling him. There wasn't anything he could do.

That night she sounded anything but broken.

Her voice drifted down the hall, light and giggly. Flirty, I'd say if it wasn't my mother. I paused in the hallway, standing outside the door. Listening to her coo—and some kind of low, deep murmur in answer—I was terrified what I'd find behind that door. After being with you, I recognized those kinds of noises. I suddenly remembered the night I'd walked in on her and Sal drinking wine.

Back in the kitchen I felt a deep and burning mad.

No longer sleepy, I put my anger to work. Using Mom's biggest pot, I mixed and boiled cornmeal and sugar. Waited for her to hear me. I didn't have Baby, but I used Mom's baker's yeast. Dared her to ask me what I was making. Wished she'd stop whatever she was doing to investigate. She didn't come out. She never saw me cooking. When it was done, I poured the mixture into one of the buckets her flour came in. Then I stored the fermenting, festering secret in the garage.

I couldn't let myself think about the sounds Mom made behind the office door. At work, Sal's booming voice and laugh grated on my nerves. The smell of his aftershave made me queasy. Roni noticed something too. "I think Sal must have a new sweetie," she said. "Thank the Lord for girls who don't mind used parts." I cringed to think she might mean Mom.

She also gave me her own kind of wisdom. "Lulu, I know Catholics don't believe in birth control. But if you and Mason..."

"We're not. We haven't."

"Yet," said Roni. "I saw you at the pool. Promise me

you'll be as smart as you should be. If you're gonna break one rule, break the other one too."

Our secret moonlight delivery turned out to be a bust. The money never showed up. Bucky was certain no one at the gas station had taken the envelope. You and Bucky went back to the drop-off spot, and it was like all those jugs had never been there. The clincher was that you couldn't get ahold of the buyer. We'd been ripped off.

"That's the way it goes sometimes," you said about a week later when I was still obsessing.

The two of us sat on the floor of your room at Saint Jude's slurping Popsicles. You were almost done fixing it up for Father Mick. The built-in bookshelves and fold-down desk fit the wall perfectly. The curved corners and the extra trim added a simple elegance. It looked so smooth and honey-golden I'd had to run my fingers along the grain.

I found it mysteriously frustrating that you didn't care about the loss of money.

"I do care," you said. "But caring doesn't change what happened."

We'd kept Aunt Jezebel working that week. You'd gotten a fresh bit of Baby and were excited that Jake had shown you how to divide her and feed her so she'd stay happy while waiting in his cabin. A stockpile of jars and jugs was hidden in the woods, since it was too much to fit in my car at the junkyard.

None of it would do me any good if we couldn't sell it.

I was supposed to leave in five weeks. It had been a little less than six since we stole Aunt Jezebel, so it felt both doable and impossible. Like I was standing on the middle of a seesaw waiting to see which side I'd fall on.

Father Mick peered in the room. "Did you need to see me, Lulu?"

I hadn't made it to confession for weeks. I was mad at God. Didn't feel like apologizing. For so long I'd tried to do the right things. I'd played by the rules. I was tired of God getting in my way, making everything so hard. Now we hadn't even gotten the money we'd earned. I shook my head and said, "I'm just here to help Mason." As if there was anything I could do.

After he left, you said, "He wants to call this the Saint Michael's Room. Because he does battle against darkness." You wrapped one of my curls around your finger, tight enough the tip turned white.

"I think we should battle the person who ripped us off."

"He'll get his," you said. "What goes around comes around."

"How can he live with himself, stealing like that?"

You smiled, still playing with my hair. "I love that you always expect the best of people."

"Do you love that I want to rip out his eyeballs and feed them to the rats?"

Could you tell I got nervous every time the word *love* was used? It seemed like it kept popping up in our conversations, making things muddled and hard to read.

Besides the moonshine worries, I was getting confused about you and me too. It was getting harder to slow things down in the dark. True to your word, you didn't push—although now I almost wished you would. Then I'd say no, for sure and for certain. Unless I didn't.

"Mason, what do you want?"

"I'm thinking another blue," you said. "But then red might feel left out."

"Not Popsicles. Something real."

"Thinking like that doesn't do me any good. When I got sober I learned to be thankful. For each day. Each moment. That's enough."

"You're working as hard as any of us. You must want something."

You traced my fingers. "I wasn't looking for anything more than getting through each day, when all of a sudden you showed up. And kept showing up until I had to pay attention."

I remembered.

"You were all fired up and burning with an idea." You paused, thinking, then said, "Seems like having someone ruin your plans for the future must be even worse than no one thinking you'll ever do anything."

I wanted to shake all those no ones who never believed in you.

"And it's been fun. Being with you, but Bucky and Roni too. Y'all didn't have a clue what you were doing when we started, but you sure were having a good time anyway."

There was something else you weren't saying. Something that rankled and bothered.

"Fact is, I love making liquor." Your eyes focused somewhere else. "I love the process. The time it takes. The steps that have to be followed. The setting and fixing. I know I shouldn't, but I do."

It felt like you were fading away a bit, lost in something I couldn't see. "What are you going to do with your share of the money, Mason?"

"Some of it goes to Seth."

"Why?"

"Like he said. I owe him." You stood up, reached down

and pulled me up. "Come on. We're taking you on the highway. We've put it off long enough."

—

I made you drive first, so I could sit back and observe. "Why are you going so fast? Aren't you over the speed limit?"

"Barely."

I couldn't understand the nonchalance that greeted me out of every other windshield. "How do you know those other cars will stay in their lanes?"

"That's the way it works, Lu. Everyone follows the rules. The way you like it."

"What if they don't? There is nothing actually there to force them in their own lane. We're hurtling down the highway inches apart and how do we know it's going to be okay?"

"Trust," you said. "Faith. Whatever keeps you going each day."

"And control," I added. "Everyone needs to keep in control."

"You can't control everything. That's when you have to trust."

"But I'm a control freak," I said.

"Maybe. Only because you see how things should be and try to get them there."

"It makes me bossy."

"I'd say strong."

"And I'm obsessive."

"Persistent. Determined."

That sounded so much nicer. It was like you saw the real me, but from a different angle. "What else do you think you know about me?"

"You like things simple, not fussy."

"So I'm plain?"

You shook your head. "Not plain. Things have to matter to catch your attention."

I hope you know how you'd caught my attention.

I finally took my turn and drove the highway. I stayed in one lane and it took me twenty minutes to reach the speed limit, but I did it. You said I could, so I did. I kept going. So long the sun and the gas gauge drifted lower.

Driving worked like a strong cup of coffee. The more miles I went, the more awake I felt. We made each other laugh and squirm over silly stories of our past. Every time you finished a story, I wanted another. You seemed to feel the same way. When you said, "I wish I could wind back time and see little, sassy Lulu," I felt an empty pang of something like hunger.

"Next exit," you said. "Time to get off the highway."

"We still have gas."

"Can't be much. Besides, we're almost at the West Virginia border. I can't take a minor over the state line."

Trying to play like that didn't rub me wrong, I said, "That's the law you're going to worry about breaking?"

"Gotta stop somewhere."

Your truck rattled and shook in protest as I hit the off-ramp and rolled onto the bumpier road of wherever we were. You directed me down the road and through a few turns. It felt like we were headed into the mountain. "Pull in here." You pointed at a large wooden building with a sign, MOUNTAIN MAGIC MEMENTOS, painted in bright orange letters.

"People come here for souvenirs?"

"And ice cream. It also helps to have the only public bathroom for fifty miles in either direction."

I needed that myself.

When I came back out, you were talking to the woman behind the counter. Seeing me, you shook her hand, then led me to poke around the displays. That shop had the tackiest plastic pieces of uselessness imaginable, but it also had real art. Handmade quilts and dolls, the most delicate wispy dream catchers, and all shapes of wood carvings.

"Aren't these nice?" You showed me a collection of wooden bowls.

"You could make those," I said. "Yours would be even better."

We wandered around looking at all the pretty things. "You could start your own shop, Mason. Maybe that's what you should do with your share of the money."

I set down the corncob pipe I'd been playing with. "You need a plan. Set a goal. That's how you make things happen."

"I have a goal," you said. Gazed at me. Leaned in close. Whispered, "Root beer float."

Mission accomplished.

After our treat, we went back in the shop, where you said, "Pick something out."

I shook my head. "Don't waste your money."

"Get something to help you remember this day."

"I'll remember, Mason. I don't need a knickknack."

You insisted. Finally, I said, "A spoon. I'll take one of those wooden spoons." Shaped from a rich red wood, they were handmade with a swirl carved into the handle.

You laughed.

"What's wrong with the spoon?"

"Not a thing." You turned to the woman behind the counter. "Show her what I set aside."

She smiled and pulled out a wooden spoon. You looked smug. "I knew that's what you'd pick."

You handed her the money, and she handed you a bag, saying, "Come back soon, now, ya hear? And here's your keys. You must have dropped them."

The sun hung low in the sky as we made our way back to your truck. Before unlocking the door, I grabbed you, pulled you in for a kiss. It had been way too many hours without. You pressed me against your truck, and I pulled you even closer, feeling greedy for the sweet taste of root beer and you.

Finally coming up for air, you said, "I don't see why you have to go all the way to California, Lu. You could run away to somewhere closer. Like this nice place."

"Where are we?"

"Here," you said, kissing me again.

I leaned back. "You know I'm leaving, Mason. You've known it all along. You can't be sad when I go."

"Now you're being bossy."

"You mean strong," I said.

"I mean rich." You handed me the bag you'd been cradling in the midst of our kisses.

I peeked inside. My spoon sat nestled into a stack of bills.

The whole day had been planned by you. You knew Jolly Ann, who ran the shop. She was going to sell some moonshine in hokey little clay jars with xxx etched in the side, and pass on the rest to her friends. She didn't want to mess with those kinds of dealings most of the time, but for old times' sake she was willing to make a one-time purchase. Paid a decent price too. You were pretty darn pleased with yourself, weren't you?

Me too. With you, I mean.

"Thank you, Mason." My words weren't enough, but the angle of the sun and the sound of jingly tunes drifting across the parking lot from the soda fountain and the soft of your T-shirt under my fingers—all of it mixed together, along with knowing I was going to leave you, made it too hard to say anything else.

"See how we did that?" you said when you dropped me off late that night. "We drove all that way and now we're back, safe and sound."

I snuggled into your neck so I missed the look you wore when you said, "When you drive off into the sunset, remember, the road comes back too."

I remember. Do you?

26

I floated into work the next day. Part of me was still humming along the highway with you, zooming up and down hills, twisting around rocky corners, passing all the luscious summer green.

Roni noticed a difference. "Mother-of-an-alien, Earth to Lulu," she said, shaking a box in my face. "Think you could land long enough to take these parts to Randy?"

"No problem, ma'am," I said, jumping up and knocking my soda into her lap. My laughter wasn't appreciated even though I offered to wipe her down with one of Sal's chamois cloths that are always turning up in odd places.

They're supposed to be for polishing autos, but as nothing ever gets polished, we are highly suspicious of them.

Fact was, I was giddy and buzzed from our day of driving, and Roni was cranky and tired. Most of the summer our moods had been the other way around, so we weren't quite sure what to do with each other in that cramped trailer.

It was almost the end of our shift when Seth showed up at the sales window. Jittery Peanut paced behind him, smoking a cigarette.

I took a deep breath and said, "Hey there, Seth. Can I help you?"

He stared so hard it made me squirm. "Hope so. I got an awful rat problem."

Seth knew about our sales.

I worked hard not to let him see how that shook me. I knew there was no way you'd want me to sell him anything. Keeping my voice light, I said, "I am so sorry to hear that."

Whenever we made a moonshine sale at the junkyard, the person ordered and paid at the window, then received a ticket to redeem. Either Roni or I would then meet him at the gate with the specially marked "poison" jar placed inside a brown lunch sack.

Those sales weren't as big as any of the ones you'd

made, but they were steady and adding up. Especially since Roni and I were the only ones splitting them: You'd said you didn't want any part of them, and Roni figured she and Bucky would share their cuts anyway. As soon as Seth mentioned rats, Roni started making up a ticket.

But when I said, "I think you can get some decent traps down at the Supermart," I saw her crumple the ticket. We were a good team. By this time she recognized him too.

"You sure you don't have nothing here?" He smiled with his lips shut tight.

"Oh, she's got something all right," said Peanut.

Still wearing my junkyard smile, I said, "I suppose we could sell you some old spark plugs to throw at them. How's your aim?"

"I was thinking *poison* might work."

I pressed my hands together to keep them from shaking. "Sorry."

He said, "I know what you've been selling here, Skip-to-my-Lulu."

"Parts is parts," I said, with a tinge of hysteria leaking out.

"You shouldn't play with things you can't handle."

Then, like a giant, hairy angel, with missing teeth and broken fingernails, Dawg appeared beside Seth, standing way too close to be comfortable. Peanut had already stepped out of the way. Dawg growled, "Cats work best. For rats."

"That's true," I said.

Roni added, "And they're organic."

Seth was smart enough to know it was time to go. As he stepped away from the window, he said, "How's Mason's truck running? Do you like that ride? Is it smooth enough for you?"

Bolstered by Dawg nearby I said, "Actually, I think Mason might trade it in. It's got a lotta miles on it. He could get something better. Something new."

I like to think I sounded pretty sure of myself. But as soon as they left I was hit with a wave of shaky trembling. Seth knew something even if I didn't know what that meant. I reassured myself that he was your cousin. Always hanging around looking for you. He was probably just curious as to what you'd been doing. I should have told you right away that he'd come by.

Instead, I decided to run away.

From you.

I couldn't let myself forget what was most important. I'd just had my best day ever with you, but that was one day. Only one day to balance out all the others. One day to match up against all the many days of sitting in the junkyard looking at rust and broken windows. Days of killing time selling to people like Seth.

I'd gotten so wrapped up in being with you, I'd forgotten what it was like to be me. On my own. I needed to go a whole day without you. To remember who I was taking to California. Me.

I talked Roni into going to the river. I was determined not to talk to you but knew it'd be easier with a solid diversion to keep me busy. Besides, I hoped it would get rid of her all-day frown.

By the time we got to the Queens' Tube Trailer Spot, a clump of ominous clouds warned of a brewing thunderstorm. I said, "We'll have to get out if thunder starts."

"I didn't think Little Miss Moonshine worried about things like lightning strikes," said Roni.

As I opened the car door, a water bottle fell to the ground. I picked it up, then saw the xx mark. "I swear this damn moonshine keeps following us around. You have any blueberry-pomegranate juice?"

"How about warm Gatorade?"

I added a few inches of Jezebel Juice to the half a bottle of Gatorade left in Roni's backseat. I took a big swallow, tasting the liquor lacing the salty sweet, then handed it to her. She looked at the bottle a minute, then said, "I better not."

I shrugged at the way we'd switched roles. Then took another chug while we waited for a group of high school boys to get their tubes. I could already feel the heat of the drink relaxing me. In some weird, mixed-up way, I thought drinking proved I was in charge of my heart, not you.

When it was our turn, Tommy Queen greeted Roni with a big hug. "I hear you're fixing to make our party something special."

"All your parties are special," said Roni.

"Nah. It's just a bunch of drunks out to pasture most of the time. With Lullaby Breaker playing, we'll be legit."

As he tied our tubes together, I asked, "What sort of drinks will you be serving?"

Tommy laughed, wiped the sweat off his forehead. "Well, it ain't gonna be no umbrella drinks. A couple of kegs, as usual."

"I seem to remember the kegs running dry at one of your parties. You're going to have a lot more people than usual if Lullaby Breaker is playing."

He carried the tubes to the river's edge for us. "That's what we're counting on."

"What if someone had in mind to offer an alternative to the kegs?"

"Lulu..." Roni shook her head.

"Because we know someone who knows someone who

knows someone who could offer a little stronger home-made something on sale." I played with my hair, feeling the little bitty buzz already. "Starts with *moon*, ends with *shine*."

Tommy eyed me, then Roni, then me again. "Would there be an incentive for the hosts?"

"We'll ask," said Roni at the same time I said, "Of course." I handed him my drink. "See what you think about this. Might be better on ice."

As we stepped into the water, Tommy sniffed the bottle, then took a sip. As we floated away he yelled, "That's got a kick. Let's talk."

"I swear, Lulu. You have one sip of that stuff and you're fearless. Not to mention a flirt. Has Mason tried getting you drunk?"

I waved off her words. She was always trying to get the scoop on what we'd been doing in the dark, and I was always dodging her questions. I didn't want her keeping score.

The water was low that day, the currents lazy. We drifted slow and easy, talking about Roni's favorite songs and the new honey-pepper barbecue sauce Mom had made. I told her how my future roommate, Ashley, wanted us to buy matching comforters that cost more than I'd budgeted for my entire back-to-school list. We talked about

Buttercup and Jimmy's breakup and how they'd get back together next time they ran into each other. We talked about how Ollie and Randy thought no one knew they were a couple. We talked about anything, everything, and a whole lot of nothing.

Except what was on Roni's mind.

When we reached the Bottoms, I asked, "Do you want to ride them? We'll have to untie."

Roni shook her head. "I don't think I should."

The timbre of her voice stopped me. "Roni, what's wrong?"

Her face puckered up, like she couldn't talk. Or wouldn't.

I paddled toward the beach. At the shallow water, I slipped out of my tube and stood in the mushy mud, holding the tubes bobbing on the surface with Roni. "Spit it out."

Her short, wet hair looked like a swim cap, as if she was one of those synchronized swimmers we used to try to imitate, making up our own choreographed water ballets. Back when we were ten and our biggest worry was deciding what to buy at the snack bar.

"I might be a little bit pregnant."

"Might be? A little bit?" I frowned, trying to clear my fuzzy head. "I thought you were on the Pill."

"I missed a few, so I quit. I've been so wrapped up in

the band and Aunt Jezebel and just everything. But"—she held her hand up—"I didn't do this on purpose. A condom broke and..." Her face didn't fit what I would have expected from someone who'd had her kids' names picked out since tenth grade. "Now I'm late."

"What does Bucky say?"

"He says we'll figure it out once we know for sure. Until I take a test, I can hope I'm wrong."

We dragged the bulky tubes onto the sand. Those rain clouds darkened the sky, making the sand look dingy and dirty.

I said, "We'll stop at Corner Drug on the way home." I'll admit the idea of doing this made my palms itch. There's always some nosy someone in there.

She bent over the tubes, trying to separate them. "I want to go to a clinic. So I can know my...options. Mason told me about one in Christiansburg."

"Mason knows?" I meant about Roni, but also about the clinic. I remembered the rumors about Cindy. That she'd been pregnant when she crashed into that tree.

"I had to ask someone who might actually help. You know if I ask Buttercup it'll be all over Dale by sunset."

She was too miserable for me to feel wronged by her keeping this from me. The fact that you knew and hadn't said a word made me realize you had your own secrets.

"I can't go around here. Not now that people notice me. I can't do that to the band. They don't need my trash mixed up with them."

"It's not trash, Roni. It's a baby."

"This is why I didn't want to tell you, Lulu. If I decide not to have it…"

Now I was on shaky ground. I said, as calmly as I could, "I thought you wanted to get married and have Bucky's babies. That's all you talked about our whole senior year. You even told the school counselor that was your ideal plan."

"I still want that. But not like this." As we wrestled the inner tubes up to the road, Roni said, "You never liked that plan of mine anyway."

I thought about your ideas. "Maybe this is what's meant to be, Roni. Maybe it's destiny."

She shook her head. "Don't you get it, Lulu? The love songs are just pretend. It all comes down to biology and a broken condom."

The rain came before the shuttle showed up to take us back to the Tube Trailer. Impatient, Roni and I walked along the road in our bikinis, rolling our tubes in front of us. I kept sneaking peeks at her flat tummy, trying to believe.

I didn't get home until after dinner that night. I'd had

my phone off all day—because of the river, but also to avoid the temptation of talking to you—and Mom was in a tizzy. Not curled up and pathetic, but more like a rubber band snapping at me from across the room.

"Where have you been all day? Why was your phone off?" Before I could answer, she asked, "Were you in public looking like that? Were you with that boy again?"

"You mean Mason? He has a name."

"You are spending too much time with him," she said.

"I wasn't even with him. Not that it's any of your business."

"Of course it's my business, Lulu. You are always my business." She took a deep breath and threw her shoulders back. "You're grounded."

"For what? Poor fashion?" It wasn't nice to laugh, but I wasn't feeling any sense of nice. "You can't ground me. What are you going to do if I leave? Chase me?"

"Your father will be home soon. He'll have something to say about this."

I looked at her, all puffed up and red with anger. Like the mother who used to keep tabs on me. Who used to see more than an arm's reach in front of her. Maybe I wanted to keep her mad, or maybe I simply couldn't hold it in anymore. I said, "Are you sure I'm what Daddy should be worrying about?" My voice shook as I went on. "I heard you

273

in the office, Mom. Late at night. I know what I heard." I turned my back on her blinking eyes and silent mouth and headed for the shower. I scrubbed myself until I stopped shaking.

That night I sorted my room into piles: for school, to sell or give away, and to throw away. I wouldn't leave anything once I was gone.

At midnight, when it was a new day, I called you. I could tell you'd been asleep, but you denied it. You babbled about lemons and sandpaper. Then, like you'd finally woken up, you said, "Hey. I didn't talk to you all day."

"Roni told me."

You knew what I meant.

"What do you think she should do, Mason?"

"Maybe Sal has it right."

"Sal?" I figured you'd fallen back asleep and were having a nightmare.

"Sometimes, when things fall apart, you get the pieces and parts for something new. Even if it's not what you planned."

Exactly.

27

The next day Roni drove me to the junkyard, but then she didn't get out of the car. "Tell Sal I'm sick. I'm going to see if Grungie wants to work on our playlist. I can't be cooped up in that trailer."

"Roni. You might not even be..."

"I'm glad you know what's going on, Lulu. But now I don't want to talk about it. I can't have you in my head while I figure this out."

I didn't want to be in my own head either. "When is Bucky taking you to the clinic?"

"He can't until Friday. He's working overtime since Mason got fired."

"Mason got what?"

"Didn't he tell you?" She frowned, but it was too late to take it back. "That night we went swimming, they caught him on the video surveillance camera climbing over the fence."

"What about Bucky? Why didn't they fire him?"

She revved the engine. Then said, "I guess Mason got in trouble before. Plus he's the one who actually opened the gate and let us in."

That was a long day at the junkyard. I wondered why you hadn't told me about getting fired, but I also knew that was something better said face-to-face. I stewed about it, knowing it was Roni's and my fault. We were the ones who'd wanted to go swimming that night.

Sal's was swamped that day. There was a big drag race coming up, and motorheads from all over southwestern Virginia kept stopping by. They mostly came to see the legendary Sal's Salvage, but once they smelled grease, they couldn't help but buy some random part. Sal stayed in the trailer all day. I don't know if he thought I might need help with Roni gone, or if he truly had work to do at his desk. He might have been simply waiting to say what he'd told Mom he would.

I'd been avoiding him as much as possible ever since I'd heard Mom giggling behind the door. A long time ago

Mom had shown me photos of Sal from high school, when he'd been hot. Even now, despite his extra padding and bountiful hair in odd places, I could see how he'd managed to lure in three wives. That day I refused to meet his eyes.

Near the end of my shift Sal said, "You got something on your mind, Lulu?"

Try several million somethings. "Not especially."

"You sure about that? Need any advice?"

"I'm not looking for junk."

"Salvage," he said, but smiled. "I know you've had a hard summer. And you must be worried about your mama."

"Daddy's coming home soon. She's always better when he's home."

"If you say so." Sal opened his desk drawer. Took out a tin of tobacco. "Do you know that spot in the river with the rapids?" He placed a clump into his lip and leaned back in his chair.

"The Bottoms?"

"Farther down."

"The Wormhole? I've seen them."

His mouth worked the tobacco into place. "Did your mother ever tell you about the time she went down them blindfolded?"

"You sure you have the right person?"

He grinned. "She was a wild one. Made all the boys crazy."

I knew he'd been one of them.

"Point is, your mother understands what you've been thinking and feeling this summer."

"I doubt that." I cleared my throat against the smell of his tobacco. I used to like that smell, but ever since I'd chewed it in the woods that day, it made me queasy.

"She doesn't want you making a mistake you can't fix." He sat up, looked around.

I handed him my empty soda can. He nodded thanks and spit into it.

I said, "Well, I'm not like her. I'm more like my daddy." I picked up my things and stood, ready to go.

"How about this boy you've been seeing? I hear he's made his share of mistakes."

"That's over and done. It's not right that everyone holds on to old news."

"Fair enough."

Then something occurred to me. "Would you give Mason a job, Sal? He's strong and good at fixing things."

"He's looking?"

"Maybe. If he is, will you talk to him?"

"I could talk." Sal grinned, showing little black flecks

on his teeth. "If he needs a job here, I guess that means he's not going anywhere."

That's what his little speech was really about. Mom thought I was planning to run away with you.

As I reached the trailer door, Sal said, "The ABC board came by this morning wanting to photograph a bit of equipment they say was dropped off back in June. It was a still. For making liquor. Copper. You know anything about that?"

Sweat immediately pooled in every one of my crevices and joints. I pressed my palms against my roiling stomach.

"Thing is, I can't find a record of any such delivery. Not in the computer, nor the handwritten logs."

I reached out and grabbed the door handle to steady myself. Self-preservation is something I hang tight to. I asked, "When was it supposed to get here?"

"Back at the start of summer. I know you girls have been distracted lately." He paused to spit. "Mistakes get made."

I sat down. Pretended to search my mind.

"Something like that is bound to be stolen. Doesn't make much difference to me. That's what insurance is for." I felt Sal watching me, waiting. Then he went on. "And as far as lawful comeuppance, I figure whoever was under the fire for this thing will either see this as a wake-up call, or else they'll keep on being stupid and get busted for whatever other lamebrained scheme they jump on. Parts and people have a way of ending up where they belong."

I picked up a paper clip, untwisted its curves, making it straight and sharp.

Tapping his fingers on his desk, Sal kept talking. "The driver, on the other hand, well, he's facing a world of trouble if we can't back him up that it got here."

You getting fired because of me throbbed fresh in my mind. "Would it have come on a trailer?" I asked, my words too full of air.

"Probably." His eyes stayed stuck on me, adding, "Besides losing his job, he might be talking to the sheriff, or maybe even the FBI."

It had been so easy to take that still. So simple to call it borrowing, not stealing.

I used the straightened paper clip to poke holes in the soda can he'd set back on the desk. I said, "I think I do remember seeing that come in. I must have forgotten to log it."

"Well, damn," said Sal. "I never even saw it. I would have put it on lockdown."

This whole summer was such a complete fluke of luck. Or what you'd call fate.

He leaned back in his chair, arms crossed and resting

on his big belly. "Of course, if I find out someone around here helped out somehow, well, I'd have to take that personally."

I nodded. Poked more holes in the can. If Sal figured out where the still had gone, it would mean a world of trouble for more than just me. Ollie and Randy knew what we were doing too. Their friends and referrals had totaled up almost as much as one big sale. They couldn't afford getting fired. There was nowhere else for them to go.

Sal said, "Well, maybe it'll turn up. Might be it's out there, hidden behind some other hunk o' junk. Stranger things have happened." He stood up and stretched. Pointed at the holey can in my hand. "Be careful, Lulu. You wouldn't want to spill that all over yourself."

I didn't know what careful looked like anymore.

28

When Daddy came home, the mash in the garage exploded.

Real fermenting buckets have air locks to release the carbon monoxide that builds up when the yeast, sugar, and corn work together. The few times I'd gone into the garage and opened the flour bucket to halfheartedly stir the glop inside hadn't done enough to relieve the pressure. You said later that the heat of the garage accelerated the process—I'd probably killed the yeast already. The things you'd made look easy weren't.

So maybe Daddy didn't cause that mash explosion; but, honest and truly, the air in our house changes when he's home. The whole house gets louder. He talks a lot. Listens to the radio. Moves furniture, reorganizes closets, throws things away. He might have caused an atmospheric shift that sped things up in the garage.

Even though Daddy is Mom's opposite—or maybe because of it—he usually soothes her in a way I can't. This time was different. The air between him and Mom seemed charged and close to sparking. I'd hear their voices, tense and intertwined, but as soon as I walked in the room, they'd go silent. Something was brewing and fermenting between them too.

You know how our house is built into the hill? So the garage meets the basement? I heard the boom of the explosion all the way up in my bedroom. I didn't know what it was—gunshot came to mind—but even not knowing, I instantly felt guilty. I was feeling guilty all the time those days, to the point it didn't mean much anymore. Then my insta-guilt turned productive, and I realized it might be something to do with the mash.

I ran downstairs and caught Daddy and Mom discussing the sound. "It must have been a truck," said Daddy. "Or construction work down the road."

"It was *in* our house," said Mom. "I vibrated." Her voice was getting breathy and full of air, the way it does when she has one of her panic attacks.

"I'll check the basement," I said.

"I'll come with you," said Daddy.

"Mario. Wait."

"Stay with Mom. I can check."

For once I was thankful for Mom's uneasy shaking. With my heart pounding, I scooted downstairs, through the basement, and opened the door to the garage.

That bucket blowing was truly mind-blowing. I never imagined what lurked in there. The force that had built up. The bucket itself had bulleted across the garage and hit the opposite wall, knocking down a shelf.

The smell was almost sweet, but closer to wrong. Everything in there—all the boxes and broken old toys and unwanted miscellaneous nothings—was splattered with the nasty glop. The gummy, gooey mess was everywhere.

Hearing Daddy's footsteps, I pulled the door shut and crept back to meet him at the base of the stairs. Because I'd become a professional liar, I had no problem finding inspiration in the basement. "Paul's golf clubs knocked into the water heater."

I started up the stairs, hoping to keep him away from the mess.

He came down to check anyway. "I need to make sure there's no crack."

I stood beside him as he moved the clubs out of his way

and then ran his fingers over the tank. Nervous, I chatted at him. The rhythm of being a daddy's girl kicked in, an easy and familiar role, even if I hadn't practiced all summer.

The bittersweet smell of exploded mash overwhelmed the air. I surreptitiously checked and rechecked my arms and hands, the ends of my hair, and even the soles of my feet, expecting to find traces of glop stuck to me. Thinking Daddy had to smell it also, I tried to distract him by saying, "Mom should make some bread. Wouldn't that taste good?"

He scanned the basement again and then turned his eyes on me. "I've missed my little girl," he said. I let him cradle my face the way he used to. He said in a slightly wobbly voice, "Your mother thinks you're in love."

That about knocked me over. "What did she say?"

"That he's polite and a good eater. The important things."

"You know him, Daddy. It's Mason. From Saint Jude's."

He frowned, his mind translating. "Father Mick's handyman?"

"He's not a handyman. Or Father Mick's."

"He's too old for you, Lulu. He's...he's not who you think."

"No, Daddy. He's not who *you* think."

Daddy never likes the boys I date, but he's not usually so surprised. Then again, you weren't the usual boy I'd dated. I didn't mind having him flustered. If he was worried about you, he might not notice real problems. Like a bucket of exploded mash.

I headed back up the stairs, knowing he'd follow me to get in the last word. Behind me he said, "I know this has been a hard time, Luisa. It's difficult to adjust your vision for the future."

I faced him. "I haven't. I'm still going to school in September."

I'd turned the page on my kitty calendar that morning. August. The last full month I'd spend in Dale. It would be a busy month for Aunt Jezebel, but come September and Labor Day, I'd be gone.

He held the banister, looking deflated. "We simply cannot afford it." Then his face brightened, grew more animated. "I'm working on something. It's quite exciting. A true opportunity. I have real hopes it could be quite lucrative. God willing."

I knew this old tune. Daddy was always looking ahead to his next big deal. The next exciting plan. His high hopes, God willing. I'd always believed him.

Until that moment.

I now knew that hopes and plans weren't always enough. Sometimes God wasn't willing and everything blew up in your face. Or garage.

"I'm getting the money, Daddy. I've already made more than half the payment." My heart thumped so hard my breaths felt shallow. I'd hoped to have this conversation once things were settled and done. "You're the one who told me I had to leave this town."

All my life Daddy had talked to me about leaving. He'd told me not to get stuck in Dale. Whispered stories about distant, shiny places. When I started dating, he'd warned me against falling in love. Told me getting stuck here would be the worst thing possible.

"But how?" he asked. "Where will you get the money?"

This was the part I was dreading. "Savings. And work."

"Is that why we received a statement from the university? I thought it was a mistake." His eyes narrowed. "Is Sal meddling in our business? I won't have you owe him, Luisa."

"No. He's not meddling in my business." I was shaking. The secrets and worries about Mom and Sal were too slippery to hold. It felt like my insides were melting and leaching out through the sweat dripping down my back and sides.

"I'm taking care of it, Daddy." My voice sounded unfamiliar. Hard, like steel. "You don't have to do anything."

"There's nothing to take care of. I canceled your account, Luisa."

Everything stopped.

I felt like I'd had my feet swept out from under me.

Like the river surged and was washing me downstream. There was nothing to grab ahold of, no way to catch my bearings. In a flash of a moment, all that I'd worked for slipped away.

I sat, with a crash, on the top stair. Stared at him. I shook all the way down to my clenched fists. Finally, I choked out, "Why?"

Because it never occurred to him that I might actually try to go.

He'd told the truth. He really had canceled all my payments. He'd told USD I wasn't coming, that I needed to defer my acceptance. He'd requested they send a reimbursement of all funds.

"That's my money, Daddy. I earned it. I worked hard to get it."

"Our situation goes beyond your schooling, Luisa. Money is tight."

"How can you trash my future? What gives you the right to throw my life away?"

"I'll make it up to you. Someday." His shoulders slumped, and worry lined his face. "Your mother has charged a lot of expenses on her credit card."

Some of those charges were mine. I'd bought jars and other supplies using her card. So, even though I felt betrayed, I still had my own guilt mixed into the situation.

I was too bewildered and dizzy to think straight. Feeling completely knocked over and beat up, I went to work trying to clean the only mess I could.

I tried to wipe down the garage. I was a whole lot better at making messes than cleaning them. The smell and the heat made me seriously woozy as I scrubbed. I had some glimpse into what you must have felt when the mash hit you so hard. The glop had snuck into every crevice and crack. Throwing our past in the trash seemed like the best idea.

Grabbing the garbage can, I tossed out boxes of old broken toys. A bag of expired seeds that Mom had ordered but never planted. Roller skates I didn't use because all the roads were too hilly and rough. All the past disappointments dumped in with the rubbish.

My future was there to keep it company.

As I climbed in your truck that evening, I felt the slop of the day slipping off me. I told the story about the mash exploding in a flip and silly way to make you laugh, trying to keep my hysteria at bay. You were surprised and confused that I'd made mash, but I still hadn't told you about hearing Mom coo behind the office door either.

When I got to the part about Daddy canceling my school account, you frowned. "Well, you gotta call and tell them to un-cancel it."

What with my head all discombobulated, I hadn't thought of that.

It was three hours earlier in California. Their office was still open. So while you drove us down to the river, I called San Diego. The woman on the other end of the line struggled to understand my jumbled words. It was hard to talk with my heart thumping in my throat. "It was a mistake," I said. "I'm coming. I'll be there in September."

"I think we have a bad connection," she said. "I'm having a hard time with your accent."

I felt like a country bumpkin. I took a deep breath and said as slowly and clearly as I could, "Could you please reactivate my account? I'll be making another payment soon."

She sighed. "I can put a note on your record to freeze your account instead of canceling. We'll hold your place. You won't be able to make any official adjustments or payments until you're eighteen. Then you'll need to pay the full amount."

I thanked her and hung up.

The only thing that could settle my restless limbs that night was wrapping myself in you.

It was a pretty spot where we parked, but we weren't looking at the view. I'd never been one to make out in a car. Besides worrying about things getting too out of hand, it's cramped and awkward. That didn't matter that night. We fit together well. And getting out of hand wasn't anywhere close to the top of my multitude of worries. You and your lips and your hands and your sweet little whispers in my ear, the feel of your skin on mine made everything else slip away.

Until the rap on the window set my nerves on fire.

You threw my shirt over me. It was a tiny thing that fit me snug and scooped low. Useless in that moment.

You pulled on your shirt, adjusted your jeans. "Keep the doors locked, Lu."

"Who is it?" I struggled into my bra, then wrestled with my shirtsleeves and the buttons that had come undone so easily yet didn't want to cooperate now.

"They don't have a warrant. They have no right to search the truck."

This was so much worse than getting embarrassed and scolded for fooling around on the side of the road.

You slammed the door behind you. I rubbed a small circle in the steamed-up window and peered out where you and two figures faced off.

They didn't look official. There was no way they were the police, which might have reassured me, but their menacing stance made my stomach drop. I felt like I couldn't get a deep enough breath. Not in the good way I'd been with you before the knock. This felt closer to drowning.

I couldn't hear what was said. You held your hands

up, palms out, as if looking to soothe them. At first you seemed to back away, but then, with a flash, you punched the shorter guy. Then I couldn't tell who belonged to what fists and legs. The wrestling clump of you moved along the road, out of my line of view.

I was already on edge that night. Fed up with trouble butting in and knocking on the window. Mad at everyone and everything except you. I was going to count to a hundred, but at fifty-seven, I reached under your seat and found your gun.

My heart pounded and my hands shook as I made my way around your truck out to the road. I should have known it was Seth and Peanut. As I crept closer, holding the gun the way you'd taught me—the only way I knew how—the punches and thuds of skin on skin slowed and the gasps and grunts grew louder. Peanut fell to his knees and stayed there. Seth sucked air while you circled, bouncing on your toes. Each of you wore bruises and cuts. Your bloody nose looked dramatic, but it seemed like Seth's swollen eye had to hurt worse.

"Enough?" you asked.

Seth backed away. Wiped his mouth, then bent over, breathing loud and raspy. His hiccups shifted, turned deeper. Somewhere along the way his gasps had turned to laughs. "You still fight like a damn weasel," he said.

"Yeah. Well, you've gotten slow." You started laughing too.

I watched; bewildered by whatever weird spell had taken over.

I realized, suddenly, Seth *missed* you. That's why he was always coming around. It wasn't a matter of owing. It had nothing to do with moonshine or money. It was you he wanted.

That was something I could understand.

I must have made a noise, because you all saw me then. And saw what I held in front of me. I wish I didn't like how you all froze.

"Give me that, Lu." Your voice was eerily calm, but I'd lost the ability to move. I couldn't remember how to lower the gun.

"Should have got a babysitter, Cuz."

Peanut laughed.

To them you said, "Y'all better get out of here. She can't aim for shit."

I guess they believed you, because they took off running.

Back in your truck, my hands felt slick but gritty too. You didn't speak the whole time you cleaned your face with a rag from the back. Then you burst out, "Did you even check to see if it was loaded?"

Thing was, even if I'd checked, would I have wanted it loaded or not?

"What were you thinking, Lu?" I'd never seen you so agitated. "I tell you what. You weren't thinking. For someone who's supposed to be smart..."

"I thought they were beating you up. It's not fair two on one." It was crazy-making how you looked so confused. "How was I supposed to know that was fun? I thought you were in trouble. What did they want?"

"Nothing."

"Why are they following you? Why'd they sneak up on us? That's not normal, Mason."

You sucked air through your teeth. "We don't have the same normal."

That's all you said until you parked in front of my house. You stared straight ahead, gripping the steering wheel. Then said, "He's my cousin, Lulu."

"I know. But I thought..." I trailed off. You were right. I hadn't been thinking. "Okay. Maybe I overreacted."

You shook your head at my understatement. I hoped you might laugh. But then, barely louder than a whisper, you said, "I was alone, Lu. Before you came along."

Me too.

I moved in close to kiss you. Smelled worry and dirt on

your skin. You kissed me back at first, then pulled away. "Thing is, I didn't mind."

It's impossible to miss what you don't know.

"But now," you said, "now it's going to be hard to go back to that."

"Don't work for Seth," I said.

"I'm not." You rubbed your jaw like it was tender. "But it's not like I'm working at the club anymore. And I'm doing fine being around moonshine."

"What about the junkyard? Sal would hire you."

"With all those broken things?" You looked betrayed.

"We'll figure something else out. You can take the money we're making and—"

You cut me off. "Lulu, you gotta get out of this town. You're right. You don't belong here."

I felt you pushing at me that night. Sending me on my way.

I was filled with a reckless, wild wish that you'd come with me. Pictured us driving into the sunset, never stopping until we reached the Pacific Ocean. But that was crazy. Impulsive. Like pulling out a gun on a group of old friends, or thinking a fixer and builder like you would ever be happy dismantling and destroying.

Impossible.

29

I'd never gone a week without talking to Roni before. She answered my texts with short and simple replies. Otherwise she avoided me. She really didn't want me in her head. She blew off work, let my calls go to voice mail, and didn't show up when Bucky called a business meeting in the gas station parking lot.

Waiting for you, I asked, "How's Roni?" What I meant was *Is she pregnant? What now?*

"Did you know Virginia Tech has apartments for married couples?"

"Is that the plan?"

He shrugged. "Still looking at options."

Once you rode up on your bike, Bucky told us about his conversation with Tommy and Jimbo Queen. My impulsive question at the river—along with the warm Gatorade bottle mixed in with our poison—had set in motion a plan for us to sell moonshine at their party.

Bucky said, "They see this as a real business opportunity. Those Queen boys know what they're doing. We could make a serious chunk of change."

You didn't like the idea. "There are already way too many people involved."

"Who would you like to kick out?" Bucky asked, putting you on the spot. "Personally, I think Lulu is the wild card at the moment. Can't begin to guess what she's going to do."

Mad, I said, "What does that mean?"

Bucky held up his hands. "Whoa. Don't shoot."

I shut up and he went on. "Roni is honestly pretty useless. But you and Roni are awfully cozy good friends these days, aren't you, Mason? So, maybe you mean me?"

You shook your head. "I meant you talking to the Queens in the first place."

"That was started by Lulu. Again, can we all say 'wild card'?"

Bucky and I were always in the same classes, same track, same learning groups. We'd worked together on numerous projects, starting with the first-place blue-ribbon all-county vermicomposting exhibit we created for the fifth-grade science fair. Roni probably told him as much about me as she told me about him. So, it makes sense that Bucky knew precisely how much I'd changed that summer. He didn't like it.

"I don't like face-to-face sales," you insisted.

"The Queens don't either. And they don't like the little rat poison jars."

I protested, "But that's good marketing."

Bucky shook his head. "They don't want a bunch of broken glass. Also, they don't want to worry about copyright infringement."

If Roni had been there, we would have laughed at that.

"One person takes the money, another pours, and someone else hands them out. No direct exchange of liquor for money. It's smart and simple."

You weren't convinced. "I have another sale lined up. Talked to him this morning. It's a big one. The guy owns several bars."

"All right," said Bucky. "We can wait and see how that goes."

Sal and his questions had been weighing on me. "We might need to bring Aunt Jezebel back to Sal's when we're done," I said.

You both looked at me like I was as deluded as I was.

Bucky moved on. "We also need to switch to a sugar-only recipe. No more corn. It's too expensive."

"Hold up," you said. "That's a bigger shift than you think."

"We need to cut costs, make as much cash as possible."

"I can't take sugar-shine on the road. I can't stand behind something like that."

Bucky stared at you like he didn't speak your language. Then said, "It's good enough for the Queens. Tommy's the one who suggested it. He can't believe we wasted money on corn."

Sometimes the simplest answer is the hardest to see. The night of the Queens' field party, way back at the beginning of the summer, that was the night of my big idea.

Everything would be different if I'd gone to the Queens to make money. That's what they do. The parties they hold in their field can't be any more legal than selling moonshine. Not that legality is something that can be weighed on a scale, but those parties are a business. They aren't playing hosts, they're working. They make money off all those drunken people stumbling around in their overgrown, rutted field.

There must be some kind of payoff to the police.

Everyone in at least three towns knows when they're having a party, and you never hear about any busts. But how many DUIs have been issued down the road out of there? It's some kind of deal that works.

It doesn't matter. No matter how much money I might have made working with them, it wouldn't have equaled working with you.

30

When it came time for the sale to Claude, I invited myself along. Each and every sale felt crucial to me, but this one mattered to you in a different way. You wanted to prove to Bucky your way was the right way. That the pay-off was worth the extra expense up front.

Claude's home was a mishmash of sleek and ominous. Outside, his mangy dogs eyed us mistrustfully from the shade, while the inside looked clean to the point of sterile. You had a sample jar of our liquor inside a brown paper bag. No whiskers or tails kind of packaging here. It was a different expectation altogether.

I wasn't expected at all, but Claude has slippery-smooth

social skills. He greeted me with a toothy smile, then raised his eyebrows in question to you.

We walked in on the top level like we were in the tree-tops. High ceilings, shiny floors, big furniture; his house reeked of money.

"Sweetie, you watch TV in here while we talk business downstairs. Sorry Barbara Jean isn't here to keep you company, but it was too nice a day for her not to go spend my money."

I started to protest, but I caught the ever so slight shake of your head.

I grabbed a magazine from the white wicker basket and sank into the cushy leather couch.

Claude upped the volume on the TV before leading you downstairs. I got the message, loud and clear. I wasn't supposed to hear whatever was being discussed.

Almost immediately, before I even got restless, you were back upstairs. Your eyes were set, firm and hard. "Let's go," you said. "Deal's off."

At the front door I forced you to look at me. "Is it because I'm here?"

"They don't trust the liquor because I won't drink it."

"That's all?"

You shrank at least a couple of inches. "I can't, Lu."

But I could. I was dressed like a shiner that day.

Wearing jeans and my heavy leather shoes. I pulled my hair out of its ponytail, unbuttoned my shirt two buttons' worth, and dragged you downstairs, stomping every step—that's not the kind of crowd to surprise.

I swallowed the queasiness I felt seeing six large men, all over fifty, sitting in the dark room that smelled of smoke, musky aftershave, and lemon furniture polish. They sat in a circle of plush chairs and couches. A long waxed bar lined one wall, and the rest of the room was for the game tables—pool, Foosball, and air hockey.

"Hey, y'all," I said, being one of Sal's best girls. I ignored their silence and plopped myself into the seat opposite Claude. I smiled and tossed my curls. "I'm awful thirsty."

"Lu," you said, standing behind me. "You don't have to do this."

"Have to?" I kept my eyes on those old men. "You mean *get* to." I grabbed the paper bag from you and pulled out the bottle. "You gentlemen at least gonna give me a glass?"

Someone handed me one.

"Thanks, sweetie." My hands were sweating, but I covered that up by taking hold of the arm next to me. "Will you please pour me a splash?"

With a low chuckle, he poured a finger's worth of the

moonshine into the glass. I picked it up and raised it to the room. "Here's to good business with good men…and good women."

I chugged the drink before second thoughts could get in the way.

It felt both cool and hot as it hit the back of my throat. The fumes burned my nose after I'd already swallowed, setting my eyes to watering. But I let loose with a "Woohoo" and laughed.

"Well, all right," said Claude. "I see who has the balls around here."

He took the bottle and sniffed. Then pulled out a mini-hydrometer to measure the proof, eyeing you as he read the numbers. Finally, he swooshed a mouthful like it was fine wine. Then he passed the bottle on to the next guy. Once the bottle made its way around he said, "So, firecracker, how about another?"

I don't think I had much choice. At least I was given apple juice as a mixer this time. The white-haired, hippie-looking guy even sprinkled my drink with cinnamon.

You watched us from your barstool, one step out of the circle. One of the men said to you, "I see why you couldn't leave your girl at home. She's way too wild to run free."

Oh, how I laughed.

You must have kind of—or more than kind of—hated

me that day. To me, it was simply getting things done. I could make a fool of myself because you were there to watch out for me.

You know better than I do how long we stayed and what was said. I don't remember leaving. I vaguely remember stopping on the side of the road and replaying the first night we met. After throwing up, I was somewhat aware of having a body again. No way could I go home like that, not at two in the afternoon. Especially with Daddy in town.

I couldn't even hide out at Roni's, since she didn't want me in her head. I was so delirious you could have dumped me anywhere.

———

I know you've felt the sickly panic of waking up in a strange place. The painful reconnecting to consciousness, the grasp to fill dark and gaping holes. The certainty that there are things you need to remember, yet absolutely don't. You know awful attempts to make sense of where you are and how you got there.

I had no idea where I was when I woke up. Besides the hideous taste in my mouth, my head pounded. A desperate, impossible thirst consumed every inch of me. When I sat up, the room spun. I fixated on the open window, but all I could see were shadows of dark greens and blues.

I felt the tiniest bit relieved to see your hat on the table beside the bed. I hadn't been left at Claude's. I had all my clothes on. But I could not remember arriving in this bed I hoped was yours.

I crept out of the bedroom, fingers pressed against the wall for support.

You sat at the kitchen table. "You need to puke again?"

"I don't know."

As soon as I stepped in your bathroom, I smelled your shampoo and shaving cream. It soothed me, until I caught my reflection. My hair was matted on one side and gone wild on the other. My eyes were red, my skin pasty. I tried to clean up, but that wimpy thing you call a comb would have snapped every tooth one time through my hair. I splashed water on my face and poked around until I found toothpaste. My mind wasn't agile enough to speculate about the box of condoms I found in one of those drawers.

Eventually I made my way to your kitchen. I sank down on a wooden chair I was sure you'd made. I rubbed my fingers along the smooth surface.

You said, "I called Roni. Your parents think you're with her." You placed a banana, toast, a cup of seltzer water, and ibuprofen in front of me. "Eat."

I nibbled at the toast and sipped the bland but fizzy drink. Once you seemed satisfied that I was following orders, you turned your back on me and put away the few dishes from the drying rack. Everything back in the cupboards, everything back in its place. Except there wasn't a spot for me.

I rested my heavy head on the table.

You sat beside me. Ran your fingers along my neck beneath my messy hair.

"What?" I lifted my head, but you pressed it back down.

"Shh." You held your finger against my neck, staring at something across the room. Then said, "Your pulse is still fine. Keep eating. You need to soak up the alcohol."

The huge hole in the day was too big to step around. "Can you tell me what happened?"

You opened a drawer and pulled out the biggest clump of money I'd ever seen. Tossed it on the table. Bills slid across the smooth surface, a few falling carelessly to the floor. "You did it."

"What will they do with all those bottles?" I put my hand against my cheek in an attempt to keep my head straight. "They can't drink it all, can they?"

"They'll sell it. At Claude's bar, and to other restaurants looking to show off our fine mountain culture. They want you to come back with more."

I groaned. "Will I have to drink again?"

"Don't you want to?" Your voice suddenly rough. "You seemed to be having fun."

"That was an act, Mason. For the sale. Those men are no different than the men who buy parts at Sal's. I was selling. It worked, right? Look at all that money."

"You'd do anything for the money, wouldn't you, Lu?"

"Not anything." I didn't like the look on your face. "Isn't that why we went there? To make the sale?"

"You're right," you said. "I'm the one who had it wrong."

I felt my own kind of wrong facing you. I'd never felt like a piece of junk under your gaze before.

You looked away, rubbing your chin. Finally you said, "There are two things I want, but can't have. And those two things spent the day together."

As you headed toward your bedroom, I sat, too miserable to move. You came back and handed me a T-shirt and shorts. "There are towels in the bathroom closet. You need to clean up."

A shower is a good place to cry yourself dry. After, feeling a little bit stronger and a whole lot cleaner, I put on your T-shirt and shorts. The shorts hung low, and I had to fold the waistband over, but I made it work. Finger-combing my wet hair was better than nothing. Now I could smell the smoke and vomit stink in my own clothes, so I shoved them into a plastic bag I found beneath your sink.

"Better?" you asked.

"Much." I swayed on my feet.

"You need more sleep." My heart thumped wildly as you led me back to your bedroom. All those cramped nights making out in your truck or my backyard gazebo, and here was your great big comfortable bed. I didn't know whether to be grateful or disappointed that you'd never brought me here.

I grabbed your arm for balance. Then leaned forward.

You backed away. "I can't kiss you, Lu. You smell like liquor."

I sank onto your mattress, curled into a ball, my arms wrapped around my knees, my head tucked into them, hiding my toxic breath.

You played with my hair a minute, then said, "Get some sleep."

I curled up in your bed while you took the couch. In my previous life I might have had trouble sleeping in a boy's bed, but that wasn't me anymore.

31

I woke up ridiculously early the next morning. You need curtains in your bedroom. Gone was the fog, the headache, the icky churning in my gut. A deep blue lump sat in my chest, but mostly things looked better in the thin, early sunshine.

You'd left the money in a neat stack in the center of the table. It seemed too dirty to be where you'd eat, but I left it alone. I heard thumping outside. Through the kitchen window I watched you chopping wood. You'd face a log sitting on the giant stump. Using both hands, you threw the ax up and over your head, down and—*thump*—into the log. Over and over.

I poured a couple of mugs of sweet tea and slipped out the back door. I sat on the steps, sipping cold, healing caffeine, and leaned against the rail, breathing in honeysuckle and sawdust, and watched you tear those logs apart.

After your haphazard pile grew considerably, you finally paused. Stretched your back, pushed up the goggles with your thick, worn gloves, and wiped your face with the bottom of your T-shirt. Then, panting from effort, you stood at the bottom of the stairs looking up at me.

I handed you a mug. "What's all the wood for?"

"It gets cold out here in the winter." You took a big swallow of tea. "But you don't have to worry about that, do you? You'll be gone."

"I don't know," I said. "Looks about fifty-fifty to me." Sitting there with my head too light, my heart aching at the look on your face, wanting to throw my arms around you, I felt fifty-fifty in every way. As we stared at each other, I worked to hold in an ambush of tears.

You hurled the ax into the pile of splintered logs. "How much money do you still need?"

At your kitchen table, I made a list. The money I'd sent to USD already—frozen until I turned eighteen, what I had stashed at home, and my share of the group account that Roni held. I counted out the newest stack of bills; it was by far our biggest intake. I wasn't as far off as I'd thought.

You sat in the chair beside me, looking over my list. "I could give you the rest."

I shook my head. "That's not fair. I can't take your money."

We'd had this conversation before. You were already doing too much for me. You had to at least make your share. You'd already lost one job. For all I knew, you were chopping that wood for extra money. You had simple needs, but you couldn't afford to give me anything more. And I couldn't afford to take it.

You said, "You're only one big sale away. I told you Claude wants more."

I suddenly wondered why you cared so much about us using corn. Why you couldn't take sugar-shine on the road. Why your reputation mattered if you were only doing this one last time.

Your phone rang then, loud and shrill. We stared at it, me not comprehending this outside interruption. You checked the screen. "It's Roni."

I took it from you. "Hello?"

"Lulu? Your daddy is about to blow a gasket. I told him you were with me but he's been trying to call you. Some man finally answered your phone, so now he's really freaking out. I told him you were in the shower. That you must have lost your phone at the movies. But he says if you're not at church in thirty minutes he's calling the police, FBI, and the U.S. Marshals."

I hadn't even noticed my phone was missing. I'd left it at Claude's. And now, with the minutes ticking by, I had nothing to wear to church. I didn't even know it was Sunday. My own wrinkled clothes smelled of smoke and vomit.

I tried to see if I tied your T-shirt in back and wrapped it just so, maybe it wouldn't look too ridiculous over your baggy shorts. You were not my size. Or gender. Looking in your bathroom mirror, I didn't recognize myself. But it wasn't only the clothes.

"He can't know," I said, pacing around your house. Panic had hit me square in my chest. "He can't know I'm here." I couldn't stop moving, couldn't catch my breath. My hands opened and closed, grasping for something I couldn't reach. "He's going to think we were..."

You left me standing there, trying to will myself back to respectable.

It wasn't the moonshine I was worried about. Not the making or the selling. It wasn't even the drinking.

It was being with you.

I couldn't bear to have Daddy think I'd been shacked up having sex with my boyfriend. When I whined, "What do I wear?" my voice sounded as young and shaky as I felt.

I headed into the kitchen as if I thought I could cook up some kind of answer.

Then you were there, standing in the doorway. With a funny look on your face and a purple something dangling from your fingers.

A dress.

I eyed it but didn't move. It was as if, if I thought long enough, the correct algorithm would pop in my head, making everything clear and logical. "Was that…" I couldn't bring myself to say Cindy's name.

"I think it'll fit," you said.

You're a problem solver. You fix and repair. You'd been in plenty of wrong situations. You'd made adjustments, excuses, cover-ups. It was clear you'd been here before.

Needing to come up with some kind of jerry-rigged, Scotch-taped paste of a fix scraped against my inner core. Being desperate enough to contemplate wearing your dead girlfriend's dress was a new low for me.

But I took that dress from you, didn't I? I didn't ask when she'd worn it. Or why you still had it. If you'd known how perfectly it would fit me. The cut shaped my curves just right. I'd never worn that color, but I should have.

Dressed, with my hair mostly tamed, I found you waiting on the porch. There in the morning light you looked so gorgeous, so close to golden. Too damn good, inside and out.

I hurried past to climb in your truck. I didn't want you looking at me in that dress.

Daddy stood outside Saint Jude's when I walked up. You'd dropped me off around the corner after a long, quiet ride. He grabbed my arm and led me into the church, where the choir was finishing the processional song. My ridiculous leather shoes made some kind of unclear statement beneath the purple dress. Grateful that we had to be quiet, I stumbled into the pew. Then numb kicked in. I didn't hear a word of the Mass. I didn't even take Communion, seeing as I was most definitely not in a state of grace. Daddy noticed. But he'd never make a scene in public. Then he'd have to admit we weren't perfect.

When the service was over, I ducked away from Daddy and headed to the basement room, hoping I'd find you.

Your beautiful room stood silent. Bits of dust swirled in the dim light. That's the room where your AA group meets. That's why you offered to fix it up. That's what you were doing at Saint Jude's the night we met. You'd stayed after the meeting to take measurements. By the time you discovered the problem with your bike, Jessie and your other sober AA friends had left. Then you saw Bucky and got stuck riding home with a couple of drunk girls. One threw up in your helmet. Why weren't you completely pissed off at God that night?

I didn't know what or how to feel that morning. I'd

made the sale to Claude and his friends but was still tally-
ing up the cost. I thought I'd helped when I drank in your
place. I knew you couldn't drink, and yet, you'd watched
me. Smelled it on me. Cleaned up after me. Then you'd
dressed me in some piece of the past you couldn't leave
behind. That purple dress was way over my budget.

Daddy never asked me where I was that morning. We
pretended I'd been at Roni's even though we both knew
he knew I wasn't. Daddy is legally blind when it comes to
problems in our family. He only sees the good, the best, his
hopes. His perpetual optimism is why he's a good salesman.
Any dark and dismal truths fester in silence. Problems sim-
mer and bubble below the surface. Like mash in a bucket.

He didn't recognize this new me, didn't know how to
talk to her. She didn't have anything to say anyway.

You didn't drive past me as I walked home in Cindy's
purple dress simply so I wouldn't have to be in a car with
Daddy. You weren't waiting on my front step when I got
home either. I didn't have a phone, but somehow I knew it
would have stayed silent. You didn't stop by and surprise
me with something you'd whittled from wood any time
during the whole long afternoon I spent lying on the couch
with my head in Mom's lap while she stroked my hair.

She didn't ask me what was wrong, and I didn't ask her
if she wished she could ride the rapids one more time.

32

I couldn't stay on the couch with Mom. The next day I woke up ready to do...something. The weather was oddly cool, making me feel like I'd lost a big chunk of time passed out in your bed.

Sitting at your kitchen table counting up money, I'd realized I might actually escape. This crazy thing we'd done wasn't just me wishing and throwing a fit. I had to keep going. I had to surge onward and cross the finish line one way or another. I was too close to quit.

That was the day I called USD and asked about work-study options. I filled out the online application even though I was told I'd be on a waiting list. You'd helped me see I needed to look at different options. Before that summer I'd imagined myself as someone special. Someone carefree and lost in higher thoughts and studies. Someone who didn't work at the junkyard.

I knew now, I was a Dale girl. Even though I needed to leave this place, I was going to take a bit of it with me. I'd never forget how to scrabble between the rock and the hard place. Working ran through my blood, made me get up in the morning. Being busy and tired helped me sleep at night. I wanted to be sure I'd be doing something hands-on to balance my book studying. Even if it was slopping food in the cafeteria or cleaning toilets.

I asked Daddy to take me to Roni's, armed with chocolate ice cream and potato chips. Without thinking, I went to the driver's side of the car. He looked at me funny as I tried to cover my mistake by asking, "Can I drive?"

"No," he said. "You don't have a permit."

"Let me anyway," I begged.

He must have been desperate to have things nice between us, because he actually let me. He was impressed by my natural talent. All thanks to you.

When Roni opened her door, I said, "If you let me in, I'll stay out of your head."

"Let me get the bowls."

Out on a blanket in a sunny spot in her backyard I said, "Mmmm," as I bit into the cold salty sweet. "Why don't we eat this every day?"

"Tell the truth, Lulu-bird. Will you eat ice cream with potato chips in California?"

"Damn straight."

She laughed. "You'll be marked as a hillbilly forever."

"That's me."

Maybe she knew I was eyeing her tummy or maybe she simply wanted to get the elephant out of the room, but she said, "I'm not having a baby."

I wasn't sure what she'd gone through to get there— whether it had been a false alarm or if it was a not any- more kind of thing—but either way I knew she'd lost something.

I wasn't in a place to judge any choice she'd made. The moments we feel most untouchable, that's when we most need a hand.

"Here's the crazy thing. Now Bucky wants to get mar- ried." She licked her spoon and looked at me. "So? What do I do?"

I set aside the rest of my ice cream and lay back on the towel. "Lie here and close your eyes. Think about each possibility. Roll it around in your head, let your mind play awhile. See how each one makes you feel."

"I was sure you'd make me a list of pros and cons. Have you been smoking pot?"

"That's another idea," I said. "Try that."

She laughed. "Did you get kidnapped by aliens or something?"

"Something," I said.

Truth was, I didn't know anything anymore. Not about love. Not about plans. Not about right or wrong.

"I need sun." Roni took off her T-shirt. We lay in her yard wearing only our bras and shorts, the way we used to do back when my parents didn't want me to wear a bikini so Roni didn't either. She said, "It's Bucky's hands."

I rolled over on my side to face her.

"I was so damn crazy for his hands." She closed her eyes. "I'd see them tapping his thigh or brushing his hair back, doing something he wasn't even thinking about, and, just like that, I'd be ready to drag him off to any dark corner. God, I loved his hands. His hands were going to lead me when we danced at our wedding. They'd hold our babies. Help them ride bikes. Point out words to read so they wouldn't end up dumb like me."

"You're not dumb, Roni."

She shook her head. Her eyes stayed closed against the bright sun. "When I told Bucky I thought I might be pregnant, I couldn't look him in the eye. Not that he could be

320

mad. He knew how it happened. But I kept staring at his hands. Wishing he'd grab me and hug me. Something."

A few tears rolled out from her lids, down her cheeks. "Then he reached out—and squashed a bug."

"Oh, Roni." I had to laugh a little.

She did too. Then sat up. "We went to look at wedding rings yesterday. Only I could hardly look at the rings because I kept seeing his hands squash that damn bug.

"Then I started thinking how I could write a really good song about hands. *Gotta hand it to you...Hand over my heart...My handy-dandy handyman...* All of a sudden I didn't want to try on any more rings because all I could think about was getting my ideas down on paper."

I didn't totally get what Roni meant. I don't know what it feels like to have a song in my head. But I could tell she was listening to a beat all her own.

Later, after we'd come back inside, Bucky showed up. He shifted back and forth like he didn't know where to stand. I kept thinking he was going to hit his head on the open cupboard door. "Where's Mason?" he asked me. "I can't get ahold of him."

"I don't know."

He narrowed his eyes. "Did you chase him off, Lulu? You just couldn't make it a whole summer with someone, could you?"

"Shut up, Bucky," said Roni, because I was too numb to answer. Too cold. The ice princess resurrected. I stood in Roni's kitchen making guesses where you might be.

I couldn't help noticing Bucky kept his hands in his pockets.

33

I didn't know relief could levitate. My heart felt a
million pounds lighter when I saw your truck outside
the junkyard gate the next afternoon. I'd spent the day
walking through skeletons of cars taking a spot inventory with Randy. All those hunks of metal seemed lonely
and useless, forgotten and left to rust. As we headed back
to the trailer, I heard the sound of your engine. Even in
the midst of all the machine groans and squeal of the air-
conditioning unit and Randy talking, I knew that rumble.

I hurried into the trailer to grab my stuff and say good-
bye to Roni. With my stomach jumping every which way, I

spritzed myself with her body spray and stole one of Sal's mints before rushing out to meet you.

You looked how I felt. Nervously close to desperate.

As you pulled away from the curb, I reached out and ran my finger along your neck, the way that gives you shivers. We didn't go far—only to the empty lot around the corner—before you pulled over. You took off your seat belt and unbuckled mine. Pulled me close.

I'd worried you might never want to kiss me again after smelling liquor on my breath. Yet here you were, warm and close. I drifted on that feeling of relief.

Until you didn't feel like you.

The rough and forceful way you kissed me, your hand on the base of my neck, was new and unsettling. I felt in danger of being devoured. Finally I shoved your chest, hard. "Stop it, Mason."

Your jagged breaths matched the fierce look in your eye. "Jake's dead."

You'd been the one to find him. Pale and gripping the steering wheel, you said, "It was awful. I've seen some things, Lu. But..."

I don't want to imagine what you found that day. You said the tools the coroner's office sent weren't medical in nature. More like garbage removal. His shack was immediately sealed and marked for demolition.

Driving again, you said, "I want a drink." Your voice sounded calm. Even and matter of fact. It took me a minute to register what you meant.

"In fact, I'd like to get drunk off my ass."

You went on, stiff and robotic. "I'd start with a shot of Jim Beam. Wash the rest of the bottle down with a six-pack of Budweiser. There's nothing like good old Bud. Not like that Coors crap Seth drinks." Now you were talking fast and driving faster. "A taste of vodka would be all right after that. Then, say, rum. Mmmmm. I forgot about rum.

"Oh, but I gots to have me tequila." You cackled. "To-kill-ya tequila. Hell, Lulu, I'd even take a glass of champagne." You looked at me, more than a little crazed, swerving your truck at the same time. "And I hate champagne."

It's hard to know what to say to someone you don't recognize. I tried to soothe you with the meaningless words of sympathy that can't begin to fill a hole. When I said, "Jake's in peace now," you barked a laugh in reply.

"Of course he's in peace. He's the lucky one."

I think that scared me more than anything else all day. But you tried to top it driving way too fast around the curves and along the back roads we'd been exploring all summer. I stayed on my side of the truck and hung on to the door handle.

"Can I drive, Mason?"

You let out a strange, twisted laugh. "This is part of your lesson, Lulu. Pay attention. This is the bootlegger way of hitting the road."

You drove reckless and too close to the edge of the road one minute, straight down the middle the next. I was sure we were going to end up as salvage. Our bodies would be burnt ashes inside your mangled truck when they hauled it in to Sal's.

The roar of your engine and the screeching of tires made it hard to think. A prayer from my childhood raced through my mind: *Now I lay me down to sleep, I pray the Lord my soul to keep.* I always hated that prayer. It's for someone who's given up.

When you skidded around a corner, I yelled, "Stop the truck or I'm jumping out."

"Why? So you can run away from your drunk of a boyfriend?"

"My boyfriend's not a drunk."

"I'd like to meet him sometime," you roared. "'Cause that sure ain't me."

I opened the door, but the force of speed and the dizzying sight of the road below made me pull it shut again, but not quite tight. "Dammit, Mason. I don't want to die slamming into some tree."

Maybe that was low of me to bring up the way Cindy

died, but you deserved it. You finally pulled off the road out in the middle of nowhere.

You slammed your fist against the steering wheel.

Even though I was burning mad, the look on your face about broke me. Before I could crumble, you bolted. Slammed the door behind you, hard enough to shake your whole truck. Then, standing in the overgrown grass of the ditch, you ranted and raved.

I got out and watched you kick the ground.

"He's gone," you said. "Like you'll be gone. But I'm not going anywhere." You threw your keys into the clump of black-and-yellow flowers at the edge of the woods. "And you sure as hell won't be looking back at me." With your face streaked with sweat and tears, you fell back against your truck, wheezing gaspy gulps of air.

I stood there, useless, until your breathing steadied and your shoulders slumped. You'd burned off the toxic rage, but misery still shone from your eyes.

"I lost my keys," you said.

Because it was easier than being next to you, I clomped through the grass and flowers, around the hidden rocks, searching through blurry, stinging eyes.

You yelled, "Watch out for snakes."

"Not helpful, Mason." But I was thankful to hear you'd come back.

"Say a prayer to Saint Anthony. He's one of my go-to guys."

"Is that right?"

"Patron saint of lost causes."

"I'm pretty sure that's Saint Jude. Or Saint Rita."

"Well, old Saint Tony helps find things. Cindy taught me about him." You laughed. "She was always losing crap because she was too wasted to see straight."

Hearing her name stopped me a second. Then I said, "Well, give him a call, because I can't find your keys."

That's what you did. Right there on the side of the road, you got down on your knees and prayed to Saint Anthony. Real sweet and polite. I guess he liked your manners. Because all of a sudden you said, "Hey! I see them." You loped out to a spot I'd already checked, but sure enough you grabbed them, triumphant and grinning like you'd never had a bad day ever. "Told ya Saint Anthony and I are tight."

I held out my hand.

You looked at the keys, then at me, back at the keys. Then gave them to me.

I asked, "Now what?"

"Now I play nice so you forget I went crazy."

I wasn't sure either of us could pull it off.

"I knew he was dying," you said. "I don't know why it hit me so hard."

"It'll be okay," I said, hoping I was right.

"I've always been terrible at good-byes, Lu. When I was little, I'd get up early and run to school on my own. Just so I wouldn't have to say good-bye to my mama."

You melt my heart when I least expect it.

"I was fine once I got to school." You bent down, picked a yellow black-eyed Susan from the side of the road, and handed it to me. "It was only the good-bye I hated. I'll be all right, Lu. Once you leave, I'll be fine."

I wasn't so sure about me.

~

Daddy and Mom were waiting up for me. "Sit down, Luisa. We must talk."

Feeling the weight of the day, I said, "Tomorrow."

"Now." Daddy's voice was firm and too loud.

"I can't," I said, heading for the stairs.

Mom was the one who jumped in front of me. Stood close enough I could smell vanilla and cinnamon, a hint of something peppery.

"Please, Mom. I need to sleep."

"We're worried about you, Lulu. You're staying out too late. Disappearing, losing your phone. Ever since you met this boy, you're different."

"His name is Mason."

"You're caught up in the moment," said Daddy. "You

don't know how the choices you make now will change your future."

I laughed, hard and sarcastic. "I wish it was all about my choices. How about the ones you've made for me?"

Daddy moved in so the two of them had me cornered against the banister. "I know Mason's history, Luisa. He's been in trouble. His past is..."

"The past, Daddy. As in over." I crossed my arms against my chest. "You don't know him. You have no idea what kind of trouble he might be. But he's not."

"We're your parents. We know what's best."

"How would you know anything? You haven't been here all summer, Daddy. You're never here." I turned to Mom. "And you're never anywhere *but* here. All you see is in this house. You don't even know about the weather. Whatever either of you think you know about me, that's done. Over. Past."

The rage and frustration that had simmered all summer burst out. "You told me I could go to college. Told me to aim high, go far. You promised I'd have a life beyond Dale. And then, when I finally got close, you grabbed it away and said, 'Not yet.'"

They stared at me, the two of them fixed on this horror in front of them.

"You took everything away from me. Left me with

nothing to hope for, nothing to do. Mason is the only good thing in my life."

Mom said, "He's not worth ruining your future. Take some time. Some space."

"When I leave I'll have plenty of space. Until then, I will be with Mason as much as I want."

She said, "Think about your soul, Luisa."

I stared at her, unbelieving. I wanted to say, *What does it do to your soul when you cheat on your husband with your high school boyfriend?* But I couldn't do that to Daddy.

I pushed past them. "I've done what you said all my life. I believed you. I trusted you knew best."

When I was halfway up the stairs, Daddy called to me, "You don't know what love is, Lulu."

I turned back and said, "And you don't know what I know."

34

$\mathcal{M}$aybe I was still too naive to believe, but I thought you and I had a good plan. We had to make the most of the little time we had left together, so we made a few agreements. (1) We were going to make one more run on Aunt Jezebel, and (2) even though you didn't like the plan, I was going to sell the moonshine with Bucky at the Queens' party. It was my best bet for selling quickly at the highest price. We both knew you being there was not an option. And all the while, (3) we weren't going to talk about California.

Daddy and Mom backed off too. They didn't know how to discipline me. They'd never had to. None of us knew how to speak the language of confrontation. When Daddy left town again, he simply hugged me and said, "Be my sweet girl," which felt impossible.

So you and I went back to enjoying each other with no talk of past or future.

Driving away from my house one night, you said, "We gotta hurry. I'm taking you somewhere special."

I couldn't wheedle it out of you, but I thought you'd made us a reservation for dinner. A tiny bit of me was disappointed. Even if you took me out of town, I didn't want to sit in a restaurant where I'd have to share you with other people. But you felt the same way.

You parked in a thicket, my window pressed against a bush. I stepped out your door, into you. "You should have told me to wear real shoes," I said, pointing at my flip-flops. "I didn't know we were going for a hike."

"It's not far." You threw me over your shoulder.

Laughing, I said, "Put me down, Mason."

You didn't. Not until you'd carried me out to that point overlooking the river. You'd gone ahead earlier and set up a picnic. A blanket spread out on the ground, a cooler filled with fried chicken, biscuits, grapes about to burst their skins, and fresh lemonade with the exact right ratio of sweet to pucker.

"Whoa," I said. "You've been busy."

You confessed. "My mama did it all."

I liked that you had a mama who cooked for you. I hated not knowing everyone that had ever known you. I wanted to know you best.

"Come here," you said, dragging me to the edge of the point. "Or we'll miss it."

It made my head swirl to see the water below us, rushing by. The sun, low in the sky, shone slanted brilliance across its surface. You'd timed it so we'd be there when they let the dam out up in Elmsworth. Something I knew happened, but hadn't given much thought. Somewhere, miles away, out of sight, water was released.

We watched from the bluff as a sudden rush of water surged up and over the banks. It whirled and raged. A moment later, the currents settled and rolled on. The water level stayed higher, but it looked like it had always been that way. If we weren't watching at that moment, we might not have realized the difference. So many changes get missed.

There was only one little niggling bit of something that kept that night from being perfect. You knew this secret place. You'd been here before. I was sure it held some kind of other memories for you.

That's why I asked, "What was Cindy like?"

You rubbed your hair, making me want to touch it too. "I don't know."

I waited, not letting you skirt the question.

"She was pretty."

I knew that. Everyone knew that.

"She loved to laugh, but she'd also get real sad sometimes. I never knew what would set that off." You put down your food. "Thing is, Lu, it's easier to stay messed up if you have someone who's worse off. They can be a marker for a low you haven't hit yet. Each of us was the other's marker.

"After she died, I had to face where I was headed." You shook your head. "I owe her, but I can't pay her back."

A little later you said, "I found this spot that day we made our first run on Aunt Jezebel. After you got so mad about the gun."

So much had changed since then.

"As soon as I saw this view, I wanted to bring you here, Lu. That's when I went back."

"I guess we have bad timing meeting now."

"Nah." You shook your head. "I think it's some kind of miracle when we met. Any earlier and I would have been too messed up. Any later you'd already be gone."

The achy feeling in the back of my throat made it hurt to swallow.

You reached into your backpack that you must have used to help haul the picnic, and pulled out your gun.

"Why do you have that?" Even when you're with

someone you trust, the silhouette of an unexpected gun is eerie, unsettling.

You clicked it open, showed me the empty chamber. "Because everything is different now." You stood up and moved toward the bluff. You hurled the gun out to the fastest part of the river. It barely splashed, and then disappeared beneath the silvery-gray surface.

Later, when we made our way back to the truck, you couldn't carry me, since your arms were full of the picnic things. You led me through the dark while I kept one finger holding your belt loop. I would have followed you anywhere.

Back home, I stood at the curb and watched you drive away. I felt wired and giddy. Too awake for the time. I skipped down the sidewalk to my front door. Then stopped.

A figure sat on the dark step. My first thought was Seth. That's because he scared me. Bucky is broader.

"Roni broke up with me."

"I didn't know," I said, sitting beside Bucky. He smelled of tobacco and sweat.

"She's going on tour with that fricking band."

"She loves singing."

"She can sing. I don't give a damn about her singing."

I couldn't help but think that was part of the problem. Roni needed him to give a damn.

"Give her some time. She's had a lot on her mind."

"Like I haven't?" He shook his head. "It's all your fault, Lulu. You've screwed everything up. For all of us. You've got us all making the wrong kind of plans. You have us looking for things we have no business wanting."

There wasn't any answer. No argument to toss back.

"It's like I don't even know you anymore."

"You've changed too, Bucky. You're the one who didn't want to marry Roni until she had something else to do. What about you and school?"

"That's what everyone else thinks I should do. Dammit, Lulu. What's so wrong with Dale anyway?"

I didn't know how to say it, but I'd learned to love Dale. More than I ever thought I could. I loved the rush of the river and the hundred different shades of green. The sun on the hills and the shadows of the valleys. The smell of the air first thing in the morning and the last breath at night. The rhythms and sounds. Also, the people who made their way through this place. Like you. And me too. We tried to make things better, but we also made do with what we had. We weren't too proud to scratch and scrape by. We knew how to spot beauty within the rough.

Truth was, sometimes the idea of San Diego was impossible to imagine. It felt bright and shiny, but flat, like the pictures I'd been staring at, trying to imagine myself within them. I didn't know how I'd fit in there.

Or, if I even wanted to.

"Lulu?" I heard Mom call from inside. "Is that you?"

"I'm talking to Bucky," I answered, then turned to him. "Want to come in?"

He stood up. "I gotta go. Just thought you should know you blew my life to hell."

Inside, Mom stood by the stairs, holding the banister.

"Are you and Sal having an affair?"

I hadn't planned the question. But after an amazing, melting, decidedly delicious night with you, then coming home to the charred wreck of Bucky's broken heart, I was a storm of confusion. What was the point of falling in love if the crash at the end was unsalvageable?

She stared at me. Unmoving. Pale in the artificial light.

"Are you?" I asked again.

"Luisa Maria Mendez. How could you say something like that?"

"Because Sal's here more than Daddy. Because I find his nasty tobacco clumps in the trash. Because..." My voice faltered.

"Sal is helping me sell my preserves and baked goods." Mom sank down on the step. "We need money, Lulu. I'm trying to do what I can to help. Sal seems to think there's a market for my more unusual recipe items. In fact, I just received my first online order."

She patted the spot beside her, but I needed to be able to bolt at a moment's notice.

Softer, she said, "Sal remembers me…from when I was different. Sometimes I need to be reminded I haven't always been this way."

"I heard you. In the guest room."

Her fingers traced the blue flowers on her skirt. "Oh, Lulu. It's hard with your father traveling so much. We get lonely."

I shook my head. I'd asked her for the truth. I thought I knew the answer. That didn't mean I was ready for her to admit it.

"Your father thought…" Her face twisted as she tried to explain. She didn't look panicky-weak. More like embarrassed. "He thought we should…"

My whole world warped to think Daddy knew.

"Don't look at me that way, Lulu. You're old enough to understand. Especially now. You and Mason…"

"Do not compare Mason and me to Sal and you."

"Sal?" She frowned. "I love your daddy. You know that."

I thought I did. But things had been so wrong lately.

"I didn't know you'd hear us." She breathed out, loud and heavy. "I know it must be hard to imagine your parents that way." She stood up, reached for me, but I moved in reverse.

"Daddy wasn't here."

"That's why we were on the computer."

My mother and father were meeting online. Doing who knows what else—I am still not ready to explore that image. It was Daddy making her coo behind the door.

"You were talking to Daddy?"

"Of course." Then, suddenly, she understood. She blinked and flushed dark red. "You thought Sal? With me? Oh, Lulu."

Finally, I sat and snuggled in next to her. "I still think Sal is in love with you."

"No, Lulu." She wrapped her arm around me. She felt solid, like she could hold me up. "But it wouldn't matter if he was. Your daddy is the only love for me."

"Why? What makes him different?"

"Maybe because there is no reason. But we're better together than either of us on our own."

If I believed in love, it might look something like that.

35

I went to see Father Mick the next morning. For the first time all summer, I wasn't at Saint Jude's secretly hoping to see you. In fact, I was relieved not to see your truck or your bike.

It used to be reconciliation was as easy as getting a haircut. I'd pop in, get rid of the bad things in my mind, say a few prayers to condition my soul, and be on my way.

That day, I didn't know where to begin. Or to continue. Or finish.

Lying was easy to admit. That, and disobeying my parents, was standard operating procedure. I needed to unload the anger I'd been carrying around toward Mom and Sal. Everything else I'd been doing was fuzzy and hard to name within my usual catalog of sins.

Most of all, I was dancing with serious temptation when it came to you. Except, that didn't feel wrong. Being with you was the one thing that felt right.

Father Mick is patient and asks good questions, but he finally got tired of my starting and stopping and talking in circles. He wasn't going to give me permission to sin. He assigned me prayers for penance and kicked me out of the confessional.

As we walked down the hall he said, "I didn't realize you'd gotten your driver's license." I don't know if he noticed the flash of guilt on my face before he added, "I saw you driving Mason's truck last week."

I couldn't answer. Lying to his smiling face above his priest's white collar and black shirt was a whole lot different than simply admitting a past lie, already done. I wondered what he'd do if he knew I didn't have my license. That I'd been breaking the law every time I sat behind your steering wheel. That could have been my downfall. Like Al Capone getting busted for tax evasion.

Then old familiar irritation kicked in. Dale was too small, too constricting. With too many eyes always watching.

Now I see it differently. All those eyes weren't looking

to pin me down, they were trying to take care of me. They saw where I was headed when I couldn't.

Outside his office he stopped walking. "I was surprised when your father said you'd decided to wait to start college," he said. "I do hope you won't wait too long."

Typical Daddy. Making disappointment sound like a plan.

I said, "You'll have to talk to him. He's the one deciding."

He frowned, looking at me. Then said, "Has Mason found a new job yet?"

I shook my head.

"He does good work," said Father Mick. "I'm sure he'll find something."

Thinking about you and the work you'd done, I went down to your basement room. Our room. The reason we'd met that night back at the start of summer. Where I'd watched you work.

The simple but beautiful furniture you'd built was sturdy and set in place. A rough wooden cross hung on the wall next to a photograph of a sunset over the mountains. Books had started gathering on the shelves, making themselves at home. It still smelled of new paint and cut wood, but I could smell something else there too. Something smoky, a hint of unfamiliar perfume. The room wasn't only ours anymore.

You know what else I discovered that morning. On one of the upper shelves, behind the statue of Saint Michael, the archangel. His prayer had always made me uncomfortable. Scared me. Maybe because I needed him. *Be our defense against the wickedness and snares.* . . .

I don't know what drew me to him then, what made me pull over a chair so I could climb up, take him off the shelf, and peer closely at his fierce face and battered wings. But when I did, I saw what Saint Michael had been hiding.

A simple box. Wooden. Handmade. Didn't look like much. If someone were to open it, and then to peek inside the foil wrapper within, she might think at first that it was nothing but a pile of dust. Or tiny pebbles. Certainly no more important than a collection of radish seeds. It's likely it would look like something that should have been tossed out long ago.

I knew that smell. Almost sour, but tempting too.

Something lived in that box. Lying dormant. Sleeping. Waiting.

My mind swirled as I left Saint Jude's. We'd only used the active liquid form of yeast when brewing. But I knew that box held the freeze-dried bit for backup. The just in case, back to the source, original start of Baby. It would take some time, some extra-special care and coaxing, but those little nothing-looking particles were alive. They were the key to the Malone family business.

As I left Saint Jude's my gut felt heavy, full of something dark and rotten. In my head I felt the desperate urge to hurry. I was running out of time.

You were too.

36

*L*ess than two weeks before Labor Day weekend, we headed out for our final push. Our last run. Countdown to blastoff. Soon I'd be on my way. We simply had to do what we'd done so many times before.

I still didn't have a phone, but I'd told Mom I was spending the night at Roni's to give us plenty of time for the run. Roni knew to cover for me. I didn't tell you I could stay out all night, because I didn't want us both thinking about that all day. It was hard enough to settle what that meant in my own mind.

I had plenty of reasons to feel uncertain that day. You did too. During the drive you were quiet and looked close to frowning. I knew you were worried about running Aunt Jezebel without Bucky now that he wasn't talking to either of us. It felt twisted and warped not to have Roni and Bucky along. But I also wondered if Baby was on your mind.

She was on mine.

I knew you'd stashed her in that room at Saint Jude's. That you'd taken her from Jake's the day you found him dead. Of course you couldn't leave Baby there when the bulldozers came to clear away his shack. She was too important to your family. I knew you couldn't turn your back on what she meant, even if you should. I got that.

Only I didn't know what you were going to do with her now. Why you'd held on to her. If your family knew you had her.

I couldn't ask questions when I dreaded what the answers might be.

You parked your truck closer to the road than usual, probably hoping not to get stuck in the soft dirt. Instead of lingering in the spot of our first kiss, you hopped out.

You charged up the hill ahead of me. I couldn't seem to muster any energy. The higher we went, the slower I moved.

I heard your curse, feral and fierce, before I knew what you saw.

The stale smell of spoiled mash filled my ragged breaths as I made it up over the last part of the ridge and took in the devastation.

Poor Aunt Jezebel.

She'd been knocked over and smashed. The branches of her disguise had been tossed aside. Someone had ripped her from her nesting spot and beaten her copper sides to crumpled lumps. Her pipes were left twisted and mangled among the trees' roots. The propane tank sat twenty feet away, lopsided and with its valve broken off, a spiderweb of cracks along the top, the gas released into the atmosphere.

You stood, silent. Only your eyes roamed.

"Who would do this?" I paced around the destruction. "Can we fix it?"

I tried to pull a piece of copper—I think it was the door to her mixing tank—from the dirt where it was wedged. It didn't budge. I kicked it. Hard. Again.

"Lulu," you said. "Stop."

I hated the calm in your voice. The concern in your eyes. The maddening dependable way you stood close by, ready to hold me up. I shrugged your hand off my shoulder.

I picked up a piece of pipe and threw it against the closest tree. The metallic *clong* sounded horribly, wonderfully, perfectly off-key. I grabbed another, bigger bit of pipe and smacked it as hard as I could against the tree.

I reared back and hit it again.

I banged and smashed and pounded and walloped that pipe—I don't know how many times—into that tree. Every bit of anger I'd felt that summer smashed into that innocent sycamore.

By the time you circled in from behind, wrapping your arms around me, forcing me to drop the pipe with a final dull thump in the dirt, my hands vibrated clear through. As the numbness wore off, a new tender set in. It matched every other inch of me.

I turned around, still in your arms, my voice thick with tears. "It's such a goddamn waste."

"I know," you said. "I know."

"If they wanted to steal her, I'd get that. Or even take her to be recycled. Sal pays good money for copper." I wrapped my hands around my head, trying to make sense of it. You stroked my hair.

"Who would do this?" I stopped my rant. Looked up at you. "Was it Seth?"

"This isn't his style."

I pulled away. Sat down in the dirt, exhausted.

I'd been so close.

Only one more run on Aunt Jezebel. Only one more load of liquor for sale. Only...only nothing. It wasn't going to happen. It was over.

Done.

No more hopes. No more dreams. No more chances or choices or maybes or mights or anything shiny at all.

I wrapped my arms around my legs and rocked back and forth.

I ached all over. Inside and out. My body threatened to disappear into the growing chasm in my chest. I didn't understand the gaspy, squeaky noises I couldn't seem to stop.

It was the waste and the mess and the overwhelming ruin. But also, I'd truly thought of Aunt Jezebel as part of our crazy, mixed-up family. Someone had left her in pieces, battered and bruised. They'd invaded our magical hideaway and made it ugly.

"I hate it here," I said.

I'd gotten so wrapped up in the pretty parts of Dale, so enamored with all our favorite spots, the places I thought I'd miss, I'd forgotten what I'd known all along. "Everything gets trashed here. There's no point in even trying. I quit. I surrender. Uncle."

"Hell no," you said. "You don't get to give up. We have worked too hard and too long—and you're too close."

"It's over." I rested my head on my arms.

"We just need a new idea. I bet it's something obvious and right in front of our faces."

I knew it was like Bucky said. Everything blown all to hell.

All summer long, from the moment Daddy broke the news, I'd been fighting fate. Refusing to see what was right in front of me. No matter what I did, no matter how hard I worked, or how low I stooped, whatever line I was willing to cross, I simply wasn't meant to go to San Diego. Seeing Aunt Jezebel smashed to smithereens had left me no more room to doubt. I couldn't lie to myself anymore. Wanting was not the same as happening.

I staggered down the hill on weak and wobbly legs. Grief and exhaustion worked like a shot of moonshine while you kept me moving in the midst of my confusion. As you drove us away, I leaned my blank and empty head against the window, steeping in my shame.

It was more than hopelessness. More than misery. More than feeling beat up and beat down and simply beat.

It was you.

All the things I'd made you go through that summer. All those trials and temptations. Risking your future, your sobriety, your best everything—all of it, for nothing.

At your house you poured me lemonade and added mint from your yard. Sat with me on your couch. "It's going to work out," you said. "We'll get your money."

I shook my too-heavy head. Then rolled over and buried my face in the cushion.

I woke up later, alone. The glass of lemonade sweated in a pool on the table beside me. I wiped the puddle with my shirt and went looking for you.

I spotted you through the kitchen window, talking on the phone in the sunlight. When you put your phone in your pocket, you looked up and gave me the crooked smile I love.

I joined you outside. A breeze ruffled the air, keeping the heat at bay. You showed me your blackberry bushes, full of plump, sweet fruit. Mom used to make blackberry cobbler every year on the last day of summer because Roni needed the sugar boost to get her through the idea of starting a new school year. I felt fall lurking behind the brambles and green leaves, but I pushed it away. It didn't mean anything anymore. There was no school to consider.

We picked blackberries and gobbled them up, staining our fingers purple. "Roni and I used to pretend this was—"

"Blood," we both said together.

"Seth and I did too."

We laughed to have one similar childhood memory.

Kisses. Hints of blackberry.

We moved back inside, still kissing, never letting go.

I led you down the hall. Into your room. You looked at me, wondering. We kissed standing, then sank to your bed.

Hands roamed, hot and heavy and everywhere. Clothes slipped away. I was unwrapped and undone. Every one of my rules was long gone, specks in the far-off distance.

All I saw and felt and breathed and wanted was you.

On top of wanting, mixed in completely, was the new place of willing.

"Wait." Your voice thick and husky. "Lu. I can't..."

I knew you meant stop. We were at the edge of where I'd said I couldn't go.

Where I now wanted to be. Had to be. "It's okay," I whispered.

"We can't do this," you said, backing away to the edge of the bed.

"We can't?" Heat and confusion swirled while I tried to catch my balance and breathe, just breathe. "You have condoms in the bathroom."

You blinked and jerked back as if I'd flicked you.

I moved closer again. But the sweet heat was gone. I said, "Don't you want to?"

You groaned. "Of course I want to." You tucked your sheet around me, turned away, and put your feet on the floor. "But this isn't how it's supposed to be, Lu. Not when you're feeling desperate and hopeless."

"At least we can be together."

"At least?"

I reached for you.

"I'm not your consolation prize."

You stood up. Pulled on your jeans, your T-shirt. Gathered my clothes, handed them to me. Turned away while I struggled back into them, unable to speak with my heart stuck in my throat.

I needed to get out of your bedroom. Away from the smell of you in the sheets. The room where, for a second, I'd pictured myself staying. Living. Being with you.

I'd been happy in that picture.

I made it as far as your couch before I realized I didn't have anywhere else to go. I focused on a tree branch outside your window, trying to calm the trembling in my hands.

You sat in the chair across from me. "Lu, I still think it's a miracle, us meeting. But..."

I guess you didn't know how the *but* in your voice pushed at me. How very far from miraculous I felt as you shut me out. I exploded. "I don't know about miracles, Mason. I don't know about meant-to-be or fate or destiny or any of those things. All I know is I can't sit around waiting for something to fall in my lap the way you do. I have to try, even if I get it wrong."

"I don't want to be your wrong!" You shook your head, frowning. "You'll never be happy here, Lulu. You're going to leave eventually. One way or another. I'm not the kind of guy you'll want once you get where you're going. Someday I'll just be one small part of what you left behind."

Your face told me it was over.

"But, Lu. Don't make me your regret."

"How can you think that, Mason? How could you ever think I'd regret you?"

"You've never told me otherwise."

I knew what you meant. I'd never told you I loved you. But how could I say it then? And how could I say something I'd never believed in?

We stared at each other. I felt the heat radiating off your skin. Or maybe that was all me. "I thought you said we were meant to be, Mason. Or was that just something pretty to say?"

There was nothing pretty about the way you looked at me. There was a sharpness to your words as you said, "This summer was our meant-to-be, Lulu. We got each other through some things. We needed each other. But it was only for this summer. We knew that all along. Now you'll go your way, and I'll find mine."

You were kicking me out of your life. The entire time I'd known you I'd been thinking about leaving. From the start, all along, in the midst of every kiss, I'd known we were headed for good-bye. Somehow I still wasn't ready for the way it felt.

We sat there, silent, each of us stuck in our own thoughts until you said, "I'm going to get you your money. You'll see." You let out a heavy sigh. "I need a minute. I'm going to go take a shower, clean up. Then we'll talk." You got up and walked away with my heart.

Your phone buzzed from the crack in the chair where it must have slipped from your pocket.

Ever since that day when I found Baby hidden at Saint Jude's, I'd known what you had planned. I knew why you were certain you could get me my last bit of money. You were going back to work with Seth. You thought taking care of Baby was a way to be part of your family's business. You'd fooled yourself into thinking you could do this one thing and stay sober.

You were choosing moonshine over me.

Moonshine was your first love. The one you'd known all your life. The one that had broken your heart. Lured you in, whispered sweet teases in your ear, made you think it would be different this time. She'd blinded you. Made you think I could never be happy with you. You loved your moonshine, but I knew she'd ruin you.

She'd never let you alone. The same way you'd tried to

resist when I came along asking for help. *Just this one thing,*
you'd said. *I'll help with this one step. Then I'm done.* I knew
how that turned out.

You'd been talking to Seth when I saw you through the
window. And now he'd sent a text: u w/ baby?

I hit Reply.

Once I know where I'm headed, I don't like to wait. As
soon as I heard the water turn on, I grabbed your keys and
phone and headed out to your truck.

I left without saying good-bye. You hate good-byes.

37

I'd driven hours and miles in your truck that summer, but never on my own.

I started it up, put it in reverse, and backed out of your driveway. Accelerated, nice and easy, the way you'd taught me. Then I got nervous. I hadn't realized how much I counted on your voice in my ear, knowing your quick reflexes would compensate for my errors.

Feeling uncertain about driving helped me to ignore my splintered heart. Gave me something to think about other than where I was headed. I coached myself along the road, coaxed your truck up to an inconspicuous speed.

I'd thought I had to choose between two perfect

possible futures. College or you. Head or heart. Go or stay. And then, in the heat of one afternoon, I'd lost both.

There was nowhere I belonged.

You didn't belong where you were headed either. I'd dragged you back into this moonshine mess, but now I was going to get you out.

I'd brought your phone along so I could keep in touch with Seth, and so you wouldn't. It meant I couldn't call you to back me up, but I needed to keep you away from the place that pulled at you.

I'd already lost everything that mattered. Already broken every rule I'd ever thought I cared about. Already learned there wasn't hardly anything I wouldn't do. I wasn't the same girl you'd met at the start of the summer. I'd been distilled into something new and dangerous. It wasn't a far leap for me to now take on the care of Baby.

Someone had to do it. The yeast was the key to your family's business. It had been carried on for generations. You'd never be able to turn your back on Baby, but that's where I came in. I could feed her. I could watch her grow, keep her safe, send her off to work when it was time. It had to be done. But not by you.

If I had Baby, I could set the rules. Any word that you were back in the mix, I'd cut off their supply. I could make sure you stayed away from the shine.

I worried I wouldn't remember how to get there, but it clicked into place. I'd gotten good at navigating back roads. I'd learned to watch for the little signs and landmarks that orient me to a place. When I saw the outcrop of boulders by the mailbox that looked like an American flag, I knew I was almost to the road you'd pointed out. A zing traveled through me—the kind of high I used to feel when I'd solved a particularly tough calculus problem.

I was still riding that blip of euphoria when I caught my first view of the ugly, squat cement building. Faded blue paint identified it as QUARRY SUPPLY CO. even though the nearest quarry had closed before I was born. A battered pickup on blocks sat in a clump of overgrown weeds. To the side of the building, a giant yellow loader sat looking lost and purposeless.

The place felt deserted. That's part of its disguise. When Seth and Peanut appeared around the corner of the building, I saw them take in the fact it was me in the driver's seat. I stuck my head out the window and waved in my very best junkyard girl manner. "Hey, y'all," I said with what I hoped was the right combination of confident and clueless.

Seth said something to Peanut, and they both laughed. Then he called to me, "This sure is a surprise, Skip-to-my-Lulu."

He sauntered over, circled your truck, peered through the windows. He stopped by mine. Said, "Get out so we can talk."

I knew that would be a moment of no return. I was already there in my head.

As I turned off the engine, my heart banged an alarm against my ribs. I could hardly blame it, but I had to play the game I'd practiced all summer. So, after I shut the door behind me, I leaned back against your truck like I was happy to stay awhile.

Seth moved close enough that I could smell his sweat and aftershave at war with each other. "You aren't packing, are ya? You already pulled a gun on me once."

I laughed, hoping he was teasing. But I also raised my hands and said, "Nope. Not today."

"Where's my dumb-ass cousin?"

"He's had a change of heart. You'll need to deal with me."

"A change of heart? You mean y'all had a lovers' spat?" Seth laughed along with Peanut. Then, in a steel-cold voice, he said, "Why the hell should I care? More to the point," he added, "why would I ever want to get mixed up with your little bitty jars of rat poison?"

"Scoff if you want," I said. "We've made a chunk of money with those."

I'd come there to talk about Baby, but now I realized I could make this my future in a bigger way. I was good at this part of the business. All those sales at the junkyard, the plan for selling at the Queens' field party; I had plenty of ideas. I said, "If we work together, we could more than double our sales. I have connections you don't know. I can sell to people you can't."

The idea bubbled up the more I worked it. I kept talking, never looking away from him. "College students are always looking for a thrill. I'd blend in, they'd trust me."

"I see why Mason likes you, Lulu. You're like a shot of lightning, aren't ya?" Seth stared at me, unblinking. "Does he know you're here?"

I didn't have to answer. He knew.

He held out his hand. "How about you hand over his keys and then we'll talk."

"No thanks. I got 'em."

Seth nodded.

Quick and hard, Peanut slammed into me, knocked me against the side of your truck. I hit my head on the glass and bit my lip. Before I caught my breath, Seth had the keys in his hand, dangling them in front of me. He said, "I asked nicely."

I wish some kind of freaky adrenaline ninja-nerves had kicked in, but instead, I stood numb and paralyzed. A fog of panic added to the bump on my head, making the world hazy and unsure. Although Seth had always made me nervous, I thought that was because of the way you reacted to him. He'd never threatened me. If anything, he'd been closer to friendly, almost flirty. I tasted blood from my cut lip, wiped it on the back of my hand. Saw the purple blackberry stains on my fingers. Wished uselessly and too late that I'd never left your house.

I was on some small, rinky-dink one of a million little roads outside of Dale and no one knew. No one would even look for me. I wasn't sure what you'd think when you discovered I was gone with your truck. You'd probably think I needed to cool off. With only your bike as a way to get around, you wouldn't be driving anywhere. Roni thought I was with you. Mom thought I was with Roni. Bucky wasn't talking to me at all. Your phone was under the seat of your truck.

Seth faced me. Not touching. But closing in. Only a snatch away. "You've had quite the run this summer, haven't you, Lulu? Beginners' luck's been good to you. But you don't get how things work."

I squinted in the sunlight, still fussing with the cut on my lip.

"It's time you see how big boys run a business."

He grabbed my arm and dragged me toward the

building. As I slipped in the gravel, his fingers dug into my skin. We approached the wall made of large metal slats, like an enormous garage door, but then he shoved me toward the smaller regular door built into the cement. He braced me against the wall as his unsteady fingers fumbled with the combination. He said, "Peanut, get this damn lock."

A few seconds later he pushed me inside, and I breathed in the familiar smell of mash brewing and corn fermenting. Though it was cooler in there, I suddenly felt parched. I swallowed against the dry in my mouth. But even as scared as I was, part of me was fascinated. We'd only been kids playing with an Easy-Bake oven compared to this setup.

Along the opposite wall were three bullet-shaped metal tanks, each one burbling and glubbing. Pipes ran from the release valves at the tops of the tanks down to where plastic buckets sat on the floor collecting thick and yeasty foam trailings. The perpendicular wall supported metal shelves stacked with various boxes, bags, and cans reaching toward the ceiling. Rows of wooden barrel ends stared back at me.

In the far corner sat Aunt Jezebel's much bigger sister.

Fluorescent lights lined the ceiling above a crisscross of pipes connecting the mash tanks to the still. Tiny windows ran along the ceiling line—the only connection to the outside world. All I could see was sky.

Keeping his knee behind my thigh and hand pressed on my back, Seth pushed me along the row of tanks, leading me to a space where a sagging brown and yellow couch faced a television while four metal folding chairs sat around a crooked card table. A microwave sat on a stained plastic counter next to a large and rusted sink.

Seth pointed at one of the chairs. "Sit."

I sat up straight, with my very best posture. I tried to act like things were going according to plan. Met his eyes that might be like yours if they weren't so glassy and rimmed in red.

I said, "This is quite a setup you've got."

"Stop acting like you know something." Seth pulled out a pack of cigarettes, turned them over in his hands.

He took one out. Tapped its end on the table. "Do you actually think I'd deal with you behind Mason's back?"

He shook his head. For a second it was almost like he felt sorry for me. But only almost. He said, "Blood comes first, little baby Lulu. Blood first." He pulled out his phone.

Keeping his narrowed eyes on me, Seth said into the phone, "Hey. I got something you might be looking for. Out here at the Quarry Supply. It smells like..."

He paused, leaned over, and stuck his nose in my hair. "Not sure if it's sugar or spice, but it's mixed with creamy buttermilk."

Immediately that idiotic song "Skip to My Lou" danced through my head. Only you would understand his riddle. Seeing as your phone was hidden under the seat of your truck—which was parked outside this warehouse—you wouldn't get that message.

As he hung up, he said, "You better hope the fly comes to sugar."

Shoo, fly, shoo.

An unfocused prayer ran on a loop in my head as I sat at the table with Seth and Peanut watching my every move. Only I didn't know what to pray for. The whole reason I'd come to see Seth was so you wouldn't. There was no way for you to get his message. And yet, we three waited for you.

I didn't know what else to do. I was doing what you suggest: Wait and see.

Seth wasn't any better at waiting than me. Between cigarettes, he checked his phone, got up and looked outside the door. All the while he twitched and fidgeted, shuffled and shifted, sweated and wiped his face with his shirt. When he hauled off and slapped Peanut for hum-ming, I started counting the cans of peaches and cherries, sugar, and bags of ground corn to help me stay quiet. I wondered what Mom could make with all those ingredi-ents. Felt desperate to think I might never find out.

Later, after he'd finally let me up to use the disgusting toilet in the back of the warehouse, I tried again. "Can we talk about a deal? Mason's not coming."

"Yes he is. He owes me."

I burst out, "Why does he owe you anything? Because of a blown deal? Did he disappoint you somehow? Don't you think you've let him down too? You want his money? Let me pay whatever he owes you. You need help? Let me work." I couldn't stop. "I know Mason's planning to work with you. But he can't. It'll kill him if he tries. You leave him alone, and I'll do whatever it takes to get the job done."

"What about you, Lulu? Are you going to leave him alone too?"

Yes.

I had to. My mind was a jumble of mixed-up uncertain-ties, but that was one thing I knew. I'd pulled you back to this place you had to avoid. I was like a rock tied around your neck, dragging you down, making it hard to breathe.

I wasn't good for you. And you knew it too. That's why you wanted to go your own way.

Seth sat beside me. "You think you're pretty smart, don't you?"

I might have, once upon a time.

"I'll admit, some of your ideas are interesting. A little girl like you can certainly get away with some things we can't." He leaned forward. Inches from my face, he said, "But you've been a thorn in my ass all summer long. Got people acting nosy and asking questions."

He spit on the ground. "Mason got it. He knew you were stirring things up. But did you know Mason's been paying us an apology fee? To make up for the mess you've made." He leaned back again, wearing a satisfied smile. "That's why he owes me. It's all because of you and your little game in the woods."

I was the reason for your debt.

Every bit of trouble we'd faced, everything that had turned sour, every single kind of wrong from every which way was my fault.

I pushed past a wave of regret and said, "Well, we're done with all that. We won't be making any more moonshine. Someone messed up our still."

The surprise on his face let me know you'd been right.

He hadn't been the one to smash poor Aunt Jezebel. I said, "Looked like someone took a bat to her."

He and Peanut broke into fierce and hysterical laughter.

"Well, Lulu. Seems to me you're out of options. You ain't got one thing that I want."

"Nothing at all," agreed Peanut, still snickering.

Once they'd quieted down I said, "I have Baby."

Seth stared at me, unflinching. Looking more amused than surprised. Uncertain what I meant. It was in that second that I realized I had it all wrong.

Wrong. Wrong. Wrong.

Seth didn't know about Baby. You hadn't promised him anything. He had no idea you'd rescued the yeast and hidden it. You must have had another plan. If only you'd told me. If only I'd asked.

When he'd sent you that text, he'd meant *me*. Little Baby Lulu.

I faltered then. I got truly good and scared. I pressed my hands against my shaking thighs. Focused on breathing. Tried not to fall out of that rickety chair. Seth ground his cigarette into the table. Flicked the butt to the floor, then scraped his chair toward me until we were knee to knee and eye to eye. He leaned forward and asked, "Who—or what—the hell is Baby?"

I didn't have it in me to make something up. I could

barely spit out the truth. "The yeast," I said. "Your family yeast. That Jake kept."

I let this sink in a minute, watched him seethe and try to settle on what to say.

"And how is it that you have it? Did Mason give it to you?"

"Forget Mason," I said, as if I ever could. But at least I'd kept you away from here. "If you want Baby, the way your family has used her for every other batch of moonshine, well, then, we need to make a deal."

He sat there, silent. Eyes flashing and mouth pinched tight. He rubbed his hair the way you do.

I said, "It has to be stored off-site. It's tricky stuff. I might have messed up some other things, but I can take care of the yeast."

"Let's talk over drinks," said Seth. "Peanut, get a bottle."

Seth poured us each a shot glass. Pushed one toward me. I knew this was how deals got made. All in a day's work.

The smell of moonshine hit me between the eyes. I could smell how it was made, where it had come from. The corn, sugar, and yeast. All mixed up and heated together. Made me think of Aunt Jezebel. Working and laughing in the woods. The good times. But the bad too. Seeped into that smell, the one that made my eyes water, was the whole summer.

You.

And suddenly, everything was as clear as the liquid I held in my hand. I couldn't make a deal with Seth and Peanut. Like you, the moonshine pulled at me, led me places I didn't belong. I had to turn away. Being nowhere and doing nothing was better than this place I'd reached.

I'd finally hit the spot where no was the only answer.

I knew, absolutely certainly, with no more doubts dancing in my head, I was done. No more moonshine. No more crazy illegal plans to get out of Dale. I wasn't going anywhere anytime soon, but I was going to be all right. I'd figure something out. Something that made some kind of sense. Something that wouldn't make me lose myself along the way.

I thought about pretending to drink. To dump it out somehow. Or to simply spill it. But I knew that was only a temporary fix. I pushed the drink back toward Seth. Braced myself for what he would do.

That's when you walked in the door.

You didn't have to get a message. Didn't need a map or directions. Somehow you knew where I'd go when I felt out of options.

Whenever I see you, my entire body responds. Each and every cell, molecule, atom, and the space in between wants to be near you. Like centripetal force. Gravity. Magnetics. An invisible, undeniable tug pulls me to you.

Even then, even there.

Even knowing I could never be with you.

"What's that?" Seth pointed to the black plastic garbage bag in your arms.

Slowly, as though you had all the time in the world, you made your way across the warehouse, eyes scanning the room, taking us in.

"Hey," said Seth. He stood up and faced you, his chest puffed out and fists clenched at his sides. "I asked you a question. What's in the bag?"

"Baby." You pulled out a five-gallon jug of foamy white yeast. You placed it on the crooked table, which swayed under the sudden weight.

The two of you stood facing each other. Same height, same coloring, same way of standing when you're ready to pounce; but like in a mirror, each one's opposite.

Seth said, "I knew you wouldn't let me down, Cuz," then flashed a grin at me, looking like he'd won a 4-H blue ribbon.

"Good enough," you said. "And now I'm all paid up. No more owing."

"I don't know about that," he said.

"I do," you said. "Baby trumps all."

You held out your hand, waiting for him to shake it. "Come on, *Cuz*."

All the hours in the warehouse were wearing on Seth.

He looked twitchy and wired. Incapable of settling in one place. But, finally, he shook your hand.

After the two of you let each other go, you reached for me. Squeezed my hand, pressing the bruises I had from beating that tree with a pipe a million years earlier that day. You pulled me to standing.

Seth said, "This means you're back, right? Like Lulu said."

We all waited for your answer.

"You know I can't do that."

"You did it for her." His face twitched. Rage simmered off his skin. "You did it all. You even fixed your goddamn truck for her. That was supposed to be for me. You were supposed to work with me."

"That's over. And now I'm taking Lulu out of here."

"Not so fast."

"I'm paid up," you said calmly. "You agreed."

"You're paid up, but she's not." His eyes darted back and forth between us, his face twisted into an angry tangle of lines.

My legs buckled beneath me. There's only so much adrenaline can hold before shaky nerves collapse.

Seth gestured around the warehouse. "She's seen too much. How do we know she's not gonna run home crying to Daddy? You think he won't call the law?"

"Lulu's got her own secrets. She won't talk."

I nodded, silent, as if to prove it.

He turned to me. "What happened to us making a deal, Lulu? You came here wanting to work with me, remember?"

You let out a strangled half laugh. "That wouldn't be good for anyone."

"I don't know. I'm sure she'd be good at *something*." He reached toward me.

You jumped between us. He swung at your face.

The table tipped, and everything fell. In the midst of tinkly shattering of shot glasses and the half-full Mason jar, Baby hit the hard floor with a thunk. At first I thought the jug survived, thanks to some kind of scientific phenomenon based on inner density and the thickness of the glass, but then the white bubbles oozed out and across the cement. A sour smell of yeast mixed with the sharp burn of moonshine whiskey filled the air.

We all stared at the chaos on the floor. Peanut, reliable as ever, let out a nervous giggle. And then said, "Shit."

You sighed and shook your head. "This is why I never should have brought you Baby. You can't take care of anything."

"We can save it," Seth said, with frantic insistence. "Peanut, go get something to scoop it up."

As Peanut left, you said, "Won't work. It's trashed."

"The hell," said Seth. He took his cigarette from his mouth and pointed it at you. Looked like he had something to say. But then, he stopped. Turned the cigarette over in his hand. Smiled. Then flicked it onto the spill.

With a roar and a flash, the spilled moonshine caught fire. I jumped back from the heat, stumbling over the chair.

It was like the rush of flame lit something inside Seth. "You have no goddamn respect for this place," he roared. "You piss on all of us. Every time you helped her, you told us we're shit. Nothing but shit."

He ran to the stash of bottles. Threw one at you. You ducked, and it hit the floor, the spill of it feeding the flames.

Again and again, Seth threw bottles. The crash and smash of glass rang around us. The smell of the whiskey burned my nostrils all the way into my throat. I coughed and choked. My eyes watered, making it hard to see much more than light and movement.

When I stepped to the side, a bottle crashed at my feet, spraying me with the liquor. Another crashed next to me. You met my eyes across the thirsty flames. The fire between us was headed toward the still.

The enormous tank of fuel.

"Stop!" you yelled, a few feet from where I cowered against a fermenting tank. "She was right, Seth. Dammit, she was right."

Seth paused, a bottle held over his head.

"I'm back."

"Mason," I said, willing you to look at me. To find another way. But you kept your eyes aimed on him.

Seth lowered the bottle but kept a white-knuckle grip hold of its neck at his side.

"I was waiting until she left town to tell you."

The way he looked at you was so raw. So full of wanting to believe you.

"Unless you'd rather burn this place down," you said.

He dropped the bottle at his feet.

"Come on. Help me get this fire out." You dragged a bag of corn toward the flames. Seth cut it open, and the two of you lifted it together, dumping the grain.

No more fire, but no more Baby either. Only the stench and a smoky haze remained. Mixed in with the smell of burnt was ripe fermentation. "Damn," said Seth. He looked to you, worried, like he finally realized what he'd done. "What are we gonna do about the yeast?"

You didn't answer right away. You made him wait to see how you'd fix it. But then you said, "I have the backup supply. It's safe."

"You what?" Seth wiped his face, spreading black smears across his cheeks. He looked like a little boy coming in after a hard day of playing outdoors. "But why?"

"You know Baby doesn't get stored here," you said. You shoved his shoulder playfully. "And you know why? *Cuz* of days like this one, Cuz."

You laughed together, the sound off-key and out of sync with my own gaspy breathing. I tasted nervous sick in the back of my throat.

Peanut came in then, carrying a bucket. He said, "What the..." and waited by the door.

You smirked at Seth. "You really thought we screwed up this time." You put a hand on his shoulder. Said, "Let's go get the yeast."

Seth turned to me. Frowned and said, "You came here ready to make a deal for our Baby. Is this a setup? Are we gonna find one of your junkyard dogs waiting for us?"

I shook my head. There was no one waiting for me anywhere.

Peanut said, "I don't like this."

That must have been the one and only time Peanut and I agreed.

"I don't know if I can trust either of you. You play too many games." Seth paced back and forth. His eyes shone wild and bright against his filthy face. He paused, spit on the ground, then said, "All right. This is how it's gonna roll. You tell me where this yeast is, and I'll go get it while you stay here. If it's like you say, then we can let little Lulu skip along home."

We weren't in any position to argue the plan, but you didn't even try. Once you gave him directions, Seth and Peanut charged out the door, leaving us alone.

I ran to the door. Over and over I tugged and pulled. Until you said, "It's locked from the outside."

I finally turned to you. "Why'd you come here, Mason?"

"Me?" Your eyes were wide and disbelieving. "I'm here for you, Lulu. To save you. Again. All summer long I've been trying to keep your ass out of trouble."

My voice shook. "But that's over, isn't it? You made it clear you don't want anything to do with me. I thought that was because you were coming back to work with Seth. But it's *me* you didn't want to deal with anymore. I don't know why you bothered now."

Your fists were clenched, the muscles along your jaw pulsed. "I guess you really don't know me at all."

There were a million things I didn't know. I folded my aching arms around myself. "All I wanted was to keep you away from here."

The exact place we were. But worse.

You let out a harsh laugh. "By making a deal with Seth? Who, by the way, now has Baby and I'm going to have to figure out how to keep him from screwing that up too! Dammit, Lulu, how could you?" You stopped. Your voice turned cold and quiet. "I told you not to get mixed up with Seth."

Of course you had. Except it was way more complicated than that. "But I've been mixed up with him all along, haven't I, Mason? Whether I knew it or not. You let me think everything was fine, when all the while you were paying him to leave us alone. Seth's right. You do play games."

But I did too.

I had to tell you what I'd done.

We'd kept too many secrets from each other. Too many truths were hidden in the shadows, slipped behind the shine we wanted the other to see. Troubles were left to sour in the dark. If we'd shared our worries, we might have carried them together.

I said, "Seth's not going to find Baby. I moved her. I didn't want you coming here. I thought I could make you see...."

You turned a pallid shade I'd never seen on you. An unfamiliar look of wretched panic filled your face. I'd never, not in one moment that we'd been together, ever seen you scared before. You said what I already knew. "We *have* to get out of here. Now."

We set off in different directions, frantically looking for inspiration. While you tried to work a crowbar at the bottom of the giant metal door, I poked around every corner, behind each of the massive burbling, groaning tanks. I tried to find a secret door in the thick cement walls. Wished a magic drawbridge would open and set us loose. As I searched, I tried to shake off the pervasive smell of fermenting mash, ripe and ready.

"Could you get to the windows?" I asked, pointing at the ladder alongside one of the silver tanks.

"Wouldn't do any good," you said. "Neither of us will fit through."

"There's nothing to do, Mason. Nothing." Panic made it hard to think.

"Hang on," you said, grabbing my hand, pulling me close. "We can't give up."

But I had nothing left to give.

"I didn't want you to see this side of me." You traced the cut on my lip. "That's why I didn't tell you. About Seth, and what he knew."

I nodded.

"You're the first person who ever thought I might be something more than moonshine, Lu."

So much more.

Your voice trembled as you went on. "I know that's what brought you to me, but then it was like you saw something different. That this was only part of me. And I started thinking that if I could concentrate on you, and us, I could make sure everything turned out all right. You made me believe in something better." You took a deep breath, then said, more firmly, "We can figure this out, Lulu. We're gonna get out of here. We just gotta have faith."

I wanted to believe like you do. Tried to pray, but was all out of words. Wished I could clear that fermenting smell from my head.

Then, like a flash, I thought of the bucket in my garage. The mess of that explosion.

I was good at making messes. An expert at destruction.

"The fermenter," I said. "What if we closed the release valve?"

It was a simple kind of solution. But hard to predict the result. No guarantee.

"Maybe someone will hear the blast," I said.

"We could get hurt."

When Seth came back, we *would* get hurt. For sure.

You would have liked more time to think about the plan. Time was one more thing we didn't have. If we were going to try, we had to act while we could.

You climbed the ladder, and I waited at the bottom, holding it steady. You leaned over the tank and turned the knob. The tank let out a sigh. The bubbles at the bottom of the pipe let out a deep *hrrumph* burp of protest, then stopped popping into the bucket.

Down on the ground again, you set the table on its side across the room from the fermenter tank that had already started to hum. "That sound means it's blocked," you said. Just the way we'd hoped.

We built a fort behind the table. We dragged over sacks of cornmeal for fortification. As a final touch you draped a tarp over our mishmashed pile, fastening it with duct tape.

"So we don't get sticky?" I asked.

You hugged me and said, "Sure. That too."

It was time to hunker down. We crawled under the tarp into our den.

I had to ask the something that still didn't add up. "If you weren't going to work with Seth, how were you going to get me more money?"

"I thought you could sell cheap vodka at the Queens' party and call it moonshine."

I still can't bear to think that would have worked.

Lying there, in the dim light, you kissed me like that first time on the side of the road. But also like it might be our last.

Each time the fermenter groaned or screeched, we'd look at each other. We held our breaths and waited. There is no one better to wait with than you. Realizing the face in front of you is the exact one you'd like to see if it's the end, well, that's something to sink into.

Beyond our cozy space, the blocked fermenter sang its one-note song, now adding some squeaky complaints. I said, "If we get out of here…"

"When," you said.

"You have to leave Dale. Promise me, Mason."

You wrapped your arms around me, squeezed me against your chest. "Seth needs me," you said. "You saw him. He's out of control."

"You can't fix him." I forced you to meet my eyes. "It's going to ruin you too." My voice was thick with needing you to know what I knew. "It's going to kill you. And it'll be all my fault. I can't carry that."

You were quiet a minute. Then said, "We all get forks in the road. But either way we turn, we eventually get where we've always been headed. It's only a question of how and when." You wrapped my hair around your fingers. "I'm just glad you drove on my road for a while, Lu. You've made me stronger. I'm different now. I can do this."

"Do what?"

"Moonshine is my destiny. Always has been."

"That's the moonshine telling you lies, Mason. It makes it hard to see what's what." The tears streamed down my face. "You have to take my money and go. Anywhere but here."

"I can't. That's everything we worked for."

"It's nothing," I said.

It was both. Everything and nothing.

"What about you, Lu? Come with me."

I shook my head against the impossible.

Turns out I do believe in love.

It's the place where faith and action meet. It's where the river takes us once we make it through the rapids. It's me with you.

And me letting you go.

As we waited, the fermenting tank shivered and trembled. It protested the gases ballooning within its walls. Rocked in reaction to the unbearable bubbles and roils. Metallic pings, bumps, and dull thunks announced the tank's struggle to stay in one place. Its metal seams stretched and slid, steel sheets scraping and screeching against each other.

When Seth opened the door to the warehouse, we were already in awe of the whistle-like shriek screaming through the air. Impossibly high and piercing. I heard him and Peanut yell in confusion.

Beneath our tarp, you smiled at me. The sweetest, most beautiful crooked smile.

Then you lunged. Threw yourself on top of me.

The tank tipped. Shot from its spot on the floor like a missile. Or a demon from hell. Like mash in a bucket.

It flew through the air—blasting through the metal door. The roar of liquid hitting air drowned every other sound.

You held me down, covered me. Your head folded over mine. I ducked into your chest. All through the chaos of the world exploding, your heartbeat pressed against mine. When the air finally quieted, and the only sounds were the echoes in my ringing ears, your eyes stayed closed, your breathing heavy.

"Mason. Get up." When you didn't respond, I rolled to the side, eased you to the floor. I sat up, ripped off the tarp, and looked around, unable to process the destruction surrounding me. When your eyes fluttered open, it gave me a burst of strength. Some kind of higher power kicked in.

I dragged you to the now-open wall, passing by two figures, one sitting up and moaning, the other coughing while lying on his back. Somehow I got you outside.

The sky was at the dusky moment when day surrenders to night. The moon and the sun, sharing the sky, both shone light on us. Your truck lay on its side from where the metal door had slammed into it. I dragged you to the loader. It seemed like a place to lay you down. Once I settled you in, I saw it worked like the one at Sal's.

Knowing I was bumping your poor battered body, I

drove the loader away from the Quarry Supply Company. At the end of the dirt road I turned and kept going. The loader creaked and sputtered, but I urged it onward. Until I found Bucky's truck parked and waiting.

That morning a man had strolled into Sal's Salvage looking for our special brand of poison. He'd been back to his childhood home for a visit. Old memories gave him a thirst for moonshine. He heard a rumor that some junkyard girls could help him out.

Turned out he knew Sal—knew my mother too, back when she was Penny Riggins. He stopped to chat and reminisce.

Hearing what his long-lost friend had to say, Sal zeroed in on Roni, asking all shapes and sizes of questions. I'm not sure she lasted twenty minutes before she broke down and told him everything. Sal, being the way he is, wanted to retrieve the still.

When they drove out to her land, Roni immediately knew who'd smashed Aunt Jezebel. She recognized that handiwork. She called to confront Bucky.

That's when Bucky noticed the missed call from an unfamiliar number. Listened to your message. Figured we were in serious trouble. Sal, who knows where to get all kinds of things, called in a few favors from friends. Managed to get pretty close to the old quarry supply store.

They'd parked to consider their options and whether it was time to call the police.

Seth and Peanut must have passed them on the road heading back to the warehouse. Five minutes later and they would have missed the explosion. Five minutes earlier they might have had time to stop what we'd set in motion. To make us pay in ways I don't want to imagine. Instead, it was somewhere in between.

They survived—riding the same miracle that saved you and me—but they were hit hard enough they couldn't take off after us. They didn't follow us down the road or to the hospital, where everyone assumed we'd been in an awful car accident. They weren't waiting when we were released late that night. We didn't see any sign of them the next morning, when we woke up together.

And then we said good-bye.

Turns out I hate good-byes too.

There was no question. Not after this. You had to leave Dale.

And I had to stay.

But that day, when I'd lost everything but found it too, Roni, Bucky, and Sal were there to circle around, lift us up, and carry us home.

Like it was all meant to be.

39

$\mathscr{E}$xcept I don't believe in meant-to-be.

It's easy to believe in destiny when everything is shiny and bright. When wishes and dreams come true. But what about the days when everything gets smashed to pieces? Or when it all explodes?

Especially when you know it's your fault. What do you do with that?

Meant-to-be might just be another excuse. A way to make peace with mistakes. One more reason to take what you want. No matter who gets shoved out of the way.

If everything is already decided, what's the point in trying? And why are there so many messes and mistakes?

Why are the very worst, most awful moments intertwined with the absolute best?

What happens when meant-to-bes collide?

Maybe it just comes down to pieces and parts. The ingredients.

Corn. Sugar. Yeast. Heat and time. That's life. The things that happen, day by day.

It's up to us to mix and shape and cook. Or brew. Sometimes we have a recipe. Sometimes we don't. But it's not what happens that matters. It's what we make.

Roni traded one kind of future for another. She's in Nashville now, searching for the brightest lights she can find. She's making that happen. And Bucky, he let his might-have-been slip away. But I know Buttercup likes the way her future looks next to him.

And me? I'm in San Diego. I made it.

Turns out Father Mick knows people at USD. He knew how to arrange for some kind of special circumstances scholarship. Once he realized it wasn't my idea to stay home, he made a few calls. That very day, about the time we found Aunt Jezebel, he was talking to Mom. Letting her know I had another option.

So, that, along with donations from parishioners, and Sal's investment in Mom's new online business, all of it mixed together—made it easy to go. Like there wasn't any way to say no.

You'd already left in the car Sal gave me for learning to drive. You headed away from the river, past the beech trees and the hills.

I'd made you promise you wouldn't look back.

My life is exactly how I dreamed it could be when I set my sights on this school. Of course I love my classes. And Ashley Jones is a close-to-perfect roommate. She's not Roni, but we get along all right. I say she's smarter than she looks, and she says I'm smarter than I sound. I caught her sprinkling potato chips on her ice cream last night.

Even my work-study came through. I have a job working in a research lab. Using distillation of all things. The professor in charge is impressed with my intuitive skills for such a complex process.

The sun is so bright here. The sky so blue. Sometimes it's almost too much for a girl who's used to shadows. But at night, the moon still shines.

Mom says she and Daddy are coming to visit me one of these days, thanks to her new antianxiety medicine. Once she managed to get to the hospital to check on us, she decided it was time to get better. If it sticks, that's one good thing that came from that awful day.

The fact that we survived at all must mean something. And yet, I wonder.

Do you wonder too?

When questions and wonderings fill up my head, making it hard to see the shine on anything, I head to the ocean. Look for hints of the rivers that end up here. The waves crash in, then ease back out. They feel the tug of the moon, even when it can't be seen.

Like me with you.

So, here it is. The way I see it. What happened and why. No more secrets.

An old friend of Father Mick's called the other day. She welcomed me to San Diego and offered to show me around. Invited me to go to church with her. It's an old church, almost as old as one of the missions. In fact, they're getting ready to restore it. They need someone to take care of the delicate wood trim. Someone to rebuild the old pews. Someone who's good with his hands. Ideally, someone who'd live on-site in the little yellow house with the hibiscus by the door.

If I did believe in meant-to-be, that's what it would look like.

Come see.

Acknowledgments

This story is my mother's fault. Thanks, Mom!

Thank you to the top-notch team at Little, Brown Books for Young Readers, but most especially to my brilliant editor, Bethany Strout. Thank you for your steady enthusiasm and for asking excellent questions.

Many thanks to my agent, Catherine Drayton, who is, without a doubt, for sure and for certain, the best. Thank you also to Masie Cochran.

I received technical advice from Derek Kermode, lead distiller of Ballast Point Brewing and Spirits, and Neva Parker of White Labs San Diego. Their patient expertise is much appreciated. Any mistakes are mine.

I am forever grateful for the community of Vermont College of Fine Arts, most especially my oh-so-reliable classmates, the Unreliable Narrators. In particular, this story benefited from the brilliant guidance of the adviser I never worked with but always wanted to: Margaret Bechard. Margaret, thank you for opening your home and my eyes, along with Ellen Howard and my fellow writer-rocks, Cindy Faughnan, Tamara Ellis Smith, and Sharry Wright. Lulu would have been lost without you all.

To my generous readers, Cindy Faughnan and Jennifer Wolf Kam, thank you for being so smart. And kind too. Thanks also to my sister, Suzanne Wones, for saying the things I needed to hear—you always do.

Oodles of thanks to Denise Harbison, Carolyn Marsden, Suzanne Santillan, Janice Yuwiler, and Andrea Zimmerman for your ongoing wisdom and silliness and persistent demands for more kissing. Special appreciation goes to Suzanne, who is also my blog partner, warden of the cornfield, and bag carrier extraordinaire. *We're gonna love it!*

To my three children: Thank you for making motherhood a joy and a delight. You amaze me. Truly.

And, finally, to my anywhere everywhere meant-to-be, Tom: Thanks for everything.